They came to a place where the ground was soaked and the fog was denser than it had been everywhere else. Accolon looked into the carriage and told them they'd be slowing down.

"Not too much, please." Merlin wanted to make Camelot by sunset tomorrow, if possible.

"We'll do our best. But the ground is treacherous."

"We're anxious to get back to Camelot, Accolon."

"Yes, sir. But—"

"But what?"

"We are being followed again."

"Splendid."

A moment later the sounds of scuffling came from outside the carriage. Swords clanged; voices were raised. Accolon shouted orders.

Merlin and Brit looked out to see they were surrounded by a dozen or more armored soldiers. Brit drew her sword and jumped out to join the fight. Slowly, patiently, Merlin stepped outside onto the soft, damp ground and reached into his pocket. When one of the attackers came at Merlin with sword drawn, he produced one of his glass globes and smashed it into the man's face . . .

THE
EXCALIBUR
MURDERS

A MERLIN INVESTIGATION

J.M.C. BLAIR

BERKLEY PRIME CRIME, NEW YORK

THE BERKLEY PUBLISHING GROUP
Published by the Penguin Group
Penguin Group (USA) Inc.
375 Hudson Street, New York, New York 10014, USA
Penguin Group (Canada), 90 Eglinton Avenue East, Suite 700, Toronto, Ontario M4P 2Y3, Canada
(a division of Pearson Penguin Canada Inc.)
Penguin Books Ltd., 80 Strand, London WC2R 0RL, England
Penguin Group Ireland, 25 St. Stephen's Green, Dublin 2, Ireland (a division of Penguin Books Ltd.)
Penguin Group (Australia), 250 Camberwell Road, Camberwell, Victoria 3124, Australia
(a division of Pearson Australia Group Pty. Ltd.)
Penguin Books India Pvt. Ltd., 11 Community Centre, Panchsheel Park, New Delhi—110 017, India
Penguin Group (NZ), 67 Apollo Drive, Rosedale, North Shore 0632, New Zealand
(a division of Pearson New Zealand Ltd.)
Penguin Books (South Africa) (Pty.) Ltd., 24 Sturdee Avenue, Rosebank, Johannesburg 2196,
South Africa

Penguin Books Ltd., Registered Offices: 80 Strand, London WC2R 0RL, England

This is a work of fiction. Names, characters, places, and incidents either are the product of the author's imagination or are used fictitiously, and any resemblance to actual persons, living or dead, business establishments, events, or locales is entirely coincidental. The publisher does not have any control over and does not assume any responsibility for author or third-party websites or their content.

THE EXCALIBUR MURDERS

A Berkley Prime Crime Book / published by arrangement with the author

PRINTING HISTORY
Berkley Prime Crime mass-market edition / July 2008

ISBN: 978-0-425-22253-9

BERKLEY® PRIME CRIME
Berkley Prime Crime Books are published by The Berkley Publishing Group,
a division of Penguin Group (USA) Inc.,
375 Hudson Street, New York, New York 10014.
The name BERKLEY PRIME CRIME and the BERKLEY PRIME CRIME design are trademarks belonging to Penguin Group (USA) Inc.

PRINTED IN THE UNITED STATES OF AMERICA

10 9 8 7 6 5 4 3 2 1

THE
EXCALIBUR
MURDERS

ONE

A DEATH AT CAMELOT

"Good heavens, look at them, Colin. They actually enjoy hitting each other. And hurting each other. I don't think I'll ever get used to that." Merlin stood at the window at the top of his tower in Camelot. A large raven sat perched on his shoulder, and another one sat on the windowsill beside him; he fed them from a pocketful of bread crumbs. Below in the courtyard knights were exercising, which meant drilling with sword and shield. The clang of metal on metal rang clearly, as did their cries and grunts.

"They slice each other to slivers, then come to me and expect me to heal them," he grumped.

"You are a wizard, after all."

"Be quiet. I am a modestly skilled doctor, no more, and you know it."

Merlin's study was large and circular. Rough stone walls were lined with shelves of scrolls and parchments. There were four chairs and a rough-hewn wooden table. Some manuscripts were spread out on it; his assistant held another one and studied it. It was nearly sundown. Two torches gave the light.

"They seem fixed on the belief that the only reasonable way to resolve a conflict is by hitting someone or something."

The assistant read without looking up. "I'm surprised more of them don't kill each other."

"There are accidents all the time."

"I mean actual murders. You know them, Merlin. Jealousy, rivalry, spite . . ."

Merlin leaned against the window. "We're a civilized court, Ni—Colin."

"Nonsense." The assistant put down the scroll and joined Merlin at the window. "I wish you'd call me by my right name when we're alone. If I'm not careful, I'll actually start to think I really am Colin. Not that I don't enjoy being him. Cutting my hair, dyeing it and donning men's clothes was perhaps the smartest thing I've ever done."

"Excuse it, please. Force of habit." Below them, one of the knights sustained a deep wound; blood flowed. Merlin turned away from the sight. "But then you wouldn't want me to slip and call you Nimue in front of anyone else, would you? You're my apprentice—my *male* apprentice—for a good reason. For several, in fact."

"I went along with this because I wanted to, Merlin. Are you saying I should never have let you talk me into it?"

"It wasn't difficult. You weren't exactly reluctant."

Merlin turned his back and made himself watch the sparring knights again. "I don't know how they do it. I didn't have that much energy, or that much competitiveness, even when I was young. The knight who was injured will be up here soon, expecting me to treat his wound."

"You're the most competitive man at court, Merlin. It just doesn't express itself physically, that's all."

"I am no such thing."

"You are and you know it. You never stop. Doing everything you can to counter ignorance and superstition. Chipping away at foolishness and wasted effort. Trying your level best to turn Camelot into a court worthy of modern Europe instead of the Bronze Age backwater it is."

He turned to face her. "You know perfectly well why I want you disguised as Colin. Morgan and the women of her court would be relentless if they knew you'd abandoned them and their assorted gods and goddesses to study with a champion of reason."

"I can handle my dear cousin Morgan le Fay."

"Do you know how many of the corpses in the cemetery thought that? She's vicious when she thinks she's been crossed. She is named for the death goddess, after all."

"You don't fool me, Merlin. You want me to pretend to be a boy for your own reasons."

"Don't be preposterous." He pulled a wooden stool to himself and sat down.

"Merlin the Wise Man. With a carefully calculated image: pure, devoted to reason, unsullied by anything as base as emotion. Or lust." She smiled and went back to her stool. Another raven flew into the room and landed at the edge of the table not far from her; she stroked its head. "You don't want people to think you might be in love with a woman thirty years younger than yourself. Or even just sleeping with her."

"For the excellent reason that I am not."

She hopped up onto the window ledge. "Besides, I think having me pretend to be someone I'm not gives you a kind of vicarious pleasure. I'm a constant reminder that the others at court aren't as clever as you."

"I don't have that kind of ego."

"You're a courtier, exactly like the rest of them. You do." She grinned. "Besides, I have my own personal reasons for wanting to hide."

He raised an eyebrow. "What would those be?"

"Never mind." She stretched and yawned. "You've been giving me too much homework. How long do you think we can get away with this, anyway?"

"As long as we need to and want to, I imagine. It's been more than six months."

Before she could respond, there was a loud knock at the door, it flew open and King Arthur strode in. Arthur, tall, athletic, virile, broad-shouldered. He had bright reddish-yellow hair; some people called him the Sun King, which seemed to fit. Middle age was creeping up on him; he was not quite as fit as he'd been in his youth. But he was beaming and alive with energy. "Merlin, we've found it!"

Merlin and Nimue jumped to their feet. Nimue bowed. "Your Majesty."

Arthur seemed surprised to see him there. "Oh, hello, Colin. How are your lessons coming?"

"Just fine, Your Majesty."

"It's such a pity you're a scholar. You've got a good strong frame. The best build of any young man in Camelot. You could make a fine knight."

She glanced at Merlin from the corner of her eye. "Horses make me nervous."

"Oh." Arthur seemed uncertain whether Colin was serious. "But you'd get used to them, surely."

"I—"

"Arthur." Merlin spoke up firmly. "As happy as I am at

your ambition for my apprentice, I can't help wondering what brings you up here."

Arthur stopped short. "It's what I said."

"All you said was that we've found it. Who are 'we,' and what exactly is 'it'?"

Arthur looked from Merlin to Colin and back. "Why, the stone of course."

"Stone? What stone? What the devil are you talking about?"

Arthur sat down, rested his back against the wall and put a leg up on the table. "The stone. The Stone of Bran. You've heard me talk about it often enough. You still let those damned birds in here?"

"Be careful of those scrolls, will you? They're not replaceable."

Arthur grinned. "I'm the king. I can replace anything I want."

"Not those."

"Anything." He said it firmly. "If we can't find them here, then somewhere else. Rome, Alexandria, Constantinople, someplace. I'm the richest man in England, remember?"

"Yes, you have enough plunder to buy what you want—if it exists. But Arthur, these books are precious. Look—this is a manuscript of Sophocles in his own hand. And this—an original Plotinus, an unknown essay on reason. There may not be any other copies in the world."

"You told me the Stone of Bran didn't exist, too. It does. We have it."

Merlin stepped to the table and carefully rolled up his manuscripts. The raven on his left shoulder clambered across his back to the right one. "There is," he said emphatically, "no such thing. For the excellent reason that there is no such being as the god Bran."

"Don't blaspheme the gods, Merlin. They have a way of getting their revenge."

"Arthur, what is this stone? I mean, who found it and where?"

Arthur smiled a satisfied smile and pretended to examine his fingernails. "Percival found it. In Wales."

"In Wales?" Merlin laughed. "What is it made of, then? Mud and onions?"

"Scoff all you like. The stone is real. And we have it."

Nimue sat up. "Am I missing something? I've never heard of this—this—"

"Stone of Bran," Arthur said patiently. "It figures in any number of ancient legends, Colin. A skull-shaped stone. Originally fashioned by the god Bran. Some even say it is his own divine skull. And it has mystical powers. It works wonders."

"Gods have skulls?"

"I only said that was one of the legends. But the stone is shaped like one. I've wanted to get my hands on it for years. Sent knight after knight out questing for it. It could actually bring peace to Camelot."

"That," Merlin said emphatically, "would be a wonder on the order of Creation."

Arthur ignored him. "It might even reconcile my wife to the fact that she's my wife."

"Arthur." Merlin adopted the tone of a stern school-teacher talking to a dim student.

But Arthur was in too buoyant a mood to be scolded. "Yes, scholar?"

"I don't doubt Percival found some kind of stone, maybe even one carved into a skull. But it is not magical. Work, study, scholarship, patience, even a bit of love—those are the things that will civilize England and stop all this constant infighting. No stone, magic or otherwise, can do that. We have to put our faith in ourselves, not a lot of arcane claptrap."

"We'll just see, won't we?"

"I can't stand it when you turn smug." He added ironically, "Your Majesty."

"I know. That's why I do it. Merlin, indulge me in this. If it doesn't work, it doesn't. I'll be the first to admit it. But if the stone is real—just think of the possibilities."

"If pie cured leprosy . . ."

"You spend too much time inhaling book dust."

Merlin was about to tell the king that he himself ought to spend more time with books when the door opened. One of Arthur's squires, a tall young man with bright red hair named Borolet, looked in. "Excuse me, Majesty."

Before he could say anything else Nimue spoke up. "Ganelin! How are you?"

"I'm Borolet. Hello, Colin."

"Oh. Borolet, then. I haven't seen you in a while."

Borolet turned to the king. "You wanted me to remind you when the council meeting is set to start."

Arthur sprang to his feet. "Just so. I can't wait to tell everyone the news." He stepped toward the door.

"Arthur, don't." Merlin was frowning deeply. "Hold off. At least wait and see what Percival actually brings."

"He who hesitates is lost, scholar."

"Fools rush in, king."

For the first time Arthur seemed deflated. "You really think it might be a—a mistake?"

"There's a remote possibility of it."

The king took a deep breath. "I've already told Mark."

"Good heavens, Arthur. You know how he prattles. And you know how superstitious he is. He couldn't keep a secret like this to save his life."

"Oh—and I sent word to Morgan."

Merlin sighed and rolled his eyes in exasperation. "Morgan? Why on earth did you do that? Arthur, when will you get the hang of kingship? Power is about discretion. About keeping secrets, if you want to look at it that way."

"She is the high priestess, after all. She deals with the gods. Even though, as everyone knows, you are a powerful sorcerer."

"Stop it, Arthur."

"You are. Everyone says so. Any man as learned as you must have entered into a pact with the dark powers. It's common knowledge."

"It may be common but, Arthur, it is not knowledge."

"Look at these birds. They do as you tell them. No wonder people think you're a kind of enchanter."

"Because I've trained a few ravens? Be serious."

"You're a wizard. It's common knowledge."

He stiffened. "It is nonsense, not knowledge."

The king chuckled. "You shouldn't let yourself grow annoyed so easily. It takes all the fun out of it. Anyway, when the stone gets here, I want Morgan to conduct some kind of ceremony, consecrating it to Camelot or England or some such."

"'Some such'?"

"She'll know the proper form. You know what I mean. It's an important relic. Its arrival here will be an event. Besides, we need something to liven this place up."

"Why not just watch the knights in the courtyard trying to slaughter each other?"

"Really, Merlin." Arthur sighed. "You're such a killjoy.

It's a good thing you're as smart as you are or you'd end up in a dungeon someplace, on principle." He put on a wide smile. "We'll talk later. Are you coming to council?"

"I'll be along."

"Good. I want you there. Mark will be there. I want to announce the news before he has the chance to gossip it all over the castle."

"Why isn't he off in Cornwall, refining tin for you? Or seducing every woman he can get his hands on?"

"He's here, Merlin. He's my chief military advisor, and tensions with the French are getting worse."

With that he rushed out of the room, leaving Merlin and Nimue to bow to the empty space where he'd been.

A moment later Borolet looked into the room again. "You shouldn't disagree with him that way, Merlin. He is the king, after all."

"And I'm his chief counselor. Disagreeing with him is my job. Evidently eavesdropping is yours."

Borolet turned to Colin. "My brother and I are going to do some wrestling later. Would you like to join us?"

Nimue stiffened slightly. "No thank you."

"Arthur was right. You're a couple of sticks-in-the-mud." He looked from one of them to the other, grinned a smart-ass grin then left, pulling the door shut loudly behind him.

Merlin sat, heavily. "You see what I'm up against? The Stone of Bran. What rubbish."

"When it gets here and he sees that it's just a stone . . ."

"He'll see what he wants to see. He's a king."

"Oh."

For an instant Merlin seemed to be lost in his thoughts. Then he looked squarely at Nimue. "You probably ought to go and wrestle with them. If you never exercise at all, they might start to get suspicious."

"Let them."

"Besides, I thought you told me once that you find him attractive."

"No, that was his brother Ganelin."

"They're twins. It comes to the same thing."

"To another man, perhaps."

"And another man is exactly what you are. Don't forget it."

"Yes, sir." She grinned impishly. "Are we going to council?"

"I am. You are staying here. I want you to memorize the first pages of *Oedipus Rex*."

"Sphinxes? Divine curses? That doesn't sound like the champion of reason you pretend to be."

"Take the scroll and go, will you? Leave me alone for a while. I need to think about this new development and decide how to deal with it."

"I can help."

"Colin, go and wrestle somebody."

"Nimue."

"Damn it, go and study." He tossed a quill pen playfully at her.

She dodged it and left. A moment later the wounded knight appeared. Merlin cleaned the wound, rubbed it with an anesthetic salve and bandaged it.

Camelot, like many another castle, had grown haphazardly for generations. It was not especially large by royal standards, but it sprawled in every direction, conforming to no architectural geometry. Wings and towers were added when and where they were needed, with no deference to a plan. Some corridors led nowhere; others wound back on themselves, confusing unsuspecting visitors. Still others rose or descended imperceptibly; a person not in the know might never realize he'd changed levels till it was too late to avoid complete disorientation. It had been built by King Pellenore, who was known to be mad.

Merlin spent ten minutes walking the halls alone, thinking. Not only would Arthur believe this foolishness about a magical stone, no one else would have the nerve to speak up and tell him how absurd he was being. For that matter, half of them would probably believe in the silly thing themselves.

From ahead of him he heard footsteps. After a moment Pellenore came into view. He was one of the petty kings Arthur had overcome on the road to power. He was a generation older than Merlin, short, a bit plump, bald but with a magnificent mustache. The loss of his lands had unhinged him, or so the story went. Merlin sometimes suspected he was crazy like a fox. But at any rate he had managed to survive untouched for years in a court notorious for intrigue. At least he was pleasant and likeable—and generally sober—which was more than most of Arthur's minions were.

He came cantering down the hall toward Merlin like a small boy pretending to ride a horse. "Merlin. Good day. Have you seen it?"

"Hello, Pellenore. You're looking well. Seen what?"

"The dragon I'm chasing. It's green."

Merlin pretended to turn thoughtful. "Green? No, I don't think I've seen that one."

Pellenore narrowed his eyes. "It came this way. There are times when I wonder about you, Merlin."

"Really? I never wonder about you."

"A wizard like you might be the one responsible for all the monsters in this castle."

Merlin leaned close to him and whispered dramatically, "Just between us, I am."

"No!"

"I swear it."

"Well, this one's green."

"So you said."

"I think it's after Arthur."

"Who isn't?"

This seemed to come as a new thought. Pellenore scratched his head and started off down the corridor.

"Are you coming to council?" Merlin called after him.

Pellenore looked back over his shoulder and shrugged an exaggerated shrug. "Keep an eye out for my dragon, will you?"

"I will."

"You'll know it—it's green."

Then he was gone. Merlin decided to walk for a few more minutes; the day and the situation called for thought, and he might be the only one doing it.

By the time Merlin reached the Great Hall, many of the others were already there. Pellenore had gotten there ahead of him and was agitatedly going from one group of people to the next, warning them about dragons, griffins and rogue unicorns. Ganelin and Borolet were playing hosts for their king, who hadn't yet put in an appearance. Sagramore, a minor lord, was complaining loudly about the heavy burden of his yearly tribute to Arthur. And everyone, it seemed, was buzzing about the reason for the council.

The hall itself was at the heart of the castle keep, the most impregnable part of Camelot. It was built of the largest, heaviest stones, and it was always claimed that not even the

largest battering ram could hope to penetrate them. This
struck Merlin as problematic; the place was full of drafts.

The room was circular as was the great council table at
its center. Though to be precise it was not a table but a series
of connecting tables, each an arc. Arthur had adopted it so
that everyone at council would feel equal with all the others,
but of course, given the court's nature, squabbles erupted all
the time anyway. It seated thirty-seven people; at larger
council meetings some people had to stand or sit behind the
others, and this caused fights as well.

Today the Great Hall was ablaze with torchlight; dozens
of torches burned in sconces along the walls and in tall
holders around the table. Drafts made them flicker and
dance. A small band of musicians played military music off
in a spot along the northeast wall. Servants passed through
the hall with trays of fruit, cheese, bread. Others carried
drinks—wine, beer, mead—for the lords and knights. And
everyone seemed to be in a celebratory mood. The hall, it
seemed to Merlin, had not seen such merry activity in a long
time.

There were the petty kings, now vassals of Arthur, attended by their retinues. The most important of them was
Mark of Cornwall, whose tin mines Arthur had taken by
main force and who was now his chief military advisor.
There was Sagramore from Kent, Bialich from Ireland and
assorted others. And there were knights—Dinadan, Gawain,
Petrilock, Bors and dozens more—most of them accompanied by their squires.

They never stopped bickering, jockeying for position in
the court hierarchy, even starting minor wars among themselves. All but old Pellenore, who was the only one of them
who had anything like a sense of humor about it all, squir-
relly as he was. Merlin had seen the court of the Byzantine

emperor Justinian, and courtiers there never ceased their jockeying and backstabbing, but at least they did it with a measure of subtlety. At Camelot, on the other hand, subtlety was all but unknown.

Everyone was drinking. Cups were huge; it wasn't hard to see most of the assembled nobles were already tipsy, not to say drunk.

Merlin had talked to Arthur time and again about this. No respectable court would try to conduct business this way, especially when there might be important decisions to be made. Camelot was gossiped about and laughed at all across Europe.

Arthur's response, as usual, was to call him a spoilsport. "They say the court of Alexander the Great was like this. You told me so yourself, when I was a boy and you were my tutor. Wine and beer everywhere. And Alexander conquered the world."

Merlin was sanguine. "Alexander didn't have Justinian and the Byzantines to deal with. Arthur, your court is an embarrassment."

"Nonsense."

Other times he tried a more direct approach. "Arthur, England is being held together with baling wire. Look at all the bickering, the feuds, the petty wars. You've unified the country, but it could come unraveled anytime. Alexander's empire splintered when he died. Letting these people get drunk every time they're together can only speed that here, too."

"Don't be such a pessimist, Merlin." The king clearly didn't want to hear this. "A unified England benefits everyone. It makes us all stronger, militarily, culturally, in so many ways. No one would be foolish enough to upset that. We are adults, here, after all."

"When have you ever known anyone to place the higher good above his own self-interest, Arthur?"

But the king wasn't to be moved. "It's only drinking, Merlin. We're only having fun. What's the point of being a king or even a knight if you can't have a little fun now and then?"

"You call self-destructiveness fun?"

"Merlin, let it go." And that was that. As often as Merlin had broached the subject Arthur ignored him.

At one side of the Great Hall, watching the others but neither dunking nor socializing with them, stood Britomart, the only female knight at Camelot. Her mere presence sent most of the men into shivers of anger and jealousy for several reasons, not least because she was a better knight than most of them. Merlin adored her.

He made his way through the throng and joined her. "Hello, Brit. It looks like a particularly big court today."

She smiled at him. "Wonderful. More councilors means more fights. Have you heard the news?"

"I live in a tower. I never hear anything."

"Don't be absurd, Merlin. Apparently Percival has found this stone everyone's been questing after. Arthur's going to make a surprise announcement."

It caught him off guard. "How did you know?"

"Everyone docs. Arthur told Mark, and you know him. He gossips like somebody's grandmother."

"That is a disrespectful way to talk about your commander."

"It's true and you know it. The news has been spreading like a fire in a hayloft."

"I hope everyone has sense enough to act astonished when Arthur springs it on them."

"I doubt he'll know the difference." She nodded toward the main doorway. "Look."

Arthur was there, and his squires Ganelin and Borolet were at his side. He was carrying the largest goblet Merlin had ever seen, and drinking freely. Apparently this was a day for celebration. Merlin realized that the king must have started to drink as soon as he left the tower; he was already unsteady on his feet.

Britomart was wry. "Should we go and pay our respects?"

"Don't be catty, Brit."

Suddenly, seemingly from nowhere, Mark of Cornwall was beside them.

Mark was the youngest of Arthur's close councilors. He was short, broadly built and had thick black hair; he wore a mustache but, unlike most of the knights and kings, no beard. Merlin often wondered about Arthur's wisdom in making someone he'd conquered his chief military advisor, but as usual the king wasn't to be moved. "I've conquered everyone in England," he would always respond. "So who does that leave?"

Mark, like nearly everyone, had been drinking. He put an arm around Merlin then tried to kiss Britomart. She pulled away.

"You two are looking even more serious than usual. This is a day for feasting."

Brit looked at the king, not at Mark. "Shouldn't you be off refining tin for England?"

"The mines are in good hands. Arthur wanted me to be here."

"The king's wisdom," she said wryly.

"Do you both know why he convened this council today?"

Merlin decided to speak up before Brit could needle him more. "We do. Arthur wants it to be a surprise. I hope you've cautioned everyone to act like it is one."

"Don't give it a thought, Merlin." He turned to Britomart. "And you declined when Arthur asked you to search for the stone."

"I did. And I'd decline again."

"Lèse majesté."

"Common sense. Hunting all over the British Isles for a rock . . ." She made a sour face to show what she thought of the idea.

"Finding the stone is a great triumph for all of us, Brit." He took a long swallow of wine. "It will unite Arthur's court as nothing else has."

"Except drinking." Merlin put on a tight smile. "Whatever our differences, we do have that in common."

Mark stepped away from him. "Most of us do. Arthur's right, Merlin. You are a killjoy." He turned to Britomart and grinned at her. "You too."

"Tomorrow morning," Merlin said heavily, "while the rest of you are sleeping off hangovers, Brit and I will be conducting the court's business."

"Alexander the Great—"

"Don't bring that up. Alexander's been dead a thousand years. And," he added emphatically, "he died young. I've seen him, embalmed in honey, resting in that glass coffin in Alexandria."

"Show-off. People say you've traveled more and seen more things than one man could do in the span of a natural lifetime."

Merlin looked past him to Brit. With a resigned air he asked her, "Why do so many people here mistake rudeness for wise self-assertion?"

Two of the knights, Bors and Accolon, got into a fight. Accolon was French, one of the men who'd come to England in the retinue of Queen Guenevere. Then, when the king and queen fell out, he had switched his loyalties to Arthur, which made him distrusted on both sides. Bors was a native-born Englishman. Ethnic epithets got exchanged, then blows. The people around them managed to pull them apart and calm them down.

Britomart was going to say something, but before she could, Arthur raised a hand to give a signal to the musicians, and they played a loud fanfare to signal that the council was about to start.

Most of the assembled crowd ignored it and kept doing what they were doing. A few, the ones who were relatively sober, moved to the round table and took seats. Merlin, Mark and Britomart were among them; they took chairs close to the king's.

Borolet and Ganelin, to get everyone else moving, took a pair of shields and began to hit them with spears. The sound echoed loudly in the stone room and finally got the crowd's attention. Arthur moved to the table, staggering slightly. People began jostling one another to reach the remaining seats. The musicians fell silent.

In unison the two squires announced, "Oyez, Oyez! Attend you all! The high council of Arthur, King of the Britons, is in session."

With that the room fell relatively quiet. Arthur sat back in his chair and smiled at them all. "Good afternoon, everyone. I know most of you are wondering why I've called this extraordinary council today. The fact is, we have important news. Momentous news."

Since most of the crowd had already heard about the

finding of the stone, this caused barely a stir. Arthur seemed not to notice. Instead, he went on to talk about Percival's quest, the legends surrounding the stone and the fact that the knight was due back at Camelot with it in a week or less. Then he added that he had requested his sister, Morgan le Fay, to conduct a public ceremony to consecrate the sacred relic to the common good of the people of England.

This, not even Mark had known. And it created the hoped-for effect. Everyone started clamoring to speak. Morgan was not especially popular with most of the kings and knights and, worse, was not trusted. All kinds of objections were raised. When Arthur pointed out she was the high priestess and therefore the logical person to conduct such a rite, ten different men demanded that Arthur's own court wizard Merlin perform any necessary rituals. Merlin buried his face in his hands and moaned.

When Arthur finally managed to quiet everyone, he asked Merlin whether he'd be willing to officiate. Merlin slowly got to his feet. "Arthur, as you know perfectly well, I am not a wizard or any other variety of wonder-worker. I am merely a well-traveled scholar, and I'm more than willing to defer to Morgan's office and expertise."

A dozen more knights rose up and agitated to be recognized.

But before Arthur could acknowledge any of them, a loud sound filled the room. Everyone looked around to see what was causing it. A thin, pale young man was spinning a bullroarer above his head near one of the doors. The sound was awful.

A few people recognized the man as Mordred, Morgan's son. There had always been rumors he was the product of an incestuous union between Morgan and Arthur. Quite suddenly, before anyone could react to his presence, all the torches in the room went out. Merlin noticed that it was several of Morgan's servants who were putting them out.

But two remained lit—on either side of the main door. And there, lit in an orange-red halo by them, stood Morgan le Fay herself. She was a tall woman, even paler than her son, and she was dressed in flowing black robes. Her manner could not have been more imperious.

"Arthur," she intoned. "You have rendered a great service to this nation in your determination to locate the Stone of Bran. With it, England will prosper. With it, your power and the influence of this court will grow ever greater. With the great god Bran as our protector, this blessed nation shall attain greatness of a kind not known since Imperial Rome."

She paused and looked around. Her appearance had caught nearly everyone off guard. None of them seemed at all certain what to make of her presence or her pronouncement. But the mention of Rome, which was always spoken of with some awe, impressed them properly. She spread her arms wide, and her enormous black sleeves seemed to resemble the wings of an ominous bird.

"Arthur," she went on, "the gods salute you and recognize your power and authority."

Merlin took in the scene, fascinated. Morgan had certainly stage-managed her entrance effectively. Her servants were placed unobtrusively around the Great Hall; they had extinguished the torches on cue. But it was quite out of character for her to acknowledge Arthur's position in any but a grudging way. What was she up to? Did she hope to get her hands on the stone for her own ends? It seemed the only likely explanation.

She went on a bit more, apparently oblivious to the fact

that most of her audience was too tipsy to follow a long speech. As she continued, people began to talk among themselves, more and more loudly. In one corner of the hall someone actually began to sing. Several times she mentioned "my beloved son Mordred, beloved of my august brother Arthur."

Her sense of audience finally told her it was time to finish; she repeated her little benediction on Arthur and England then raised her arms again to signal that the torches should be relit.

The hall broke out in loud talking, arguing, ranting. Everyone seemed to have reacted to Morgan differently. Arthur, wine goblet still in hand, got to his feet, took Merlin by the sleeve and crossed to where Morgan was standing with her son. The royal siblings hugged in a way Merlin had never seen them do before.

Close-to, Mordred looked even worse than he had at a distance. Thin, short, rickety, pale as flour, with pimples and a runny nose he kept wiping on his sleeve. He was, Merlin knew, the same age as Nimue—nearly twenty—but his small stature made him look years younger.

"Morgan, I didn't expect you here today." Arthur smiled a political smile.

Morgan, the would-be queen named for the death goddess, smiled in return. "Arthur, I know it. But the god moved me to attend. How wonderful all this is." She turned to Merlin. "And Merlin. It is always so interesting to see you."

"And you, Morgan. When was the last time?"

"It has been nearly a year." She brushed him aside. "When will the stone arrive here, Arthur? And when do you want the ceremony?"

"I was thinking perhaps at the end of October."

"The thirty-first! A day of power, of magic. That is quite appropriate. But why not till then?"

"There are some preparations I want to make."

"Such as?"

"In time, Morgan. I'm sure you'll approve."

"This sacred object must be treated with proper reverence, of course."

Merlin couldn't resist. "Maybe we can have it conjure up a handkerchief for your son."

Mordred took a step behind his mother and sniffled. "Mother says you keep ravens, Merlin. You should be more observant, then. The god Bran sometimes takes the form of one."

"If he shows up, I'll give him some extra corn."

"Mother says you're not really a magician."

"That is nothing, Mordred. I say the same thing."

Mordred sniffled.

Mark made his way through the crowd and joined them. "Hello, Morgan." Like most of Arthur's men, he didn't like or trust her.

"Mark. How nice to see you. But you must excuse me. The full moon will be rising shortly. I really must be going."

With that she turned and swept out of the hall followed by Mordred and the servants who'd worked the "magic" with the torches.

Merlin watched her go, frowning. "Are you honestly impressed by all that flummery, Arthur?"

"She is the hereditary high priestess, Merlin. And my sister, a member of the royal house. These things matter."

Mark spoke up. "What was it you wanted to ask me, Arthur?"

"Ask you?" He drank some wine.

"You told me to find you after council, remember?"

He didn't remember and it showed. The strain of thinking was evident in his face. Then it came to him. "Oh—metal!"

"Metal?"

"You have skilled metalsmiths in Cornwall, don't you?"

"Yes, of course, but—"

"Send for one of them. The best of them."

Merlin was as baffled as Mark seemed to be. "What on earth do you need a tinsmith for?"

"Not tin, Merlin," he said in a loud stage whisper. "Gold or silver."

"What on earth—? At least wait till you're certain the thing's real."

"I want to have a precious shrine made to house the stone. It's the least a divine relic deserves, don't you think?"

"Oh, naturally." He didn't try to hide his irony.

"You need to learn reverence, Merlin. It ill becomes a man of learning to be such a cynic."

"The Cynics were a respected school of philosophy in Greece. 'The Cynic questions everything in order to learn what is true.'"

"This is not Greece."

"I'll say it isn't."

"Even though we drink like the court of Alexander the Great."

Mark got between them. "I have a particularly skilled metalsmith in my service, a Roman named Pastorini. I'll send him to you as soon as I get home."

Merlin found it too exasperating. "If you'll excuse me, Arthur, I'm due to give Colin a lesson." He added sarcastically, "In Greek."

"Go, then." He handed his goblet to a servant. "Get me more wine."

The weather stayed warm and dry despite the change from summer to autumn. The knights were able to keep up their outdoor exercise much later in the season than they would have normally. But thick banks of black clouds were beginning to build up in the western sky. That more than anything else—more, even, than the trees turning color—seemed to presage the coming winter.

Borolet and Ganelin were exercising in the castle courtyard. Except for the fact that Borolet's hair was a lighter shade of red, they were quite startlingly identical, so much so that Nimue could only tell them apart when they were standing side by side. Of the two, Borolet was much more somber and taciturn; it was Ganelin she found appealing. He had the better physique and was the better athlete. He almost always had the advantage over his brother.

She sat on a stone bench and watched them wrestling, stripped to the waist and covered with sweat. The light of the half-obscured sun, dimmed as it was by the clouds, lit their bodies sharply, outlining them in brilliant detail. She couldn't take her eyes off them.

"Colin, you should come join in. Exercise is good for you." Borolet wiped some sweat from his eyes and took a deep breath. While he was off guard Ganelin caught him by one leg and dropped him to the ground.

Nimue laughed at the sight. "I'm no athlete, Borolet. If Ganelin did that to me, I'd crumble."

Ganelin got a headlock on his brother. "You would. But you'd love it."

"Not as much as you'd think."

Borolet pulled free and pinned Ganelin. "Why'd you come down here, then?"

"I enjoy seeing half-naked twins." She laughed.

"If I thought you meant that . . ."

"Yes?"

"Never mind."

Britomart came walking across the courtyard to them and sat down beside Nimue. "Hello, Colin." There was a slight sneer in her voice when she said the name. "Enjoying the show?"

"How could I not? They're the most beautiful men at Camelot."

Brit was wry. "Except for the king, of course. He's the handsomest by definition."

"Of course."

The brothers said hello to her then went back to their contest. Brit leaned very close to Colin and whispered, "You ought to be more careful. You'll give yourself away."

Caught off balance by this, Nimue stammered, "I don't know what you mean."

"No." Brit grinned. "Of course not." She got up and crossed quickly to where the brothers were wrestling and caught Ganelin in an arm lock. He struggled, apparently mortified that a woman had gotten the drop on him.

Borolet came and sat down beside Colin. "You really ought to work out with us, Colin. You could make a good knight."

"I'm a scholar, Borolet."

"You could be both."

She shrugged. "That would be a good novelty, at least. Will the two of you be at the consecration ceremony?"

"Of course. We'll be attending the king." He smiled. "It's an important occasion and we'll be part of it."

"Don't you ever get tired of waiting on him?"

He seemed puzzled by the question. "He's the king."

Britomart was applying severe pressure to Ganelin's arm. Finally, he cried out in pain and she let him go. Rubbing his arm, he sat next to his brother. "Serving the king is an honor, Colin. You should know that."

"An honor." Nimue was deadpan. "Of course it is."

Robbed of her diversion, Britomart waved lightly and went off to join another group of knights.

"Yes," Ganelin said emphatically. "We're virtually the only ones beside the king himself who have access to his private chambers." He gestured toward Camelot's tallest tower, which everyone simply called the King's Tower. "He keeps all his most precious things there, even Excalibur. How could we not be honored?"

"And he's going to keep the Stone of Bran there, too." Borolet was caught up in his brother's enthusiasm. "Have you seen the shrine Pastorini's making for it? Pure silver, all worked in intricate designs. It's an exquisite thing, and Arthur will be placing it in our care."

"Silver? Where on earth did he get it?"

Borolet shrugged. "Arthur's the king."

"Suppose it turns out to be just a stone?"

He didn't like the sound of that at all. "It won't."

"I envy you your simple faith, Borolet." Nimue looked up at Merlin's tower. He was there at the window, watching them and scowling. She waved at him and he pulled back inside.

"I think I'm due for my Latin lesson," she announced to the twins. "Merlin's looking stern."

Borolet looked up at the tower; Ganelin head-butted him. "Stay and wrestle with me."

"Thanks, but I really have to be going."

"You should train. Don't you want to be a knight?"

"No." She said it with heavy emphasis.

"You talk like a girl."

She bristled at this. "Which girl did you have in mind, exactly?"

Abashed, he apologized. "Sorry."

"I'll see you both later." Nimue crossed to the castle's entrance and climbed the stairs to Merlin's tower. He was there, waiting for her. Three of his ravens were perched in a row along the edge of the table as if they were scolding her for paying more attention to a red-haired, bare-chested twin than to her lessons.

"Merlin, Britomart knows about me. Did you tell her?"

"Of course not. How do you know?"

"She as much as told me just now."

"I'll talk to her and see." He gestured to a scroll on the table. "See how you do translating that."

"What is it?"

"Ovid. *The Art of Love.* I don't think you have to worry about Brit. I know her pretty well, and she can be trusted."

"I hope so."

"She's my closest friend. And she's politician enough to know that if you spread a secret around it loses its value. But I promise I'll talk to her as soon as I can."

"Thanks. I'm having too much fun to have this end and go back to Morgan's court." She wrinkled her nose at the scroll in her hand. "*The Art of Love.* Why does that seem out of place at Camelot?"

He scowled at her. "The king's marriage is the king's affair. Mind your Latin."

"Yes, sir."

"That's difficult stuff. You'll have to concentrate." But after a moment he couldn't resist asking. "Are you smitten with one of the twins?"

She nodded and smiled, grateful for something to focus on other than Augustan Latin. "But don't worry. It's my mind I want to develop right now. I'm not ready for another betrothal, and I won't be for a long time."

This caught him by surprise. "You were betrothed?"

"Yes." Her voice took on a bitter edge. "To Mordred."

"Good God."

"Exactly. Why do you think I fled Morgan's court?"

"I had no idea. Mordred! What a ghastly marriage that would have been."

"We'd have been as cold and distant as Arthur and Guenevere." She smiled sweetly.

He frowned at her again, even more deeply, but rose to the bait. "Theirs was a political marriage, not a love match. Her father, Leodegrance, is a minor king in France. He thought the union would open up opportunities for grabbing land and money here. And Arthur thought the same thing in reverse. It wasn't long before they reached a stalemate."

"Poor Guenevere."

"Poor, nothing. She went into it with her eyes open, as an agent for her father's interests. As soon as she realized she would never get one up on Arthur, she moved out, found a convenient castle and set up her own court. Why she chose Corfe . . ." He wrinkled his nose. "Is there an uglier castle in England? They don't call it the Spider's House for nothing."

"At least she had the good grace to realize that a queen of England ought to live in England. She could easily have returned to her father. Give her credit for that."

"I understand there is bad blood between her and her mother, Leonilla. But she never stops scheming, Nimue. I spend half my time trying to anticipate her plots. She'd do anything to bring Arthur down. And it isn't just a matter of her father's business, now. It is personal."

"I hear she's coming for the consecration ceremony."

"Splendid. As if we won't have enough chaos to deal with." One of the ravens flapped its wings and flew out the window. "Guenevere has a pet ape. It is always with her; she keeps it on a silver chain. A lot of people have fun trying to tell the difference between it and Lancelot."

"I've seen the queen but never him. Is he . . . ?"

"An athlete. Tall, blond, strong, handsome and dumb as a sack of rocks. In one way it's not hard to see why she took him as her lover. In another . . . I've never understood why so political a woman as Guenevere would choose a man with no connections. No thoughts."

"Maybe she enjoys the change." She held out the scroll. "Somehow this isn't the kind of thing I want to read just now."

He turned thoughtful. "No. I suppose it isn't." He searched the scrolls on the shelf nearest him and held one out. "Here, this might be more the thing."

"What is it?"

"*The Golden Ass.*"

She laughed. "Are you talking about this book or Lancelot? Or Arthur?"

"Stop it. I tried to make friends with Guenevere when she first came here. She's a smart woman. Very. But when it became clear she'd never stop working against Arthur—against *us*—I put some distance between us. There is a lesson there for you."

"Yes, sir." She turned her attention unhappily to Latin.

• • •

The weather turned harsh and stormy. Percival had been expected at Camelot within a week or so of sending the news about the Stone of Bran. As it turned out he was delayed at the Mersey River, which was swollen and impassable, for nearly ten days. Then he contracted influenza and was confined to bed for another five.

Arthur grew more impatient each day without his relic. "Where is he?" he grumbled to Merlin and Mark. "Everyone's on edge."

"Try and look at it in a positive way," Mark counseled him. "If nothing else, the delay is giving Pastorini time to construct a shrine that's genuinely worthy of such an important artifact."

"And to waste more of the country's treasure." Merlin couldn't resist adding it.

Arthur glared at him. "I want my stone. It will unify us all, it will stop all the fighting and bickering. I'm so tired of it all. No one knows that better than the two of you."

"Cheer up, Arthur. If the stone really is what you say it is, maybe it will work a miracle, cure Percy and transport him here."

"Stop it, will you?" He turned to Mark. "There was a report of a French raid on Dover. Guenevere's father, most likely. Is there anything to it?"

"No. It turns out it was just a trading ship that was blown off course. You know the weather in the Channel."

Merlin decided he had needled him enough. Arthur's desire for some peace at court was quite understandable if not exactly realistic, given his style of governing. But it seemed politic to let him find it out on his own. When the stone arrived and proved to be . . . a stone, Arthur would realize quickly enough how foolish this enterprise was.

Then finally, more than two weeks after he was expected, word came that Percival was about to arrive at Camelot.

He had always struck Merlin as an unlikely knight. Short, plump, heavily bearded, he was not exactly the picture of chivalry. And he was not over his illness; he coughed nonstop.

But he had the stone with him, and that was all Arthur— or most anyone else—cared about. The king and a small circle of his closest advisors waited anxiously in Arthur's chambers in the King's Tower. Arthur paced; the others watched him.

There was always a guard on duty outside the rooms and another at the foot of the spiral steps that led up to them. People filed past them one by one, to wait in the king's private study. It was where he kept his most precious belongings. In a case fronted with leaded glass rested Excalibur, the sword that was the emblem of his kinghood. It was crusted with gemstones, and somehow, improbably, a shaft of light lit it brightly.

Percival left his horse in the care of a servant and went directly up to Arthur's rooms. He carried the stone in a flour sack, which hardly seemed the way to transport a powerful relic. Arthur, Mark and Merlin were there, attended by Nimue, Borolet and Ganelin. Out of breath from the climb and covered in dirt, Percy said nothing but produced the thing with a flourish.

And it was not impressive: roughly skull-shaped, caked with mud and soil.

Merlin touched a fingertip to it and scraped away some of the dirt. "I think it might be some dark variety of quartz, or perhaps obsidian. Not the easiest stone to carve. Assuming it is carved, that is."

"So you admit it might be miraculous?" Arthur was

pleased with himself and his knight and the stone he'd found.

"I admit it might be carved. Let me see it work a miracle. Then I'll admit that."

"In time, Merlin, in time. Morgan is studying all the old legends about it. She'll know how to unleash its power."

"Of course." He didn't try to hide his exasperation. "Arthur, how can you trust her? She never stops plotting. She wants to be queen."

"She's a member of the royal house, Merlin. Plotting is what we do. I can handle her." He grinned. "I always have."

Mark picked the stone up and tossed it in his hand a few times. Some of the dirt flaked off. "It's heavy." He looked at Arthur. "Like gold."

Percival seemed pleased that the king liked his find. "It was buried in the corner of an old ruined barn."

"How miraculous." Merlin grinned sarcastically.

"Stop it, Merlin." Arthur took the stone and handed it to Ganelin. "Here. Place it in the cabinet next to Excalibur. It will be safe here."

Ganelin took it, unlocked the wooden case and placed the stone carefully on a shelf.

Arthur beamed. "The Stone of Bran. I never really believed we'd possess it. But just look at it." Torchlight glistened on its surface. "The ceremony is in five days. I need to check with Morgan and see if she needs anything special for it."

"I'll go to her," Mark volunteered.

"She doesn't like you."

"I know." He smiled impishly. "But the stone gives us a common interest."

Before Arthur could respond to this, Merlin spoke up. "Then go, by all means."

And so with no more fuss the gathering broke up. On the way back to his tower Merlin told Nimue, "Miracles. He wants miracles. Well, it will be one if we get through this without all looking like fools."

The night before the ritual Camelot was full. People had come from all over England to see the spectacle. Knights and nobles were packed in like the poor, two and three to a bed. They grumbled; such accommodations were beneath their station and dignity. But there was nothing to be done.

Merlin was in his tower, reading. A raven perched on his shoulder; two more rested on the table in front of him. He heard someone on the stairs. There was no knock, but the door flew open rather violently. He looked up, startled; the bird on his shoulder flew away. "Guenevere. You came."

Imperious despite her short stature, dark as Arthur was fair, the queen looked around as if she'd never seen anything as strange as the contents of the room. She was approaching middle age but looked younger. "You've taken over my old apartments." Though she had been in England for years her French accent was still strong.

"You moved out." He got to his feet and added in an ironic tone, "Your Majesty."

Guenevere had her pet ape with her. It scrambled to the table and chased the two remaining ravens, which flew away in alarm. Then it tried to jump at Merlin, but its chain was too short.

Merlin scowled. "You ought to teach that beast better manners."

"I shall," she announced imperiously, "require my rooms while I am here."

"You wouldn't like them anymore, Guenevere. The bed only holds one."

She ignored the dig. "Nevertheless, you will please take your things and go."

"Arthur assigned me this tower. I'm afraid it's up to him."

The queen glared. "This is a royal order."

"Not from my royal. This isn't Corfe, Guenevere. You're a guest here, not a queen, not as far as I'm concerned."

"Merlin, I am ordering you out of these rooms."

"And when Arthur seconds that order I'll obey it."

The ape lunged at him again, and Guenevere pulled on its chain. The creature returned to her unhappily.

"This will all crumble someday, Merlin."

"Camelot is as solidly built as any castle I know."

"Not the castle. You know perfectly well what I mean. Arthur's little empire. He's not fit to rule. No one here is. And when Arthur falls, I will be waiting at Corfe to pick up what's left and reassemble it. And I promise you, there will be no room for scholarly quasi-wizards."

"Fair enough. But I can't shake the feeling you're always doing what you can to hasten that fall. Aren't you?"

She smiled a tight, patient smile. "I will have these rooms again, Merlin. Just wait."

"Perhaps. Perhaps not. As I said, it's Arthur's decision. Good-bye, Guenevere." He couldn't resist adding, to the ape, "Good-bye, Lancelot."

She froze; she turned to ice. "Do you really think there is any point throwing that in my face? Do you honestly believe you can make me feel ashamed? We could populate five counties with the bastards Arthur has fathered." She sneered. "English morality."

"Is it worse than the French kind?"

"I am living for the day when I can prove it."

With that she turned and left, pulling the reluctant ape after her. She did not bother to close the door. Merlin did so; it wouldn't do to have his ravens fly that way and get lost in the rest of the castle.

Morgan took over the Great Hall. Her people, under Mordred's supervision, arranged the torches and candles according to some prearranged but mysterious plan. A high dais filled one side of the room, with three steps leading up to it. Chairs for the audience were carefully arranged, apparently with the object of giving everyone a good sight line.

Merlin and Nimue watched the preparations for a few minutes, not certain what to make of it all. Seeing them, Morgan joined them.

"You're turning this room into a theater worthy of Aeschylus." Merlin was suitably impressed. "Is it for the Stone of Bran or yourself?"

"You expect a tragedy?" She focused on the arrangements, not on Merlin.

Nimue, standing just behind Merlin, spoke up. "The question is, what do *you* expect? Is all this really necessary?"

"Arthur wants the ceremony to be as impressive as possible," Morgan told Merlin. "This is as much a political event—a state occasion—as a religious one." Then, suddenly seeming to notice Colin, Morgan looked closely.

Nimue moved farther behind Merlin. Happily, Morgan seemed not to recognize her through the disguise. A loud noise from the dais caught Morgan's attention, and she rushed to see what had fallen.

"You ought to get out of here, Colin," Merlin whispered. "We don't want her recognizing you."

Nimue was going to protest that her disguise was too good, but she thought better of it.

Then Merlin decided to leave as well. "Wait—I'll go with you. I don't want to see how she rigs her magic tricks. That would take all the fun out of it."

The two of them left Morgan to oversee her preparations. A moment later they ran into Arthur. "Come with me," he told them. "The kitchen staff are making special treats for tonight. We get first taste."

"No thank you, Arthur." Merlin was grateful the king wasn't drinking.

"Colin, then. You have to like honey cakes—a boy your age."

"No thank you, Your Majesty."

Arthur sighed, exasperated. "You two never want to have any fun."

"Different people derive fun from different activities." Merlin was offhand. "I get mine from thinking."

"Well, come on anyway. You haven't seen the shrine yet, have you? Pastorini did a splendid job with it. Let me get a few cakes and I'll show it to you."

This, Merlin couldn't resist. They went with Arthur to the kitchen, watched him eat three fair-sized cakes then accompanied him up the spiral stone stairs to his chambers.

As always, there was a guard posted at the door. There was a large anteroom, a sitting room and a bedroom off to one side of it. Windows looked out in every direction. Beyond was the study where Excalibur and the Stone of Bran were kept among Arthur's other treasures. Jewels glistened; gold and silver glinted.

The shrine was evidently too large to fit into the shelved

cabinet that held the crown jewels. It rested on a small wooden table in one corner of the room. And it was a fine piece of work, much more so than Merlin expected and more so than anything else he'd seen in England. It was cubical, more than two feet on a side. The walls were made of burnished silver; silver filigree covered most of it, and carefully placed rubies provided bright accents. With no special lighting at all, it gleamed.

Merlin and Nimue were duly impressed and said so.

"But, Your Majesty, shouldn't it be locked securely away?"

"Of course not, Colin. There's a guard here and another at the foot of the stairs. Besides, no one would ever dare come in here without permission. No one ever has."

"My grandfather never died," Merlin said dryly, "until last year."

Arthur scowled. "This is a big day for me, Merlin. For all of us. Try not to dampen it too badly, will you?"

Merlin ignored this and bent down to inspect the shrine more closely. "This really is excellent workmanship. As good as some of the things I saw at the court of the emperor Justinian." He had also seen much better ones there, and in Rome, in Jerusalem and elsewhere, but he decided not to mention the fact. "How did Mark ever lure a craftsman this skilled to Cornwall?"

"There is money in Cornwall," Arthur said, pleased by the thought. "All Europe buys our tin for their bronze. They need it."

Merlin ran a finger along one edge of the shrine. And he found he couldn't hold his tongue after all. "And Pastorini is probably a second-rank metalsmith or he wouldn't have come here. Imagine what a really first-rate one could do, a Roman or a Byzantine."

"Nothing better than this." Arthur beamed.

Merlin decided not to press the point. There was no politic way to do so without pricking Arthur's sense of importance. But he wanted to learn what he could about the art of metalworking. "Where is Pastorini? I'd like to congratulate him."

"Back in Cornwall."

"You're not letting him attend the ceremony?"

"Tonight is for the stone, Merlin, not the shrine."

"Still, it seems unfair to deny him recognition for this."

Arthur shrugged. "He's been paid. That's the kind of recognition artists like best. I'm going down to the courtyard to exercise now. To burn off some of this energy. Would you like to do some fencing, Colin?"

"No thank you, sir."

"Oh." He seemed puzzled by the refusal. "I'll never get used to the two of you. Well, I'll see you both tonight in the Great Hall. The ceremony starts promptly at eight."

Something occurred to Merlin. "I haven't seen Percival anywhere lately. He will be there, won't he? In a place of honor?"

"His influenza has turned to pneumonia. He's infected half a dozen people already. I don't wanting him spreading his sickness any further."

"Maybe you should have him share quarters with Guenevere."

"Don't give me any ideas."

"I can't help it. Guenevere inspires them. Well, we will see you tonight, then."

"Till then." Arthur beamed, pleased they were duly impressed, and reached for a fencing saber.

"Aren't you going to show us the stone?" Nimue couldn't hide her disappointment.

Merlin could never resist needling him. "You know—the really important object?"

Arthur ignored him and addressed Colin. "Oh, that's right. You haven't seen it yet, have you?"

"No, sir."

Voice lowered, he said, "Here it is." He scowled briefly at Merlin, as if warning him not to make any impertinent comments, then turned his attention to the shrine. Slowly, carefully, almost reverently, he slid the door open on its hinges.

And there it was. The stone had been polished since Merlin last saw it. It was perfectly smooth, perfectly brilliant; a sleek glass skull, four inches high. It caught the light; dark as it was, it seemed almost to glow.

Colin's eyes widened with wonder, and even Merlin seemed impressed.

"It's beautiful, Your Majesty." Colin reached out a fingertip to touch it but Arthur caught his hand and moved it away.

"No! I don't want that finish ruined. Pastorini spent hours polishing it."

Merlin looked around the room to see if there was a light trained on it; there was none. Then he moved close and inspected it carefully. "It is beautiful, Arthur. But is it magical?"

"We'll know soon enough, won't we?"

"What miracles has it worked so far?"

"Stop it, Merlin." Carefully he closed the shrine. "The rite begins promptly at eight o'clock." He smiled and made a little salute to each of them. "Till then."

The Great Hall was crowded, even more than it had been on the day when Arthur announced the finding of the stone.

People had come from all over the country; entire noble families with their retainers wanted to see the Stone of Bran. There were nowhere near enough chairs; many people were standing. Tapestries depicting the exploits of Bran had been hung all along the wall. The court musicians played festive music. Servants circulated with cakes and ale. This was a holiday, it seemed, even if it wasn't official.

Mordred and his servants had done a fine job of creating the proper mood. The hall was mostly dark, lit only by occasional candles, except for the dais, which was ablaze with torchlight. There were two thrones set up, a large one for Arthur and a smaller one for Morgan, who was of course not merely the high priestess but Arthur's sister, a member of the royal family. Between them stood a table elaborately carved from blackthorn on which the shrine would rest.

Merlin and Nimue had a good dinner together then headed to the hall. Nimue decided to stay at the rear near one of the entrances just in case either Morgan or Mordred seemed suspicious of her. Merlin, too late to get a seat, circulated among the crowd, much more interested in seeing the people and their reactions than in the relic.

People stood talking in small groups, wondering loudly just what they were going to see. Arthur had shown the stone and its shrine to only a handful of people, and there were all sorts of rumors about its precise nature. It was a skull made of solid gold, or silver, or the alloy of both called electrum. Or it was made from wood from an ancient prophetic oak. Or it was an actual skull, encrusted with jewels and somehow endowed with miraculous powers by the god. There were skeptics, though not many, who argued that it was all hokum. Wagers were being made.

Pellenore was there, warning people, more or less at random, not about his usual dragon but about a malevolent water sprite. Merlin avoided him quite carefully and ambled about the hall, eavesdropping, pleased that not everyone had been taken in.

When he found Nimue, he told her so. "All this flummery . . . I can't tell you how it disgusts me."

"Yes, you can." Nimue was wry. "And you have, several dozen times."

"You have an annoying habit of being contrary, Colin."

She smiled sweetly. "I can't imagine who I got it from."

Just at that moment Mordred walked by and nodded at the two of them. For an instant he seemed to recognize Nimue; then he seemed to think better of it, shrugged and kept moving.

"He's going to realize who I am sooner or later. He has to."

"Do you think so? I don't have the impression he's any brighter than he needs to be."

"All he'd have to do is drop a suggestion to his mother, and . . ."

"I'd worry about her, not him." Merlin looked to the entrance where Morgan and Arthur would be coming in. There was no sign of them. "Morgan and her boy don't come here often. After this nonsense is over, I'm sure they'll be going back to their own castle."

She glanced around nervously. "I hope you're right."

Mark of Cornwall joined them, in a festive mood. "Have you tried the honey cakes? They're wonderful."

"I'm dieting," Merlin said irritably. "How is Percival? He should be here."

"His pneumonia is getting worse."

"I'll go and see him after the ceremony. I am the court physician, after all."

"He asked for a doctor who believes in the gods. He says someone like you could never cure him."

"Some things," Merlin said dryly, "aren't curable."

Nimue smiled. "Merlin has an annoying habit of being contrary. Have you ever noticed, Mark?"

"Everyone has." He scanned the crowd. "There's Britomart. I have to talk to her about a new drill I want to introduce."

"I'm going to get as close to the dais as I can, Mark. Why don't you join me there?"

Mark nodded, then shouted, "Brit!" and disappeared quickly into the crowd.

A moment later the musicians played a fanfare and then a slow, solemn march. Servants extinguished some of the lights, as they had at the council. The crowd fell nearly silent. Then slowly, majestically, Arthur and his sister came in.

They were dressed in their best court finery, Arthur in white robes trimmed with gold and Morgan in black ones with silver trim. They climbed slowly to the dais and stood in front of their respective thrones.

Ganelin and Borolet stood at attention just beside the platform. Arthur nodded to Borolet, and the squire left quickly, presumably to fetch the shrine. Merlin elbowed his way through the crowd, trying to get closer, without much success. He found himself standing next to Britomart. "Mark is looking for you."

"I know. I'm avoiding him."

Suddenly Guenevere swept into the hall, followed closely by Lancelot and several lesser retainers. She went

directly to the dais and began to climb the steps to it, clearly
expecting to have a place there. Ganelin blocked her way.
There was an exchange of words; Merlin couldn't quite
hear what was being said, but it was fairly plain she wanted
to take her place on the second throne. At least she had
decorum enough not to raise her voice.

Lancelot, who was built like an athlete, slender and fit,
ten years younger than the queen, moved past her to confront the squire.

Arthur got quickly to his feet to join his squire and his
wife. Morgan did not budge. There were more words. Then
Arthur signaled that a third chair should be brought for the
queen. A servant brought one, and Ganelin placed it carefully on the other side of Arthur's throne from Morgan. The
queen, trying without success to not look slighted, walked
slowly to her makeshift throne and sat. Lancelot turned, descended the steps and disappeared into the audience.

Pellenore, evidently in a great hurry, pushed his way past
Merlin and Britomart and disappeared into the crowd as
well. Merlin looked around for Mark, but there was no sign
of him.

Several moments passed. Arthur bent down and whispered something to Ganelin, who looked around the hall,
evidently worried. Morgan sat perfectly still, staring directly ahead. The crowd began to grow restless; they started
to talk and move about. When the noise level began to be
quite noticeable, Morgan frowned; this was not seemly behavior at a sacred rite. Where was Borolet? Merlin wondered why, with all her careful preparations, Morgan hadn't
made provision for the shrine to be brought more quickly,
or better yet to have it brought before the ceremony began.

More time passed. More people ignored the royals on the

dais and talked, drank, ate or whatever. Merlin and Brit
made their way to the platform. Arthur bent down and told
Ganelin, "Go and see what's holding him up."

Merlin was enjoying it all. He whispered to Britomart,
"Maybe it will transport itself here miraculously."

"Something's wrong, Merlin. For once why don't you
keep your thoughts to yourself."

"Yes, ma'am."

Borolet's delay was now quite pointed, quite unmistakable. No one could have failed to realize things were
not going as planned. The assembled audience was getting
more and more restless. Several people took extinguished
torches and relit them from the ones that were still burning.
A servant came and told Arthur the cakes were almost gone.

Then Ganelin rushed back into the hall and climbed to
the dais. He was pale and agitated. He whispered something
to Arthur, who turned pale as well. The king looked around
the hall and called out, "Mark? Where is Mark of Cornwall?"

There was no response. Arthur looked uncharacteristically grave. He gestured to Merlin and said, "Come with
us." The three men left the Great Hall quickly.

Camelot's halls were nearly deserted; only servants
came and went, each bowing deferentially as the king
passed. In a matter of moments the little party reached the
foot of the stairs to Arthur's chambers.

The guard who had been stationed there lay on the floor.
Merlin rushed to him and did a quick examination. "He's
unconscious, not dead."

They climbed quickly. The guard at the top, outside the
king's rooms, had been knocked unconscious, too.

"In here," said Ganelin, his voice shaking. He led them
quickly through the outer chambers.

Blood covered the floor in the study. In the center of a large pool of it lay Borolet's body. He had been hacked to pieces, evidently with a broadsword. The silver shrine was gone. The Stone of Bran was gone. And so was Excalibur.

TWO

MERLIN TAKES CHARGE

They identified the body from the hair color and the shreds of clothing.

Of course the ceremony was called off. How could it not be? Arthur, trying not to look ill, mounted the dais in the Great Hall and moved to the front of it. He ignored both Morgan and Guenevere. The crowd, noticing something odd in his manner, quieted without him asking them to. He announced softly that the ritual would be postponed, perhaps indefinitely. "Please, all of you, return to your rooms."

And slowly the audience dispersed. Only Arthur and his close advisors remained.

Merlin approached him and put a hand on his arm. "Arthur, you should have asked them to stay here."

Seemingly dazed, Arthur gaped at him. "Why, Merlin? Why, for heaven's sake?"

"Until we could take account of who's here and who isn't. Now there's no way we'll ever know for certain."

"Does it matter?"

"There's been a murder, Arthur. We have to find who did it."

Sadly, the king said, "I suppose you're right. That poor boy. He was an excellent young man, Merlin. He and his brother. The best, the most promising I have. Had."

Ganelin had been listening; he looked even more stunned than the king. "Thank you for saying so, Your Majesty. That would have meant a lot to him."

They were now nearly alone in the hall, Arthur, Merlin, Mark, Britomart, Nimue and Ganelin. Nimue stood back from the others, not knowing what to say or do. All of them watched Arthur, waiting for some indication of what he was thinking and feeling.

Mark moved close to the king, looking grave. "We'll find him. We'll find the assassin."

"Will we?" Arthur muttered. It was not so much a question as a resigned statement.

Merlin had never seen his king look so lost. "Arthur, I—"

"I want to be alone. All of you, please leave me. I want to take a walk and think."

Britomart spoke for the first time. "Are you certain that's a wise idea, Arthur? There's a killer loose in Camelot."

"He got what he wanted. He got the shrine and the sword and the crystal skull. He killed the boy with my sword. What more could he want?"

"We don't know why the killer did what he did. He could have had any motive at all."

"Brit is right, Arthur." Merlin forced himself to keep his voice calm and steady. "There are a dozen reasons why this might have been done. Out of greed, for political advantage, out of hatred or jealousy of you . . . Stay inside. Stay in your rooms, guarded."

Mark added, "I can have guards posted immediately. We have to keep you safe. If we should lose you . . ." He let the thought trail off unfinished.

Arthur looked from one of them to the next. "Come walk with me, then. I need fresh air. I need the night."

"It's getting cold outside, Arthur." Brit took a step toward him then seemed to think better of it. "Stay here where it's warm."

"Do you suppose it's warm where Borolet is?"

"Let us get swords, then." Mark spoke forcefully. "Let me call guards. I won't have you wandering around alone."

"All right. Get them." He looked to the rest of them as Mark went. "I never thought I'd need guards in my own castle. In my wildest imaginings I never thought such a thing."

Britomart and Ganelin said they were going to their rooms to get weapons, leaving Merlin and Nimue with the king.

Suddenly, Arthur turned animated. He rushed to the nearest wall, took a torch and began going about the room, lighting the ones that had been extinguished. "We want light. What happened, happened in darkness. With more light the boy would be alive."

"Arthur, stop it!" Merlin caught him by the arm. "That isn't so and you know it."

He pulled free violently. "Let me go! I want light in here!"

Merlin stood back, alarmed, and let the king go on lighting the room. By the time the others got back it was ablaze with torchlight. Lit, it seemed vast and much more empty than it did in near-darkness.

Mark returned with a dozen soldiers; he left them by the door and rejoined Merlin.

"I'm worried, Mark." He kept his voice low. "This isn't

at all like Arthur. We've seen him in crisis before. He's lost battles, lost whole regiments and not acted like this."

"That was out in the world." Mark studied the king. "Not in his home. The dead were anonymous, not his squire."

Suddenly Arthur turned to them. "Let's go."

Six of the soldiers took the lead. Arthur, Merlin and the others followed, trailed by the remaining guards. The party moved quickly through Camelot's winding corridors. There was no talking.

The halls were filled with people. Somehow news of the murder had leaked out; presumably, one of the guards had said something. Everyone was buzzing about it, speculating, gossiping. They stood, some in small groups, some in larger ones, watching the king's progress. No one seemed to take it as reassuring.

From nowhere Pellenore came galloping down a hallway, directly at the king. "Beware, Arthur, beware!"

Arthur's party stopped and waited for him to reach them. He had, to appearances, been running all over Camelot; there was sweat on his forehead, and his clothes were soaked with it. Arthur caught him by the shoulder and made him stand still. "What the devil is wrong with you? For once, Pellenore, try and act like a normal man."

"Normal?" The old man staggered a bit and Arthur steadied him. "How can anyone behave normally? Don't you know what's happened?"

"I know only too well. I—"

"The beasts, Arthur, the beasts. They've begun to kill. If we don't vanquish them, we'll all be dead before long."

Merlin planted himself in front of the mad old man. "We'll all be dead eventually anyway, Pellenore. Let the beasts do what they will."

"No! I have to stop them. No one else can. And no one

will believe me." With that he drew his sword and sped off down the corridor.

For a moment everyone stood looking at one another, unsure what to say or how to react. Finally Nimue spoke up. "Poor old man."

"Poor old man, nothing," Mark said. "I often think he's only pretending to be mad, and now I'm sure of it. How else could he know about the death tonight?"

"Everyone knows." Merlin sounded tired; he wanted all this to end.

Arthur got between them. "Come. We're on our way outside, remember?"

At the main entrance two other guards stood on duty. Mark had a quick word with them and left two more of the cohort with them for extra security.

The courtyard, unlike the castle, was quite empty. The night was cold, unseasonably so, and no one had thought to bring winter clothing. There were heavy clouds; the moon was a bright pale patch through them. Merlin felt a drop of rain and looked up; the sky was ominous. "Winter weather," he muttered. "Too soon."

One of the guards from the front gate said to Mark, "She hasn't left yet, sir, if that's who you're looking for."

"She?"

"The queen. Her party is assembling at the back of the castle, by the stables."

"The queen?!" Merlin shouted. "We mustn't let her leave."

Sparked into action, Mark took two men and went to look. He came back quickly and walked straight to the king. "She's leaving, Arthur. She, Lancelot, all their servants. The horses are being loaded now."

Loudly, Merlin said again, "She mustn't. Arthur, you

can't allow her to go. Not till I've had time to question her and her people about the killing."

"Guenevere is a vindictive, loveless woman, Merlin. But I wouldn't like to think she's behind this."

"Don't be naïve, Arthur. She—" He was going to remind the king how much his wife hated him, but he caught himself. "If not she herself, then Lancelot or one of her servants. Any of them could have a hand in this."

Sounding even more sad than before, Arthur told him, "You're right, I suppose. Let's go and talk to her."

Mark spoke up. "I'll have the guards close all the gates. They won't get out."

At the rear of Camelot, Guenevere was overseeing preparations for the journey home. Her carriage, small but ornate, was harnessed to four black horses. Packhorses were being loaded. Two dozen servants worked busily. One carried an unfurled banner bearing the queen's arms.

She herself stood on the carriage's step, watching, giving orders, making certain everything was done to her satisfaction. Her ape perched on her shoulder and cried, apparently unhappy to be in the cold. There were torches; the rest of the courtyard was in darkness made deeper by the clouds.

"James," she said loudly to one of the servants, "get me another cloak."

Lancelot, ever the chivalrous gallant, took his own off and wrapped it around her shoulders. The ape jumped onto his back.

"Guenevere!" Arthur tried to resume a tone of command, not quite convincingly. "I must ask you to remain here for the time being."

"Why, Arthur! How nice of you to come see me off." She was the picture of sweet composure.

A sprinkle of large, heavy drops of rain came and went

quickly. Merlin looked to the sky again. There would be a storm. Guenevere looked skyward as well. "I wish I had time to talk, but we really must be on the road before the rain comes."

"Did you hear me? You are not to leave."

She let out a girlish laugh. "Is that authority you're trying to convey? You lost the right to talk to me that way years ago. Arthur, I have to return to Corfe. I have a castle of my own to tend to, remember?"

"The guards will not let you out of the courtyard, Guenevere. Send your people back to their rooms."

"But, Arthur." She feigned innocence well; she was every inch the French coquette. "Camelot is so crowded."

"Even so."

Mark took a step forward. "Your Majesty must know how unwise it is to travel by night. There are bandits—cutthroats."

"Then perhaps you'll be good enough to provide me with guards." She lowered her eyes. "My poor throat is so delicate."

Before Mark could respond to her irony, Lancelot stepped forward from among the servants where he'd been seeing to his horse's saddle. "We can handle any brigands who might dare attack the queen's party."

Then for the first time Arthur spoke like a king, with a sense of command in his voice. "Your swordsmanship is precisely the issue, Lancelot. Guenevere, you are not to leave. This is an order." He smiled. "Departure will not be permitted."

"Don't be a fool, Arthur. There are three times more people than the castle can hold. Food is running out already."

He turned to Mark and ordered him pointedly to post

more soldiers. Then to the queen he said, "Go back to your rooms, Guenevere. If you don't go now, and voluntarily, you will do it under guard."

Lancelot stepped toward him, his hand on his sword, obviously angry. Two of Arthur's men drew their own swords, as did Mark, Britomart and Ganelin.

Guenevere stepped serenely between them and put a hand on Lancelot's arm. Servants scrambled to get behind one another. "You would never dare hold us prisoner, Arthur," Lancelot snarled.

"Do you think I'm afraid of the scandal? If I can weather the gossip about you bellying the queen, I can certainly weather this."

Looking more than mildly alarmed, Lancelot and Guenevere stepped into the carriage and talked hastily. A moment later she emerged, smiling lightly, and told her husband she would remain for another day, no more. "But I warn you, Arthur, we are to be treated as guests, not prisoners."

"Is that a threat?"

"Let us say it is a request. A firm request."

Arthur turned to Britomart. "Take two of the men. Go and spread word that the queen will remain in residence."

Smirking, Britomart asked him, "As a guest?"

"As a guest." Glancing at the queen he added, "A royal guest."

Merlin leaned close to Nimue and whispered, "A royal pain would be more like it."

The rain began to come down steadily. Mixed with it were occasional particles of ice. It stung faces and hands.

Arthur watched as his wife, her lover and their servants were herded back into the castle by his soldiers. To Mark he

said, "I should have let her go. This storm will get bad.
She'd never have gotten far in it, and I'd have had the pleasure of hearing her ask for shelter."

"Would you have given it?"

"Not until she begged or became waterlogged."

A moment later everyone went back inside. Arthur asked
them all to meet in Merlin's rooms the next morning, to discuss what had happened that night and plan how to find the
assassin. "I won't rest till we find him. Borolet must be
avenged."

"Suppose it was the assassin who you just sent back into
your castle?" Merlin asked.

It caught Arthur off guard. In fact it seemed an impossible thought for him to confront. "Would that be worse than
letting her go free?"

"She was trying to leave for a reason. To leave by dark of
night," he added emphatically. "And without saying a word
to you or anyone else. Is it wrong of me to find that suspicious?"

"You find everything Guenevere does suspicious."

"Only because it is."

"I'm going to bed, Merlin. I need a good night's rest. We
all do." To everyone he announced, "We'll meet after breakfast. In Merlin's quarters."

After midnight the rain became heavy. Then a cold wave
blew down from the north and turned it to ice and snow.

Like all castles Camelot was full of drafts. Cold air
rushed through the halls and chambers, wailing mournfully
like an invasion of ghosts. Tapestries blew in it; rickety old
furniture wobbled noisily.

In his bedchamber Merlin woke, freezing. He got up,

threw four logs on the fire, which gave the only light in the room, then opened a huge old wooden chest and rummaged about till he found a coverlet made of wolf hides. It was thick and warm, and he wrapped it around himself as he walked back to the bed.

But the wind was howling too loudly for him to get back to sleep easily. He got up again, went and stood by the fire, rubbed his hands together and wondered aloud why people ever chose to live in places where the weather got this un-pleasant.

There came a soft knock at the door. He opened it to find Nimue, wrapped in a blanket and shivering. "I'm sorry to wake you, Merlin."

"You didn't."

"The fire in my room went out and I don't have any tin-der to relight it."

"Come in. Mine is burning high and hot."

"Thanks." She entered hurriedly. "Say what you will about Morgan, she always keeps her castle warm."

"That's a good trick. How does she manage it?"

"Only she and the gods know."

"Let me get us some wine." He opened a cabinet and took out a bottle and two cups. "Fire only warms the out-side."

Nimue took the wine gratefully. "I hate winter."

"And it's not even here yet. This is only a foretaste. I hope it doesn't mean winter itself, when it gets here, will be worse."

"What an awful thought." She drank deeply.

"It must be my age, but every year I have a harder time believing spring will actually come."

Nimue drained her cup then walked to the window. "Where would you live, given the choice?"

"I don't know. Alexandria is warm but noisy. There's something wrong with every place, I suppose."

"I hate winter." She looked outside.

"You might stop saying so."

Camelot sat atop the highest hill for miles around. There was a wide, wonderful view of the surrounding hills and forests, all white from the weather. And there were breaks in the clouds though it was still snowing. The moonlit world was ghostly.

Then something caught her eye. "Merlin, look."

Fifty feet away from them rose Camelot's tallest tower, the one where the king resided. Two windows looked from his bedchamber out over the castle and beyond. And both windows were lit brightly. The figure of the king was unmistakable in one of them.

The sight startled Merlin. But he told her, "He's restless, that's all. You saw how the murder affected him."

"Yes."

Then another figure appeared beside him, male, shorter than he. For a moment they stood side by side. Then they embraced.

Seeing it made Merlin uncomfortable. "I have a flint and some wood shavings. Let's see if we can't get your fire re-lit."

Nimue lingered at the window for a moment, fascinated. She watched as the two figures pulled apart and the light went out. Then she went with Merlin. Her room was just below his in the tower, but her windows faced the opposite direction. He was glad of that. When he managed to reignite the fire, he said good night and went back up to his own chambers.

The room was warmer now. He put another log on the fire, hoping the warmth would last, got into bed and wrapped himself in wolf fur. But sleep would not come. Too much was happening. Too much that was unexpected and made no sense.

Early the next morning they began to arrive at Merlin's chambers.

The snow had stopped, but occasional flakes still danced in the air, glinting in the grey diffuse light from a heavy cloud deck.

Most of the windows in Camelot were either unglazed or permanently sealed shut with glass. The glass was crude, not at all smooth or clear, which made windows inconvenient. But Merlin had contrived to have the window in his study hinged, for the ravens. They would come and peck at it to be let in or out. Sometimes the hinge would stick and the window would have to be forced, and sometimes as a result the glass would crack and need replacing. But in weather like this he was glad he'd installed the hinge.

First thing that morning all three of the birds were outside the window, tapping earnestly. He let them in and fed them some stale bread crumbs. Then they gathered near the fireplace, though not too close.

Mark arrived first. He gave every indication of having slept well and soundly despite the night's events and the pervasive chill. "Good morning, Merlin."

"It is not a good morning. This is only the beginning of November. It's way too early in the season for this kind of weather."

Mark beamed. "I love the cold."

"You're a dangerously unbalanced man."

"Relax, Merlin. It'll warm up again."

"Maybe the weather will. I'm not at all certain that I

will myself. Cold has a way of settling deep in my bones. When that happens nothing warms me up but soaking in a hot tub of water for a long time, which I find equally unpleasant."

Mark pulled up a stool and sat with his legs up on the table. "You're getting old."

"Arthur always tells me I was born old."

"He has a point." For the first time he noticed the ravens, huddled a few feet from the fire. "You're still keeping those damned birds."

Merlin scowled. "Colin is supposed to bring some warm spiced wine. That'll help warm us up."

"Wine always helps everything."

"You're one of Arthur's men, all right."

As if on cue the door opened and Nimue came in, carrying a large pot of steaming spiced wine. "Good morning. Let's put this near the fire before it gets cold."

Mark sprang to his feet. "Not till I get a cupful for myself."

The ravens scuttled away, watching Nimue warily. There was an iron hook at the fireplace. She hung the wine pot then walked to the window. "Look at it out there. The world has turned white and pure."

"The world," Merlin said carefully and pointedly, "has not been pure since Pandora opened her box."

"Who?" Mark looked into is cup. "There's too much cardamom in this. Who on earth is Pandora?"

"A myth. Never mind."

Britomart knocked and came in. "Morning, everyone."

"I'm glad you didn't say *good* morning," Merlin grumped.

"I just met Pellenore in the hall as I was coming here. Even he's unhappy about the cold. He says his dragons have gone into hibernation, like bears." She smiled. "So now he doesn't know what to do with himself. Is Ganelin coming? And Arthur?"

Nimue stirred the pot. "They should be here soon. Would you like some hot wine?"

"Please. Anything warm."

At the window Merlin looked down to the courtyard. There was some activity. It took him a few seconds to realize Morgan and Mordred were there with their servants. Apparently, they were trying to leave, exactly as Guenevere had the night before. But the guards had been doubled and given strict orders. No one, not even the high priestess, was going to get out of Camelot today.

He turned to the others. "It looks as if another of our suspects is trying to get away." He explained what was going on below.

Brit swirled the wine in her cup then tasted it. "Morgan can't be a suspect, can she? I mean, she was there in plain sight the whole time—on the dais."

"But Mordred wasn't," Nimue volunteered. "I saw him leave the hall just after his mother took her seat."

"Maybe he had to use the privy, Colin." Mark got up and refilled his cup. "I did."

"And did you see him there?" Merlin asked.

"Don't be absurd. You know how many loos there are in Camelot."

"I've never actually counted."

Brit took a seat across the table from Mark. "I wish we didn't have to deal with this. I wish . . . I don't know . . . I guess I wish Borolet was still alive."

Merlin crossed to the fireplace and got wine. "He was in training to be a knight. That more or less precludes a natural death for most people."

"I'm still here." She took a long swallow of wine. "There's not enough cardamom in this."

There was the sound of footsteps on the stairs outside. Whoever it was was walking slowly and heavily. Then the door opened and Arthur came in. He looked as if he hadn't slept; he was pale and drawn, and there was nothing like his usual energy. "Morning, everyone. Cold day."

"Shrewd observation, Arthur."

"Why don't you save the sarcasm for once, Merlin? I've had a terrible night."

Merlin and Nimue exchanged glances; it was tempting to comment on what they'd seen at his window, but they both kept tactfully quiet about it. She asked Arthur, "Is Ganelin coming?"

"Yes. I want him here. But he may be late. I think he had an even worse night than I did. What happened is only beginning to sink in for him."

Suddenly, Merlin was in his element. "He has lost not merely his brother but his twin. That must be devastating for him. Philosophers have theorized what accounts for twin births. The usual explanation is that they are halves of a whole, and that neither is ever quite complete without the other. If Ganelin is feeling that—"

"Whatever he's feeling can't be pleasant, Merlin." Arthur avoided looking at him. "The question is, who could have wanted the shrine and the stone badly enough to kill Borolet so horribly to get them?" He looked around the room hoping someone would answer, but they were all watching him and waiting for him to go on. "Do any of you have any ideas?"

No one else spoke up, so Nimue did. "I think we all know who the suspects are, sir. At least the obvious ones."

"And who are they, Colin?"

She hesitated. "Well . . . Guenevere and Morgan."

"My wife and my sister." His voice broke. "No, each is a monster in her way but I can't believe that of either of them." Then he brightened slightly. "They were both there in the Great Hall, in front of half the nobles in England. How could either of them—"

"They weren't alone, Arthur." Britomart got to her feet and began pacing. "They have servants. Friends. Devotees. I saw Lancelot leave the hall myself. Other people saw Mordred go."

"Mordred? That spindly, watery, spidery bas— nephew of mine? He could barely hold a broadsword like Excalibur let alone wield it properly."

"What about Lancelot, then?" Mark looked into his empty cup, thought about getting more wine then put the cup on the table instead. "I mean, he's dense and everyone knows it. But this was hardly a crime that required much thought."

Arthur was looking more and more out of his depth. "I'll ask Guenevere about it."

"She'll defend him." Merlin was surpassingly firm. "She'll never admit her stud knight could have done this. Especially if she told him to."

"Even so. I'll talk to her. What else can I do?"

"While you're at it, then, ask her why she tried to sneak away under cover of darkness. Even if she wanted to leave, the sensible thing would have been to go by daylight and in better weather."

The king fell silent. After a long pause he said, "I want you to find this killer, this assassin, by Midwinter Court. I want to announce then that he's been brought to justice. Do what you need to do to find him."

"I want to help." Without anyone noticing, Ganelin had

slipped into the room. He stood pressed against the door, looking sad and frightened.

"Ganelin." Merlin smiled. "Come in and sit. Let Colin give you some warmed wine."

"No thank you, sir. But I heard what you said about my losing not just my brother but my other half, my other self. That is so true. I can't remember a time when he was not there, beside me. My memories stretch all the way back to the cradle and our mother, Anna, and there was always Borolet next to me, warming me, comforting me with his presence. Last night the world seemed completely empty to me. If King Arthur"—he nodded in his direction—"had not held me and calmed me, I would have gone mad."

So it was Ganelin they had seen in Arthur's window. Nimue and Merlin exchanged glances but kept silent.

"So you see," the squire went on, "it's important to me to help find the one who did this . . . this awful thing. Please, let me help."

Arthur stood up and gestured to his seat; Ganelin obediently sat down.

"I can help, really I can. I can find out things none of you can."

Mark wanted to laugh; it showed in his face. Happily, Ganelin didn't notice. "You're a boy. A squire, not even a knight. What can you do that we can't?"

"I know people who would never talk to any of you. Not willingly, anyway."

"Who?" This time he did laugh. "The other boys who carry our spears?"

Softly, Ganelin said, "The servants." He looked around. Now no one was laughing. "We were practically raised by them. Our mother pledged us to the king's service when we were ten. The servants raised us, taught us court protocol—taught us everything. We learned who matters and who doesn't. Who to obey promptly and who we could safely ignore. The servants know everything that happens in the castle. If there are alibis, they are the ones who can corroborate them or give them the lie."

No one was at all certain how to respond to this. But it made perfect sense.

Ganelin turned to Merlin. "Please, let me help. They trust me; I'm practically one of them myself. I want to help bring my brother's killer to justice."

Arthur looked at Merlin, who looked back. Neither of them could think of a reason to keep Ganelin out of the investigation. Arthur put a hand on the boy's shoulder. "Yes, of course we want you to help. But you must remember, Ganelin, you have other duties as well. You are still my squire."

"I won't neglect my duties, sir."

"And you must promise to share everything you learn with Merlin, and to do so immediately. He is in charge of this investigation." He looked around the table. "That goes for the rest of you, too."

There was a general murmur, though neither Britomart nor Mark seemed happy about it.

"Promise me, all of you."

They did so, one at a time.

"I don't want any of you working alone. Whoever did this is vicious, maybe even mad."

"Like Pellenore?" Brit said, voicing her suspicion.

"Pellenore?" Arthur frowned, obviously not liking the thought. "He's a harmless old fool."

"Is there such a thing as a harmless fool? In the town

where I grew up there was a fool, a complete imbecile, who used to go wild when he saw the gleam of precious metal. How do we know Pellenore isn't the same?"

"He's been here for years, Brit. We'd have noticed by now."

"There isn't much point to us investigating if you're going to reject possibilities out of hand, Arthur."

He took a deep breath. "I know it."

"Pellenore left the Great Hall before the ceremony got under way. He was galloping about the castle as usual, screaming about bogeymen. And in his day he was a warrior. He knows how to handle a broadsword."

"Why not let us investigate," Merlin interjected, "and bring our results to you? We could spend the whole day spinning theories. But we need facts."

Arthur took a deep breath. "I want all of you to be careful. This is a killer, after all, and possibly a madman. Don't let anyone know you're investigating."

"When we start asking questions," Brit said, "they'll know."

"We must never ask directly what we want to know." Merlin was in teacher mode. "We must be clever. Indirect. We must learn what we want slyly, carefully."

Arthur turned thoughtful. "Exactly. And—suppose this. Suppose I make an announcement that Mark is conducting an official investigation in my name? He will conduct one for show, and that will leave the rest of you to do the real work."

"Am I in, then?" Ganelin sounded quite unsure of himself.

"Yes, Ganelin. You are one of us." Merlin smiled. "And I'm certain you'll be a great help."

"Good. I mean, thank you. If I might say something . . . ?"

"By all means, Ganelin." One of the ravens flapped to Merlin's shoulder, and he stroked its head.

"Well, sir, it seems to me you're making some assumptions that might not be valid."

Mark laughed. "Oh really? What are they?"

"Be quiet, Mark." Brit shushed him impatiently.

"Well . . ." Ganelin looked uncertainly around the room. "You're assuming the criminal must have been after the skull and the shrine and the king's sword out of greed. Is that necessarily so? And you're assuming it must be someone who left the Great Hall."

"He can hardly have committed the crime while he was still there." Mark laughed again. Merlin crossed the room to him and took the wine cup firmly, pointedly, out of his hand.

"No, sir," Ganelin went on. "He—or she—couldn't. But there were certainly people who simply never went to the hall."

Everyone looked at one another, startled and abashed that it hadn't occurred to them.

"I mean, unless someone was keeping a roll of who attended, that is."

"You're right, Gan." Brit seemed pleased he had thought of it. "Everyone who matters—everyone who is anyone— was at the hall. We think. But—"

"It's the kind of thing the servants will know, if anyone does. As I said, I can be a help to you all."

"I don't think there's any doubt about that at all." Arthur glared at Mark, warning him not to make any sarcastic comments. Then he took another cup of wine and drained it in one swallow. "I have to go. I have to preside at court today. There are sure to be peasants squabbling over livestock. I have such important matters to judge."

They all bade him good morning, and he left. Mark took his wine cup again. Everyone in the room turned to Merlin.

"It seems we have several clear suspects." Ticking them off on his fingers, he went on. "Morgan and her party, especially Mordred. Guenevere and hers, particularly Lancelot. Pellenore. But there must have been others who left the hall before Borolet was—before the crime happened. And as Ganelin rightly suggested, there may be key people who simply avoided the ceremony. We need to find out who."

Nimue had been listening, taking everything in. "I'm fairly certain I saw Gawain heading for an exit."

"Good observation. Did anyone else notice anything?"

"That damned Frenchman, Accolon. He left." Mark had never trusted him.

"Good. And anyone else?"

They stared at one another blankly.

"I think we have to assume there must be one or two more." He turned to Ganelin. "Can you ask among the servants, then, and see if they can tell us where any of the suspects were? And whether there are any others?"

"Of course. I'll be happy to. Give me a day or two, all right?"

"That will be fine. Meanwhile, the rest of us can begin to question the various possible culprits. Obliquely, indirectly. We don't want anyone to know we're investigating."

"People will guess." Mark sounded impatient with it all. "A crime has been committed at Camelot. At the seat of government. That makes it much more serious than any ordinary murder. Whatever the motive, this strikes at the heart of England's government and stability. We must find the assassin and bring him to justice as quickly as possible."

"Of course, Mark." Brit was finding him annoying. "I'm sure we all share those concerns. They must have occurred to each of us. Until we find the killer, Arthur himself is in danger, and so is everyone else at court."

Mark started to bicker with her, but Merlin got between them and dismissed the little council. "Thank you all for coming. I'm sure Arthur is grateful to have us working together." He hoped his point wasn't lost on Mark. Then he gestured to the window. "We're lucky in one way, at least. Look—more snow. From the look of the black clouds in the west, another storm is coming, possibly worse than the one last night. If I'm right, no one will be leaving Camelot for at least a few more days."

"Splendid." Mark slammed his cup down on the table and got to his feet. "More of this damned overcrowding. I'm sharing my quarters with two elderly knights from Dover. They smell of flounder."

"It is a gift, Mark. Let us take it and use it to our advantage."

Mark scowled and stomped out the door. For the hundredth time Merlin found himself wishing Arthur's knights wouldn't drink so heavily. He asked Brit if she had anything more to add, but she said no and left. To Nimue, she said, "Thanks for the wine, Colin." She said it with a wink, and Nimue looked at Merlin as if to repeat, *She knows about me*.

Ganelin lingered by the door. He seemed to be screwing up his courage. "May I ask you something, Merlin?"

"Yes, of course."

"Well, why can't you just use your magic powers to divine who did the—who—who did that to my brother?"

Merlin rolled his eyes skyward. "I am not a wizard, a magician, a sorcerer, a shaman, a warlock or anything else of that sort. When am I ever going to convince people of that?"

"All the knights say you are. They say for anyone to be as wise as you—to know as much as you do about so many things—is unnatural. It could only come from something dark, something hidden."

"The knights are fools, most of them. And drunken fools at that. What they don't understand, they make mysterious. But reason—understanding—is the key to every mystery. Even your brother's death. You'll see."

"I—I'm sorry. I didn't mean to offend you."

"You didn't. But the next time the knights start spreading rubbish about me, you tell them the truth, all right?"

"Yes, sir. Thank you again, sir, for letting me join the hunt." And he left.

Nimue took a seat at the table and unrolled an old scroll. Merlin turned toward the window. "The snow's coming down more heavily already. This will get bad. I don't know whether to be pleased."

"Maybe you can use you magic powers to stop it."

"Shut up and study your Greek."

"Yes, sir."

As Merlin expected, the storm got bad. Waves of ice fell, coating everything. Soon all of Camelot was encased in it. When he looked out his window, Merlin could see it glistening; it was almost blinding in the early light. Then came snow, more and more of it. At times it fell so quickly it was not possible to see more than a few feet ahead. Within two days there was nearly a foot of it. The world was soft, white and horribly cold.

It was sufficiently early in the season that the servants had only just begun to prepare the castle for winter. They went to work energetically, hanging tapestries, distributing extra firewood and blankets, plugging up the sources of the worst drafts.

Because of the ice and the frozen ground it was not possible to bury Borolet. Merlin saw that his remains were placed in the deepest, coldest storeroom in the castle basement, not far from some unoccupied dungeons. With luck they would keep there till the ground thawed.

By evening of the third day Arthur and Merlin began to realize that food was running low. Winter supplies had not yet been laid in. Arthur ordered rationing, which of course made the castle's occupants even edgier than they'd been.

Just before dusk that day Guenevere tried to leave again. Merlin warned her she wouldn't get far, but she was determined.

"Arthur won't permit it, Guenevere. The gates are locked."

"My men will deal with the guards."

"There is no point."

"I am the queen. That gives it point."

Her people met in the stables, saddled the horses and loaded the pack animals with what provisions they could collect.

But the party was not halfway across the courtyard when the horses began to lose their footing and panicked. One of them slipped, fell and broke its leg. It whinnied horribly with the pain, trying to get up; but the more it struggled, the greater its agony. Finally, Lancelot got a large knife, stood over it and cut its throat. The animal's blood steamed in the cold air and turned the snow on the ground bright red. It kicked fiercely, but its energy soon drained away and it was still.

Merlin watched it all from his window. And it seemed to him that Lancelot had taken unnatural relish in what he'd done. The knights were all trained to kill, and they all seemed to enjoy it, or rather the prospect of it. Lancelot seemed born to it.

A while later Arthur asked Merlin to join him as he visited the queen in her chambers. She had had a suite of three rooms assigned to her. Blankets were spread on the floor for servants; two young men snoozed, undisturbed by the people around them. In one corner several packs were stacked, apparently unopened.

She was dictating a letter as they arrived. Arthur asked who she was writing to and what about. She was cold. "Private correspondence is exactly that—private."

Arthur looked around. "Privacy? You're joking."

Her face was stone. She said nothing but took the letter and waved her secretary away.

"Guenevere, I must ask that you not try to leave again until weather conditions improve. My knights and the castle staff are busy enough dealing with all this. There's no reason they should have to enforce common sense."

Her ape scampered into the room and jumped to her lap. Then it turned to Arthur and Merlin and let out a sinister hiss.

"How can you keep a creature as disagreeable as that? It's a little fiend."

"That is no way to talk about my pet, Arthur." She stroked the ape's head and it nuzzled her.

"A fine pet. Why not simply get a cobra?"

"We tried to leave because we are miserable. Sleeping on floors, rationing food . . . A fit ruler would have planned for this."

"You think it's possible to control the weather?"

"No, as I said I think you should plan for it."

One of her servants rummaged through one of the packs

in the corner. Merlin watched as the young man took out a piece of cheese and ate it happily. "Arthur, look."

Taking in the scene, Arthur turned on Guenevere and bellowed, "Food?! This is your idea of roughing it? Guenevere, you are the most staggeringly dishonest human being I have ever known. It's no wonder you shattered your wedding vows."

"Lower your voice, husband. Remember your royal dignity, will you?"

"I want to talk to Lancelot."

She was offhand. "I'm afraid I don't know where he is."

"Guenevere, I am warning you. Do not attempt to leave Camelot again until I give permission. I plan to double the guard at the gates. There is no way you'll get out."

"You are holding me prisoner?"

"If you want to think of it that way. I have more—and more important—things to deal with than your comfort and convenience. If you wanted everything to revolve around you, you should have stayed in Corfe."

Slowly, she put her letter aside and stood up. Even more slowly, she walked to a little table and picked up some knitting. She took one of the needles and pointed at her husband with it. "Do not threaten me, Arthur. Do not even think you have the power to frighten me. I shall leave when I choose to leave, and neither you nor your men nor this would-be wizard will stop me. Understand that."

For the first time, Merlin got between them. "Guenevere, this is for your own safety. You saw what happened when you tried to leave a while ago. It is treacherous out there."

"We can calculate our own risks."

"Then think of it this way. A crime has been committed. At least one of your men is under suspicion. It is to your benefit to remain till we can clear his name."

"No clearing is needed, as I see it." She looked to the king. "Arthur, you know you can't keep me here against my will. Do you think my army would stay at Corfe then? We will leave when we choose. If you expect otherwise you are a bigger fool than I thought."

"You think your knights would go to war over a suspected murderer?"

She bristled. "So it is that. I had nothing to do with it. Nothing."

"And Lancelot?" Merlin asked.

"And Lancelot, and his squire Petronus, and my maid, and the assistant pastry chef." She paused then said emphatically, "We were not involved."

Arthur sighed loudly. "A young man is dead, Guenevere. We will find the killer. And your behavior here has only made me more suspicious that you and your lover may be involved." He put on a sarcastic grin. "Understand that."

He and Merlin turned and stormed out of the room before she could respond.

The snow and ice stopped, but the weather remained cold. Arthur sent a male servant out to try to reach a nearby village for food; the man never came back. No one knew what to make of it.

But as Merlin had said, the snowy weather gave him and the others in his investigative group the chance to learn what they could. He and Nimue stalked their suspects relentlessly, seeking them out on various pretexts, making casual conversation, dropping subtle references to the crime to see what reaction they got.

There were several more encounters with Guenevere, who grew colder and more distant each time. Pellenore proved as unstable as ever; none of his reactions made a bit of sense.

Then finally, they managed to corner Lancelot. He was exercising in one of the unused dungeons, repeatedly lifting over his head a heavy stone he'd found. A torch he'd wedged into a crack in the wall gave the only light. Nimue, holding another torch, whispered to Merlin that the dungeon might be a harbinger of things to come for Lancelot.

"Why, Lancelot. How interesting to find you here."

He put down his rock. "Hello, wizard."

There was no use arguing the point. "Do you know your way around here? Arthur asked me to find a manuscript in the palace archives, but I'm afraid we're quite lost."

"You should see the lower levels of Corfe."

"Will you walk with us for a while? Just to be sure we don't get lost? These passageways can be so confusing."

The knight looked at his stone as if he might miss it. "Well . . . all right. But I really need to get back to my workout."

"We wouldn't dream of keeping you a moment longer than we need to."

So the three of them took their torches, left that dungeon and walked the dark, musty corridors of Camelot's basement. Merlin made a show of opening one door after another, pretending he really was searching for something there. All the while he made offhand conversation, trying to get a rise out of Lancelot.

"There's not much traffic down here since Arthur abandoned torture."

"Arthur is a fool."

"You think extracting false confessions from innocent people is a desirable thing?"

"I think it works. Criminals confess."

"Under torture, everyone confesses. Besides, you should be glad we don't do that here, if only for Guenevere's sake."

"Guenevere is the queen."

"Even so."

"What crime could she be suspected of?"

Instead of answering, Merlin paused, pushed open a door, looked inside then closed it again. "A broom closet."

Lancelot answered his own question. "That boy. That squire." He said the word with faint distaste, as if squires were beneath his notice.

Merlin tried another door, but it was stuck.

"Guenevere couldn't have killed him. She was with Arthur in the Great Hall the whole time. You know that."

"Oh yes, that's right." Merlin looked thoughtful for Lancelot's sake. "But what about her servants?"

"They're servants. Who knows what they do?"

"And—and—" He convincingly acted as if he were having a new thought. "Where were you during the ceremony?"

Lancelot narrowed his eyes. "I was there."

"Someone saw you leaving the hall. I was only wondering where you went, that's all."

"That's none of your business."

"Of course not. I was only making conversation, nothing more."

Lancelot didn't know whether to believe him, and it showed.

"Well, there don't seem to be any archives down here. Arthur must have been mistaken. We'll leave you to your exercise, then. We've never really talked before, Lancelot. This has been nice."

The knight looked around. "Where are we? I've lost my bearings."

"I told you, it can be terribly confusing down here." He smiled a benign smile. "Just head back that way. And have a good workout."

They left him standing in the passageway, looking bewildered. Whether he was baffled by the castle's layout or the encounter he'd just had—or both—was impossible to say.

But as they were climbing the stairs back to ground level, Nimue whispered, "You're right. Guenevere has two apes."

For all this time, Mark was conducting his "show investigation," asking pointless questions, bothering everyone he could, in hopes of diverting attention from the ones who were really probing the crime. Merlin, Nimue and Britomart were prying as subtly as they could, asking a pointed question here and there then backing away from it, trying to get some idea who might have killed the squire. But they had no more success than Mark, who wanted none.

Meantime Ganelin was making his inquiries among the castle servants. He followed Merlin's suggestion and never asked too directly. And he trusted Mark's show investigation to provide cover and keep people from getting suspicious. But by making conversation with select maids, grooms, valets, pages and suchlike, he began to piece together a tentative picture of the situation in Camelot on the night of the ceremony. Not only had a lot of the servants seen one suspect or another, but the ones who hadn't had heard gossip from the ones who had. So it wasn't too difficult to learn what he wanted to.

Among the people who would normally have been expected to attend the gathering but didn't, there was only

Percival, and he had the alibi of illness. Ganelin went to visit him on the pretext of checking on his condition for Arthur. He found the knight coughing uncontrollably.

"Can I get you anything, sir? Or can I summon the court physician?"

"That charlatan?" He hacked. "He claims to be a magician, but have you ever seen him work any wonders?"

"Pardon me, sir, but I think he claims *not* to be a sorcerer."

"Nonsense. He's seen more, done more, learned more than one man could do in a normal lifetime. He has sold his soul, and everyone knows it."

There was no point bickering. "I see. Well, if you don't need anything, I'll leave you to your phlegm."

"Please do."

As for the people who had gone to the Great Hall that night then left again, Ganelin was able to confirm the ones that were already known—Lancelot, Mordred, Pellenore—and he was able to add several of the knights to the list. Then one by one he began making oblique queries about where they went and what they did.

It would have been odd indeed for someone to move about the castle unnoticed by any of the servants. And in fact he was able to construct tentative accounts for each of the guests—except four.

He made careful notes on everything he'd learned about the various suspects' movements that night. Then he reported to Merlin. "I think I know who might have done it, sir. There are four whose activities I haven't been able to verify."

"Excellent work, Ganelin. Tell me, then."

"I'd like a few more days, if it's possible. I haven't quite tracked every possible source of information. I want to be as certain as possible before I name names."

Merlin smiled. "Said like a scholar, not a knight."

"There's no need to be rude, sir."

"It's just my sense of humor. How much more time will you need?"

"As I said, a few days."

"No more than that? Are you sure? Arthur wants the assassin brought to justice before Midwinter Court, remember."

"I'm sure I'll know much sooner than that."

In the following days the weather began to warm. Snow and ice melted; roads turned to mud and were nearly as impassable as when they were frozen. But people started to leave Camelot nonetheless.

Guenevere, Lancelot and their party were first to announce. Lancelot said arrogantly that he'd dealt with worse than mud before this, and the queen was anxious to return to Corfe.

Then Morgan and Mordred announced they would be leaving the next day. Soon Sagramore, Bors, Gawain and Accolon said they'd be going, too. Arthur sent parties out to the surrounding towns to buy provisions for the ones who would be remaining longer.

Merlin watched most of the preparations from his tower. By this time tomorrow the castle would be livable again. His ravens were happy of the warmer weather.

Some scrolls he had sent to Antioch for, months before, finally arrived. He unpacked them, unrolled them on his table and began to inspect them. A large cup rested on the edge of the table; he accidentally knocked it off, and it clattered loudly on the floor.

Nimue knocked and entered. "Merlin, there's trouble."

"Look at this. An eyewitness account of the Trojan War by a Phrygian named Dares. There are copies all over the Mediterranean, but I think this one may be Dares's original."

"Merlin, will you listen to me. Something has happened."

He forced himself to focus on her, not the scrolls. "Yes?"

"Ganelin is dead."

THREE

ANNA

Stone steps spiraled upward along the inner wall of Merlin's tower. Halfway up sprawled Ganelin's body. Britomart waited to guard it while Nimue fetched Merlin. The squire had been stabbed through the heart with a sword, and his right arm and leg had been slashed. She was thankful that, at least, the body was nowhere near as badly mutilated as his brother's had been. But that was not much to be thankful for.

The steps had been worn down in the center from years of traffic; blood trickled from one down to the next; before long it would reach the main floor of the castle, and people would know something had happened. Brit watched its downward flow, wishing there was some way to stop it. But she had nothing that might be of help; it would take mops or swabs or, at the very least, a great deal of cloth.

She could not resist the impulse to bend down and touch the boy's body, hoping for signs of life even though she knew there would be none. Ganelin's cheek was still warm; the flesh was tender and resilient.

Just at that moment Merlin and Nimue came down from above. Merlin said nothing; he glanced at Brit then bent down to examine the corpse. "What happened?"

Brit answered, "As you can see . . . We only just found him a few moments ago."

"Thank goodness," Nimue said softly, "he isn't cut to pieces the way his brother was."

"I think he would have been." Merlin got up and reached around to rub his back. "It looks like the killer started to but was interrupted."

"There's no place he could hide, Merlin," Brit said. "If he fled when he heard us approaching, the only way he could have gone is up to your rooms."

He looked at her then turned his attention back to the body. "That's a good observation. But something must have interrupted him."

"Did you make any sounds up there? Sounds that might have scared him off, I mean?"

"I dropped a goblet. I'm not certain that would have been loud enough to panic the killer, though."

"It must have been."

"Poor Ganelin." Nimue's face was blank. "I always liked him. Poor Ganelin . . ." she repeated. "I never knew how passionate he was till after Borolet died."

"We must have some servants take him and place him by his brother." Suddenly Merlin sounded very sad; the reality of what had happened was sinking in. "I suppose we'll bury them together. Let us hope the cold earth will permit that sometime soon."

It was Brit who brought up practical matters. "We'll

have to ask Arthur to delay all the departures. We can't have the suspects leaving now."

"I'll talk to him. But I'm not certain how wise that would be. We know now the lengths this fiend will go to. I had let myself hope privately that Borolet's death was a singular event. But now . . . The rest of us are vulnerable. Do we really want this killer at large in Camelot any longer?"

"But—but we'll never know who it was if—if—"

"I understand your concern, Brit. But . . . but I'm just not sure what to do. Arthur will decide. Has anyone been sent to tell him about this?"

No one had.

"He'll want to know." He looked down at Ganelin and let out a long, deep sigh. "I'll go and tell him. You don't know how badly I want not to, but . . ."

From below came a shout. "What on earth is going on up there?"

It was Mark. He had been passing below and apparently had noticed the blood seeping down.

"Be quiet, Mark. Come up here."

Obviously in an unpleasant mood, Mark climbed the steps to them. "What—?" Then he saw. "Oh. Oh, no."

"We've been fools, Mark. We naïvely assumed your sham investigation would provide cover for us. But . . . but . . ." Helplessly, he gestured at the body. "We've bungled. We've been too smug."

"Arthur will be unhappy."

"So will everyone. Everyone who knew Ganelin."

Nimue said, "If only some of the suspects were gone already. At least that would make things easier for us."

"I don't know." Merlin looked down the steps at the still-flowing blood, not at her. "They could have left someone here. Or bribed someone. Or—I don't know. I can't think now. I have to find Arthur."

"Do you want me to come with you?" Nimue asked.

"No. No, you go and find someone to move this—him. I'll be all right in a moment or two."

Mark said, "Let us hope their ghosts rest as soundly as their bodies."

"Ghosts?" Merlin couldn't believe he was hearing it. Not knowing what to say, he turned to Brit. "Will you please stay here with him till we can have him moved? And make certain he's handled properly, with respect. I don't want the servants—"

"The servants liked him, remember?"

"Oh. Yes. Yes, well . . ."

Slowly he descended to the ground floor. Occasional servants passed, going here or there, some apparently busy, some not. But he couldn't bring himself to talk to any of them. He had made a terrible mistake, a terrible misjudgment, and Ganelin had paid for it. How could he tell Arthur?

The king was going over an old map, in his study. He was too caught up in it to notice Merlin's mood. "I'm glad you came, Merlin. I was about to send for you. I've had a few thoughts about our hunt for the killer."

"Arthur, something awful has happened."

"I don't want to hear bad news just now, Merlin. I just came from Guenevere. That was unpleasant enough." Finally he noticed the pain in his counselor's face.

"There's no way to avoid it, I'm afraid. Arthur—"

"Don't, Merlin. Whatever it is, it can wait."

"No, it can't. Arthur, Ganelin has been killed."

There was a long silence. "Oh."

"I'm sorry."

"Oh. The poor . . . How did it happen?"

"He was on the steps going up to my room. I think he was on his way to tell me who he thought the killer was. He had said—"

"How was he killed?"

"Like Borolet. Stabbed, hacked. Not so badly as his brother. But he—"

Arthur put his map aside, got up and walked to a window. "Look out there. I own it all. It's mine. You helped me take it. Remember all the dreams I had about a place of goodness and light? Remember how naïve I was?" He looked at Merlin then quickly turned away again. "Merlin, what's wrong with us? This isn't the kind of country we wanted to build."

"England is a good place, Arthur. Strong and getting stronger. These murders—"

"These murders give the lie to what you just said."

"Human nature doesn't change, Arthur. We're a race capable of goodness. We are even more capable of evil, and much of the time many of us embrace it. You are a good king and your England is a good place."

"No!" He pounded a fist into the wall. "This is not what I meant. I wanted a land where things like this don't happen. Those poor boys."

"I know how fond of them you were. They were good young men. But, Arthur, you can't let grief run away with you like this. You're the king. You have duties. One of them is to remain in charge, of yourself and of the government, of public affairs. You've always understood that. I taught it to you at a young enough age."

Arthur turned to face him. "They were mine, Merlin. They were my sons."

Merlin fell silent. After a long interval he said, "Oh. I see."

"Do you? Do you know what they meant to me? Guene-vere has never given me children. I daresay she never will. And I don't want her to anymore, now that I know what she is. But Borolet and Ganelin . . ." He looked away again. "I met their mother on a progress through the fen country. Beautiful young woman. When she came to me later and told me we'd made twin sons, I actually remembered her. Of all the women I had in those days, she was the one I re-membered. I told her to bring them to me when they were ten, that I'd raise them and teach them and make them wor-thy of their heritage."

Softly, Merlin asked, "Did they know?"

"No. Never. I think they must have suspected now and then, but they never asked and I never told them. But I think they knew they were being raised for some special destiny. And now . . ." There were tears in his eyes.

"Arthur, I'm sorry."

"I know. I know. We should have done better by them, Merlin. *I* should have. When I lost Borolet, I told myself, at least I still have his brother. I will raise him up, make him a good, worthy man—a good, worthy heir. Now . . . what do I have of them? What?" He sat down again. "Bring me a cup of wine, will you, please? And the bottle."

"This is no time for drinking."

"I have never known a better one."

Merlin filled a cup for him, and Arthur drank it quickly. Then he took hold of Merlin's arm and squeezed tightly. "I want you to find him. The killer. Merlin, these deaths have diminished all of us, all England, even though no one knows that but you and I."

"Arthur, you're hurting me."

He let go. "I'm sorry. But you must promise me, Merlin,

that you will do everything in your power to find whoever slaughtered my sons."

"You know I will."

Arthur got up, crossed to the table that held the wine bottle and poured himself another cup. "Burial. We must see that they're buried with all proper dignity."

"They were squires. People might find it odd."

"Do you think I give a damn?"

Merlin said nothing.

"And their mother. I don't even know if she's still alive. I want to find out."

"She is. Ganelin talked about her." He hesitated. "Shall I have Mark make the preparations for the burials?"

"Yes, he'll do a good job. I think he even suspected the truth about the boys. He asked me once or twice, but I always avoided answering. Now he'll understand. And I'll have to ask Morgan to officiate at the funeral."

"You want her in this?"

"They were her nephews, even if she didn't know it."

"Of course. Will you tell her? Do you think she might have guessed?"

"I don't know. I need to think. And drink more. Will you set everything in motion?"

"Certainly, Arthur. I'll get to work right now."

"Good." He paused, then looked Merlin directly in the eye. "And thank you. Even though this place is defective, even though it is tainted with human evil in a way I never imagined, I could never have begun to build it without you. And I want you with me now."

"I'm not certain what you mean, Arthur."

"Tomorrow."

• • •

The next morning Camelot's courtyard was filled with activity. Morgan's party, and Guenevere's, and several less illustrious, were packing their animals, checking their weapons, making certain they had provisions enough for the trips to their various homes. Merlin had pressed Arthur to detain them, but the king was reluctant. "There are no grounds. And I want them gone. I want them out of my house."

"It may make finding the killer more difficult."

"Merlin, I want them gone."

It was just warm enough for a thaw. The landscape was dotted with puddles of water and thick mud, and a steady drip fell from the top of the castle. Now and then chunks of ice peeled off the roof and battlements fell to the ground below, alarming the horses, even occasionally striking someone. Outriders had been sent to make certain the roads were passable and came back to report that they were, but barely so.

Arthur walked among them, enjoying the chaos, and happy of the departures, with Merlin at his side. Camelot would be their home again, not the mass hostel it had been.

Nimue followed them, making note of everything she saw, bidding farewell to acquaintances. Arthur had asked her to keep an eye out for petty theft. "It's to be expected. They will take anything they think we won't miss."

Unlike the king and her teacher, she was slightly intimidated by all the people and the hustle. "Do you think it's advisable to let them all go, Your Majesty?" She lowered her voice. "We may never have all the suspects together again. Solving the mystery will be that much more of a challenge."

"I don't see that we have any choice, Colin. Camelot can't support this many people. You've seen how scarce food became, and how quickly. Besides, I don't really have the authority or the pretext to hold them all here. I want our society to be based on laws, not force.

"They'll all be back for Midwinter Court. It's the time for them to renew their vows of fealty to me. Anyone who doesn't come will be counted a traitor." He shrugged. "More or less."

"I see. But still—"

"For goodness sake, Colin." Merlin was impatient with her for questioning the king. "We're getting rid of them. That's a blessing in more ways than one. Do you want a mad killer on the loose here permanently?"

"But—"

"We'll get to the bottom of the killings. And we'll do it by Midwinter Court. Just be patient."

She resigned herself to it, glumly.

Arthur made a show of saying good-bye to the most important people, particularly Morgan and Guenevere. Guenevere actually seemed in a pleasant mood for once, and Arthur commented on it.

"And why shouldn't I be? I'm leaving my husband's house. What wife wouldn't be overjoyed?"

"You are the picture of domestic bliss, aren't you?" He kissed her perfunctorily on the cheek, not the lips, and moved on.

To Morgan, he made a special request. "We'll be burying Ganelin and Borolet within a few days."

"Highly advisable. They won't keep long, even in winter."

He ignored this. "Morgan, I'd like you to preside at the funeral."

"For a pair of squires? Your sense of humor can be so alarming, Arthur."

He leaned close and whispered something to her; Merlin thought he knew what. Then he pulled away and added, "Please, Morgan."

Reluctantly she agreed, but she added that she was doing Arthur an enormous favor and he owed her for it.

Then, after all the official and unofficial business was out of the way, Arthur led Merlin and Nimue to a small gate at the rear of Camelot. Britomart was waiting there with horses and a cohort of six guards. Arthur asked a waiting servant, "Do you have it?"

"Yes, sir." He handed Arthur what looked like a sable cloak, carefully folded. Arthur took it, placed it in his saddlebag and quickly climbed onto his steed. "Come on, all of you. Let's get moving."

Nimue looked to Merlin and Brit. "Where are we going?"

It was Merlin who answered her. "You're not going anywhere. You have some Homer to translate, remember?"

"But—"

"You're not dressed warmly enough to travel on a morning like this. Go and do your Greek. I'll tell you about it later."

Glum and puzzled, she went inside.

Brit jumped onto her horse. "Nine of us? Arthur, you said you wanted this to be inconspicuous."

"Would you rather we travel without guards?"

"Of course not, but—"

"It's unlikely anyone will see us leave, Brit. There's too much activity out front for that."

The others mounted their horses, two more guards opened the rear gate and the party left. Arthur rode at the head of the column, flanked by two of his men. None of the three talked very much except for occasional orders or directions. Brit and Merlin followed with the rest of the guards. Arthur had ordered them to bring an extra horse; no one seemed to know why.

The morning was uncomfortably damp. Wisps and streamers of mist floated in the air. The sun shone, a pale ghost of itself, through heavy clouds above. After a few minutes the entire party fell silent.

The landscape changed from low hills to flat, featureless terrain. Merlin looked back over his shoulder to see Camelot on its hilltop retreating into the distance more quickly than seemed quite right.

Brit reined her mount next to his and whispered, "Do you have any idea where we're going? He told me to arrange the party but nothing more."

"I can guess, but I don't know for certain."

"What's your guess, then?"

He looked thoughtful. Arthur had not told anyone else but Morgan that the dead young men were his sons. It seemed advisable not to spread it. "In time, Brit."

An hour later the land had turned to moor. Sprigs of heather grew here and there, but not much else. Toads and snakes slithered out of their way. A guide was waiting to steer them through it; how Arthur had arranged for him, Brit could not fathom. One of the guards' horses slid into some quicksand, and they all had to work to pull it and its rider out. The man was shaken; Arthur sent him back to Camelot with a companion to take care of him.

Another hour passed. Brit found herself growing impatient, but she knew there was no point trying to get information out of either Arthur or Merlin if they didn't want to share it. For nearly the entire trip Arthur had said virtually nothing.

Then ahead of them there was a small village, not much

more than a hamlet—ten or a dozen tiny shacks on either side of the track, most of them made of mud and twigs. Arthur raised his hand and the party stopped. The guide pointed to one particular hut. Arthur dismounted, walked to its door and knocked.

A woman opened it a crack and looked out. She was in early middle age, and her features reflected her hard life. It was immediately clear she recognized the king. She pulled the door open wide, Arthur went in and she closed it behind him.

The rest of the party dismounted. The guard in charge told them to make themselves comfortable; there was no way of knowing how long the king would be. They had brought food, which he passed around. The guide walked a few paces away from the rest of them and watched them without eating or talking to any of them.

"Merlin, are you going to tell me what this is about?" Brit tore a piece of bread and bit into it aggressively.

"You know as much as I do."

"Nonsense. I want to know. Please."

He took a deep breath, seemed to consider the possibilities then sat down on a relatively dry patch of earth. "She was their mother."

"Oh. And Arthur—?"

"Yes. Exactly."

"I see. I've wondered about that. He always seemed so attached to them."

"The attachment has been severed."

They ate without saying much more. Finally, Brit said, "So it's that much more important that we find the killer, then."

"Yes, Brit."

"If the killer knew about his sons, somehow . . . these

may have been dynastic murders, intended to do more harm than most people realize."

"I don't see how anyone could have known. I didn't know myself until Arthur told me yesterday. He said Mark had guessed, but Mark and he are close friends."

"But—but if these killings were a strike at the royal house . . . I wish we had something definite to go on. No one who might have done it has a verifiable alibi. Mordred told me he went to use the privy then got lost in the unfamiliar corridors. I have no idea whether to believe him. And Lancelot says pretty much the same thing. Pellenore . . . well, you know, he was being Pellenore, charging around the castle chasing phantoms. I wish I could trust him as much as you seem to. We need to know more."

"I know it, Brit. But how?" He looked to the woman's hut; there was still no sign of Arthur. "If only Ganelin had told me what he'd learned from the servants. Or some of it, at least."

"We'll have to question them ourselves. There's no other way."

"Ganelin had a point. They won't open up to us the way they did to him."

"Then we'll have to force it out of them."

"No." His voice took on an uncharacteristically hard edge. "No torture. That is not the kind of land Arthur wants to make."

"Then how do we—"

"We'll find a way."

The hut's door opened. Arthur came out, followed closely by the woman, who was crying. Her dark features were made worse by grief. He took her by the hand and led her to where the others were waiting. From his saddlebag he got the sable cloak and placed it around her shoulders.

"No, Arthur, please. It doesn't matter. I'm numb anyway."

He wrapped it more tightly around her. "Don't be foolish. It's a cold, wet day." He looked to Merlin and Britomart. "This is Anna, who might have been the mother of kings."

They said soft hellos to her. She averted her eyes.

"Come, Anna. I chose this horse for you myself. She's the sweetest, gentlest in my stable."

"Like me?" Her voice was bitter with her sorrow.

"Please don't talk like that." Then he turned to the others. "Anna, this is Merlin, my most trusted advisor, and Britomart, one of my senior military aides."

It was all so completely unexpected. Uncertain what to say, they made simple greetings to her, trying, not very successfully, to sound friendly and pleased she was with them.

He helped her up then mounted his own horse. "Come on, everyone, let's get home."

And so the party returned the way it had come. There was not much more talk on the return trip than there had been on the ride out. At one point Britomart reined her mount next to Anna's. Anna gaped at her, not seeming to remember their introduction.

"Hello. I'm Brit. It's a pleasure to meet you."

"Thank you." She avoided looking at her.

"You've been to Camelot before?"

"No. Never. Arthur wanted to take me. But I don't belong in a place like that."

"Just between us," she lowered her voice to a confidential whisper, "no one does."

Anna smiled shyly. "I want to see the funeral. I want to see my boys buried. I told him I'm coming home after that."

There was an awkward silence. Then, "Do you love him?"

"I don't know. It's been so many years. He told me he loved me when we first knew each other. He says that he's never stopped. But he's the king and I'm a woman from the midland swamps."

Brit tried to make more conversation, but Anna was badly out of her element and shaken by her grief. Brit determined to make the woman feel as much at home as she could, once they reached Camelot.

At one point on the long ride to the castle, she noticed that Anna had begun to cry again. Was it for her boys, or for what might have been with Arthur, or some combination of the two? There didn't seem much point in asking.

Late that night, Nimue, Brit and Merlin sat before a roaring fire in his study with more spiced wine. None of them seemed to have any idea how to proceed.

"Where's Mark? I thought he'd be joining us." Brit yawned and stretched.

"He's packing for the journey back to Cornwall." One of Merlin's ravens tapped at the window, and Merlin got up to let it in. "He's done as much as he can here, and he does have his own fiefdom to govern."

"Does it occur to you," she asked, "that kingship is now firmly established in England?"

Merlin swirled the wine in his cup. "I'm not certain what you mean."

"Not so long ago queens ruled here."

"And you're saying there are at least two women who would like to see the country revert to that." It was a statement, not a question.

"Exactly."

Nimue took a long drink. "But no one likes either Morgan or Guenevere. No one would ever submit to their rule."

"Suppose they ruled through a puppet at first? A lover or a son?" Brit got up and stretched again. "It's been a long day. Too long."

"That hadn't occurred to me before, Brit." Nimue looked at Merlin to try and guess what he was thinking. "But you have a good point."

"We should have thought of it before now. And if one of them learned somehow that the squires were Arthur's sons and presumptive heirs, it would have given them the motive for . . . for what happened."

"I can easily imagine Morgan ruling through Mordred— and Mordred going along. Guenevere and Lancelot—that's another matter." Merlin started to drink then seemed to think better of it and put his goblet on the table. "The thought of King Mordred makes my blood run cold. There couldn't possibly be enough wine to warm it again." Like Britomart, he yawned. "You're right, Brit, the day has been too long and too busy. We'll think more clearly in the morning. But I think we will need to visit our suspects on their home ground. Their guard may be down then."

He got up and poured his wine into the fireplace. "The king's wife or his sister. A fine pair of suspects we have."

They said their good nights and parted company. Merlin sat in his chair, stroking the raven's head, till he fell asleep.

It rained on and off for three more days, and there was constant fog. Merlin watched from his tower, as always. At times the rain was so heavy his ravens wouldn't leave the study.

"When I was young, I lived in Egypt for three years," he

told Nimue. "In Alexandria. Studying at the great library, or what is left of it. It hardly ever rained there; the weather was warm and lovely almost all the time. It was the happiest time of my life." He turned to face her. "I had to come back to dear old England."

"You love England and you know it."

"This is not a fit place for someone who likes to think."

"Is any place?"

"I don't know. Perhaps I've romanticized Alexandria. Our memories do that to us. Did you know there are catacombs there? The dead are buried in underground chambers. You should see the catacombs sacred to the goddess Nemesis. It is a vast complex, all carved from the living bedrock. Athletes from the stadium are buried there, and even their horses."

"Charming."

He sighed. "Why do the young always sneer at everything they don't know?"

She shrugged. "It's hard to resist. It's hard to imagine that you didn't do that when you were young."

"I suppose I must have. Memory fails."

Camelot's burial ground was an eighth of a mile behind the castle, beyond a stand of blackthorn trees, distant enough to be out of sight, close enough to be nearby when necessary. The gravediggers kept trying to dig a hole for the dead squires, but the walls kept collapsing; even when they didn't, the graves filled with water. With winter approaching, no one was certain when or even if the young men would get a proper burial.

Their mother, Anna, had become a disconcerting presence in the castle. She wandered the halls, distracted, dis-

traught, holding imaginary conversations with her dead
sons and, to appearances, hearing them answer. Now and
then she would go down to the basement room where their
remains lay and would stroke what was left of their bodies.
Arthur ordered the room to be locked.

But she kept up her long, mad walks and the fancied conversations with her boys. No one seemed able to make her
see what she was doing. Even Pellenore found her alarming. And Mark was more shaken than most. "It's what I told
you. Their spirits are uneasy. I'm glad I'm leaving for
home." He departed the next day.

Arthur asked Merlin to talk with Anna, to counsel her in
her grief. "Understand, Merlin, the life she's had. Her boys
were everything to her. She lived in mud. In filth. But knowing her boys were here gave her hope. That is gone now."

"You could have brought her here before now, Arthur."

"She wouldn't come. It was all for Ganelin and Borolet."

So Merlin tried talking to her, tried to make her understand how erratic her behavior had become. But it was no
use. "Honestly," he told Brit, "I'm at a loss. How can I know
what to say to her? I don't know her, don't know anything
about her. For all any of us knows she's been half-mad her
entire life."

"Isn't there something you can give her? Some drug to
calm her?"

He shook his head. "I've had the servants put a small
dose of valerian in her food. It has no effect at all."

"Poor woman."

On the fourth day the rain stopped, but the clouds per-
sisted and the world remained a bright, cold grey. If the rain
didn't begin again, a funeral should be possible soon.
Arthur sent word to Morgan. "Come in a fortnight." He
voiced his hope repeatedly that the weather would hold—

no more rain, no more freezing till after the boys were laid to rest. Merlin's ravens were happy to be able to get outside again.

No one had inspected the bodies in the basement to make sure of their condition. No one much wanted to. Finally, Merlin offered to take some servants to prepare them. They took soap and water to clean them and winding sheets of the purest white linen from the king's own stores. Fortunately, the cold had preserved the corpses fairly well. Even so, it was an unpleasant duty.

Woodworkers fashioned two caskets from birch wood. Both were intricately, elaborately carved; at Arthur's insistence, both bore his own royal crest. A summons was sent to Pastorini in Cornwall to come and make bronze handles for them. Oddly, Mark sent word that the metalsmith was unable to come, but he made handles there and sent them.

A few days after that, Morgan arrived for the funeral, attended by her son and a dozen servants. They took over most of a wing of the castle. The first night they were there, as Morgan was going to the refectory for her dinner, she encountered Anna in the hallway. The two women, twenty feet apart, stared at one another for a long, silent moment. Then Anna moved on, looking presumably for what had always mattered in her life— her boys. Her melancholy affected Morgan, who did not say much during her meal.

Then the morning for the burial finally arrived. Well before dawn, Merlin was wakened by a persistent knocking at his door. He climbed out of bed, wrapped himself in a blanket and walked to open the door. "Yes?"

It was a boy, fourteen, maybe fifteen, with black hair, olive skin and large dark eyes. "Merlin?"

"Yes. Who the devil are you?"

"I'm Greffys, sir. The king's new squire."

"You are." His voice was neutral.

"Yes, sir. He sent me to make sure you're ready for the funeral."

"It isn't even sunrise."

The boy's face was blank. "I know that."

Merlin looked him up and down. "Why did Arthur choose you?"

"He says I'm the best athlete among the squires." The kid smiled with pride.

"It wouldn't have occurred to him to choose the best scholar, would it?"

"Uh . . . I don't know what you mean, sir."

"No. Of course not. Go and tell him I'll be ready."

"Yes, sir." The boy rushed down the stairs without bothering to close the door behind him.

A few minutes later Nimue arrived. "You're up."

"Arthur sent his new squire to rouse me." He smiled sarcastically. "Kings."

"I've brought some hot soup. Here, you'll need it."

"I'm dreading this. I wish I had a plausible reason to stay in bed all day."

"At the very least," she said, pouring the soup from a pot to a large bowl, "we'll have a chance to observe Morgan and Mordred. We were so focused on Guenevere before, we more or less ignored them."

"Stop talking sense. This is going to be a terrible day."

By the time Merlin had eaten, washed and dressed, Britomart had come to his rooms as well. He found her warming herself by the fire in the study. "You're coming to the funeral?"

"Of course. Arthur should be surrounded by his friends, don't you think?"

"Yes. But who are they, Brit? I wish I knew."

"You're in a dark mood."

He shrugged. "Funerals do that to me. Let's go."

They assembled at the rear of Camelot. Arthur was there, and Greffys, and Anna, Morgan, Mordred. Sagramore, Gawain, Bors, Accolon and the rest of the knights attended. Gossip had spread about the dead squires' connection to the king; the royal crest on the coffins seemed to cinch it in most people's minds. Pellenore was noticeably missing, but no one had expected him anyway. Twelve pages served as pallbearers, carrying the two coffins on catafalques. The court musicians were there, playing mournful tunes. The music echoed loudly and clearly through the morning air and mist.

The party left the castle by the same rear gate Arthur had used when he set out to find Anna. They walked slowly, solemnly, accompanied by more dirges by the musicians, who brought up the rear. Fog swirled among the trees. At times the light was so dim Arthur called for torches. Pages ran back to Camelot while the procession waited. The torches, when they arrived, showed brilliant yellow-orange among the mist and trees.

At the burial ground the two royal gravediggers were still at work, shoring up the sides of the hole and bailing out water. Arthur went to them. "I thought the ground was dry enough."

"So did we, sir. But it's saturated much more than we thought."

"Do what you have to do quickly."

"Yes, sir."

Everyone formed a circle around the coffins. Morgan raised her arms in supplication and voiced a prayer to the goddess Arianrhod, begging that she guide and protect the souls of these two valiant young men. Merlin found himself looking around at the assembled mourners. Someone was missing.

Then he saw him, standing off among the trees, watching it all the way a naturalist might watch wild animals. It was Mordred. He was only half-visible through the mist. But at one point, when the air cleared momentarily, it seemed that he was smiling.

Merlin nudged Brit, gestured toward Mordred and whispered, "He seems to be enjoying this much too much."

"We always knew what a morbid little creature he is."

"I wonder if it's only that."

Morgan finished her prayers. The coffins were laid in the grave side by side. One by one the mourners lined up to sprinkle handfuls of earth on them. But the soil was too damp; it formed muddy clumps and thumped unpleasantly on the caskets.

Through it all, Anna had managed to maintain her composure. Now she began crying uncontrollably. Arthur put an arm around her to try and comfort her, but it did no good. Merlin looked to see what Mordred was doing, and the boy was smiling even more widely than before.

Two days later the weather broke. For the first time in days the sun was shining and the air was warm, or at least warmer than it had been. Knights wrestled and exercised. Everyone from the castle tried to spend time outdoors, walking, running or just enjoying the bright day.

Merlin climbed to the roof and walked the perimeter,

chatting with the sentries he knew. The countryside was still dotted with patches of snow and ice. Winter would be settling in in a serious way soon. At the far end of the roof, Arthur and Greffys wrestled playfully. Arthur let the boy get an arm lock on him, then pulled free. The funereal mood had evaporated.

The forest around Camelot was black, nothing but bare branches, and the landscape was still dotted with patches of white. The migratory birds had long since gone, and there seemed to be fewer of the ones who stayed year-round. A few sparrows and cardinals scratched at the roof stones, looking for food. Two of Merlin's ravens followed him about; the third one had disappeared.

Find the assassin by Midwinter Court: the charge had been repeated more times than Merlin cared to remember. But there was so little to go on—practically nothing but suspicions and obvious motives for too many suspects. Not that Arthur's wish was a command; he was not that kind of monarch. But there were good reasons for finding the killer as soon as possible. The idea of order must be maintained.

A cloud covered the sun briefly; then it emerged again. Merlin shaded his eyes.

Then from behind him he heard a voice.

"Where are my sons?"

With a start he turned to find Anna just in back of him. He said hello. "How are you today?"

There were tears streaking her cheeks. "Do you know where my sons are?"

Uncertain what to say, he pretended to study something in the distance. "The air is still a bit chilly, Anna. Shouldn't you be wearing a cloak?"

"I've been cold all my life." She peered at him. "Where is Arthur?"

He pointed.

"I have to find Borolet and Ganelin. I have something for them. He'll know where they are."

It was so awkward. What would be best, to let her delusion continue, or to try and bring her back to reality? To let her disturb the king with this, or to find some way to keep her away from him? He found his resolve and said, "They are not here, Anna. You saw where we took them, remember?"

She looked confused; her eyes darted about as if trying to focus on something but she was unsure what. "They are here. I sent them to be with the king."

"No." He said it gently. "They are gone. Anna, you must remember."

"The night he made love to me I knew I'd bear him sons. I never told them who their father was, but they guessed."

"Anna, please."

"Arthur will take care of them. He is their father, you know. He won't let any harm come to them."

It was so futile. And he felt so sorry for her. He wished Brit or Nimue were there; women were so much better at handling these things.

"They will be kings one day themselves, you know. He promised to make them his heirs. But they haven't been home for so long . . ." She was fighting back tears; it was plain to see.

"Anna, they were good boys. Bright, helpful, energetic. They were the best; Arthur said so often enough. But they are gone." One of the ravens flapped onto his shoulder; he brushed it aside and it quickly flew away. He watched it go. "I sometimes envy my birds, do you know that? Their lives are so simple yet so full."

Arthur broke off wrestling with his squire and moved to

join them, with Greffys following behind. From ten yards away he called, "Merlin! Anna! How good to see you both out here on this gorgeous day."

"Hello, Arthur." Merlin was grateful for the interruption. "You don't seem to have worked up much of a sweat."

"It was only horseplay, not a workout." He turned to Anna. "Good afternoon, Anna. Are you feeling any better today?"

"No." The word seemed to weigh a ton. "I'm looking for Ganelin and Borolet. Do you know where they are?" Instead of Arthur, she peered directly at Greffys.

"No, ma'am." Mildly alarmed, the boy took a few steps backward and pressed himself against the battlement.

"Where are my sons?!" She shrieked it and rushed toward Arthur.

He caught her wrists and steadied her. "Please, Anna. Try and remember what happened, and why I brought you here."

She pulled free and turned to Merlin. "Where are my boys?" she wailed.

Then suddenly she lunged toward Greffys. "What have you done with them? Where are they hidden?"

He barely managed to step aside, and the madwoman plunged over the edge of the castle roof to the ground below. Her impact made a terrible sound. As she had rushed past him, Greffys was knocked off balance and nearly fell himself, but Arthur caught him by the arm and steadied him. The boy clung to Arthur frantically; it was clear Anna had been trying to push him.

Merlin and Arthur moved quickly to the edge and looked to the courtyard below. Anna was lying in a pool of blood, not moving. People were beginning to gather round her. Gawain looked up and saw the king; then he spread his arms wide apart and shook his head. The woman was dead. It was over that abruptly.

Arthur turned his back on the scene. "Good God, Merlin. Not another one."

Merlin watched the activity below, hoping she might show some sign of movement, but there was none.

"Three. Three deaths now, Merlin. The man who killed her sons killed her, too."

"She was out of her mind, Arthur." He spoke softly. "Something would have—she would have—"

"She was always a bit mad. But not like this. The killer pushed her to it. Three deaths are on his head now. Find him, Merlin. Find him and deliver him to my justice."

The next day, the second of Merlin's ravens disappeared. It flew off in the morning, seemingly healthy and happy, then . . . simply didn't return. The third and last of them perched on his shoulder that night as Merlin sat in front of the fire, thinking about the killings again and again.

Anna's death had unsettled him. Not that he hadn't seen death before; Arthur had fought too many battles for that to be possible. But the conviction that it was self-willed and not an accident—that madness could lead to a yearning for release from life—that bothered Merlin. Even if she had managed to push Greffys, she would have gone with him.

He reached up and idly stroked the bird on his shoulder. Unexpectedly, it nuzzled him and rubbed his cheek with the top of its head. It was the first time any of his pets had ever shown him special affection beyond the mere fact of staying with him when there were other choices.

"There, there," he whispered. "We're not alone. We have each other, sweet thing."

Someone knocked at the door. He wanted not to be bothered that night, but he got up, crossed to the door and opened it. "Greffys."

The squire looked tired. He was wearing a shoulder bag. "Good evening, sir. I hope I'm not disturbing you."

"I'm not busy at all. My little bird and I were just sitting and thinking."

"Oh. Should I—?"

"No, come in. How are you feeling?"

"Still shaken, I'm afraid." Suddenly he seemed self-conscious. "Oh—don't tell anyone I said that, will you, please? I'm training to be a knight. We're not supposed to—"

"Don't give it another thought. What can I do for you?"

He shuffled his feet, still feeling awkward. "The king asked me to come."

"I see. Is there some message?"

"Not exactly, sir. I have this—"

"Sit down, please. Make yourself comfortable. Would you like some wine?"

"Thank you, no. I just ate."

Merlin resumed his seat. The raven had not left his shoulder all this time. "I was just thinking that I really ought to give my pet a name. Do you have any ideas?"

"No, sir, I'm afraid not. Everyone says I never have any ideas."

"Do you?"

The boy shrugged. "I don't know. I'm not sure what it would feel like to have one."

"Not very pleasant, to tell you the truth. There are times when I wish . . ." He looked away; it was his turn to feel self-conscious.

"Oh. Then I guess I must have a lot of them."

Merlin leaned his head toward the raven and it nuzzled him again. "Hmm . . . what about 'Roc'?"

"Roc, sir?"

"It's the name of a fabulous bird. Probably a myth, but . . . I heard about it when I lived in Egypt."

"Egypt?" Greffys face was blank. "Where is that?"

"It's a magnificent land at the far end of the Mediterranean. Colossal ruins. Strange, wonderful art."

"The—?"

"The Mediterranean." He had to remind himself to be patient; Greffys was only a boy. "The great sea that separates Europe from Africa."

"Africa?"

"Never mind. Why did Arthur send you here?"

The boy seemed relieved at the change of topic. "Well, I've found something."

Roc flapped from Merlin's shoulder to the window and pecked at it. Merlin got up and opened it, and the bird flew off into the night. He turned to face Greffys. "They come and go in the most incalculable way. I keep studying them, trying to find some pattern, but I'm not sure there is one."

The boy was completely lost. He reverted to the comfortable topic. "I'm moving my things into Ganelin's room. You know, just below the king's chambers in the tower?"

"Yes?"

"I felt something odd in the bed. And there it was."

"It?"

He opened his shoulder bag and produced a large scroll. "Here. I showed it to the king, and he said to bring it to you."

Merlin unrolled it on the table then lit a large candle. It was a roughly drawn, barely decipherable diagram. Merlin studied it for a moment and decided it must be a sketch of the castle. At the center was a large circle; a square had been drawn inside it, against one edge, with three smaller squares inside it. Various lines branched off the large circle; along them were strings of odd symbols: +, X, ★, and ▼.

"You found this in Ganelin's bed?"

"Yes, sir. His majesty said he couldn't guess what it might be. Can you?"

"I think so." Merlin went to the window and took a deep breath. "Were you at the Great Hall the night Borolet was killed?"

"Yes, sir, I was With the other pages."

"What do you remember?"

He thought for a moment, pretty obviously trying to guess what Merlin was after. "A long wait, then confusion."

Brit knocked at the door and came in. Merlin was glad to see her. "Brit, look at this. Greffys found it in Ganelin's room."

She inspected it, lit two more candles then inspected it again. "The Great Hall and the corridors around it."

"Exactly."

"And this square with the little squares inside it—it must represent the dais and the three thrones."

"Certainly. And all the little symbols in the halls?"

She looked it over again. "They could mean anything. This could be some game he was playing with his brother, or—"

"I don't think so. I think this is a diagram he made to keep track of what he learned about the movements of our various suspects that night."

"A cross, an X, a little star and a triangle? Why would he—I mean, why wouldn't he use their initials or something obvious? These things could represent anyone."

"Point taken. But how well did you know him?"

"What do you mean?"

"Do either of you have any idea if he could read and write?"

Greffys and Brit looked at one another. Greffys was plainly lost. Brit said, "Probably not. He was training to be a knight, not a poet."

"You're a knight, Britomart, and you're one of the best-educated people in the country."

"I'm the odd one, remember? The woman? Learning to read couldn't diminish my status the way it would a man. Reading is for clerks." There was a slightly bitter edge to her voice.

Merlin turned his attention back to Ganelin's diagram. "There were four people Ganelin suspected—four people he learned enough about to make their movements worth noting."

"Excuse me, sir." Greffys was quite out of his element. "I really don't know what you mean. Or who."

"No, of course you don't. I was forgetting. Why don't you get back to your room and to bed. Brit and I have a lot to talk about."

Not certain whether to be offended, the boy said good night and left.

"Well, Brit. Look at the way the symbols are arranged. They run in lines down various corridors, leading away from the Great Hall."

"If we're right and this *is* the Great Hall."

"We have to assume it is. How else can we proceed? I think the little symbols must trace the movements of our suspects."

"That could be. Or they could be arranged according to some other pattern that isn't occurring to you."

"Possibly, but . . ." He rubbed his chin, furrowed his brow and went over the diagram still again. "I think we have to assume this charts their movements until that assumption becomes untenable or something stronger occurs to us. There are four symbols. That means four suspects he learned enough about to think they were worth concentrating on."

"Four." She leaned next to him and studied the scroll. "Mordred and Lancelot. Those are the obvious ones. And . . . Pellenore?"

"Maybe."

"And then . . . who is the fourth?"

He stood up and exhaled deeply. "How well do you know the servants?"

"Better than most of the knights, I think, but not really well."

"Will they talk to you? Open up to you the way they did to Ganelin, I mean?"

"I don't know. I can try." She hesitated. "We can always force them to talk."

"No, Brit. Arthur has banned that. It is out of the question."

"And if there's no other way?"

"There is. And we have to start confronting the suspects. Gently. Obliquely. We don't want anyone panicking, and we certainly don't want any more murders. But if we can put what the servants know together with what we learn from the suspects themselves, we should be able to match each symbol to the right person. Once we've eliminated the ones we can account for, the one left is the killer."

"It's cold in here." She walked to the window and started to close it.

"Don't. My raven will come back soon."

"Raven? One? What happened to the other two?"

"A hawk got them. Or they got sick or had an accident. I don't really know."

"Merlin, we can't assume Ganelin identified every possible suspect." She crossed the room and stood by the fire.

"We can't assume anything else, not till there's a reason to."

"People left the hall for the privy. Even Mark told us he did that."

He rolled up the scroll. "This is all we have to go on, Brit. At least for now. If we work slowly, steadily and carefully we can solve this."

"A star, an X, a triangle . . . It's like some mystical code."

"It *is* a code, but there's nothing mystical about this. With thought and reason and careful analysis we can unmask the truth."

"Does truth need unmasking?"

"It rarely needs anything else."

FOUR

THE INVESTIGATION
BEGINS IN EARNEST

The next day Merlin went to Arthur and explained what he thought Ganelin's chart represented. They were in his study, the room where Borolet had been killed. "So you see, by learning what we can from the servants and putting it together with what we learn from the suspects, we may be able to discover the killer's identity. I think we have a very good chance."

"Suppose these symbols mean something else?"

"They may. There's no way of knowing till we investigate."

The king listened patiently, frowning occasionally, examining the chart, trying to follow it all. "How long will this take?"

Merlin smiled. "How can I know that? Weeks. Possibly longer. If you want prophecy, consult Morgan."

"Her prophecies are always wrong. Well, nearly always."

"Heavens, I can't imagine why."

Arthur bristled. "You're not going to make any friends being skeptical of religion, Merlin."

"This isn't a matter for Morgan's hokum. If we're going to find the killer we must rely on reason. The more so since Morgan is under suspicion herself."

"You cannot go around accusing the nation's chief priestess of murder. Not without firm evidence. *Irrefutable* evidence."

"If you want the murderer unmasked, it hardly seems wise to place one of the prime suspects off-limits to the investigation, Arthur."

He sighed. "I'm not placing anyone off-limits. And you have every right to be as skeptical of the gods and their priests as you please. But you have to understand, it's not a prejudice most people are likely to share."

"Fine. Point taken. But I need you to promise me your full support if I'm to go ahead with this. As you've pointed out yourself, the queen and the chief priestess—the king's wife and sister—are under suspicion. This will take some delicacy."

"Delicacy? Is that really the word you mean?" Arthur suddenly turned to the door and cried out, "Greffys!"

The squire came running. "Sir?"

"There's no more wine. Rush and get me some, will you?"

He went.

Merlin brought him back to the subject at hand. "Perhaps you should do the investigation yourself, Arthur. No one could question its 'delicacy' then."

"Don't be foolish. You're the wisest man here."

Merlin narrowed his eyes. "You don't want to deal with this."

"Of course I don't." Uncharacteristically, Arthur exploded in anger, pounded the table and began to shout. "My boys are dead—horribly so. Their mother is dead. And every time we talk about it you tell me either my wife or my sister is probably behind it."

"You can always tell me to abandon the investigation completely."

"I wish I could. But . . . but . . . I don't know what to do." Deflated, he picked up the diagram, glared at it then put it back on the table. "You're my chief advisor. Tell me what to do."

"You know what I think is necessary for finding the assassin. Let me do it."

Arthur stared at him without saying anything.

"And then," Merlin went on, "there is the bigger question of what might be done to prevent this kind of thing from happening again."

Arthur sat again. This was obviously a new thought to him. "Yes?"

Softly, Merlin said, "Education."

"I beg your pardon?"

"Education. Schools."

"What the devil are you talking about?"

"Education always pays off—always enriches a society. It makes things run more smoothly."

"You have a way of making me feel dense, Merlin. I'm not following you at all."

"If Ganelin had simply noted the names of the suspects, we'd have the killer already. Instead he used these little symbols."

"What of it?"

"Arthur, the boy couldn't read and write. This cryptic chart is the best he could come up with. We should be glad we have it at all, but even so . . ."

"Guenevere can read. Morgan and Mordred can read. Yet you suspect them of villainy."

"Learning increases the potential for crime, yes. But it also increases the odds of solving the crime. Arthur, teach your pages and your squires. Establish a school here. Teach them about Rome and Athens, about the magnificent things mankind can accomplish. If nothing else, learning about government—about the benefits it brings us, the order, the stability—will make it less likely anyone will strike at your kingship in this way again."

"You've been trying to get me to do that for years. You know the risk—the knights wouldn't like it. Focus on finding the one who killed my sons. We don't even know that these killings were an attempt to 'strike at my kingship.' It may have been simply theft. We'll talk about schools later."

Greffys came back with a skin of wine and poured a cup for Arthur. The king drank, satisfied, thanked him and told him to go. Then to Merlin, he said, "Have you tried this? Mark's people have taken to cultivating vines in Cornwall. He says it's the only part of the country suitable for wine-making. It's pretty good. With luck we won't have to import our wine from France much longer. Guenevere's father will be most unhappy." He grinned like an impish boy. "You are going to have Mark work with you on this investigation, aren't you?"

He'd been hoping it wouldn't come up. "Not right away, no."

"What the devil do you mean?"

"Once we've cleared him—"

"Cleared him?" Arthur bellowed it. "Do you mean to say he's under suspicion, too? My military commander? Is there anyone near me you don't suspect of murder?"

"He was seen leaving the Great Hall at the start of the

ceremony, Arthur. He's even admitted it himself. And he was not seen to return."

Arthur got up and started pacing. "What will you need? And who? I want this ended as quickly as possible."

"I'll have to visit the various suspects on their home ground. I'll need plausible reasons for that. With Mark, we can come up with some reason for me to inspect the tin mines. Perhaps we can concoct some story for Morgan about wanting to go over the ceremonies for Midwinter Court. For Guenevere—I don't know. Nothing convenient occurs to me. Do you have any suggestions?"

"Not offhand. She's likely to be suspicious of any story, anyway."

"A fine wife."

"What do you think wives do? She has her fortieth birthday coming up next winter. Perhaps we can tell her we want to make it a national feast or something, and you're going to visit her for preliminary discussions."

"Do you want to make her birthday a national feast?"

"Don't be absurd, Merlin. But I'd be surprised if the idea hasn't occurred to her already. So there's nothing to lose. Maybe we can invite her father and then imprison him."

"Provoke an international incident?"

"He's as minor a king as you could find in Europe. I doubt if anyone would mind. And it would give Guenevere a reason to start behaving herself." He drank. "For once."

"Well, fine, then. Let's give all of this some more thought, though, shall we? There's no sense stirring things up more than we have to."

"I thought you liked stirring things up."

"Don't *you* be foolish, Arthur." He stared at the chart. "There has to be a way to decipher this." Then he looked at Arthur again. "I want Britomart. I know her and trust her.

And I know she can't be the killer. She was with me in the Great Hall the whole time. Can you do without her for a time?"

"Fine, yes, take her. Who else?"

"My apprentice, Colin. I know I can rely on him."

"Fine. And who else?"

"I may need Greffys. Or at any rate someone who's on good terms with the servants. I suppose any of the pages would do. But since Greffys is already involved in this, I think . . ."

"Fine. Anyone more?"

"No, I don't think so. We'll need horses for ourselves, and a few more to carry luggage and supplies. And I think that should be all. For the time being, at least. I don't think we should travel with an armed escort. It will be better to keep a low profile."

"Good. Go and get started. Remember, Merlin, I want the killer exposed by Midwinter Court."

"I'll do my best, Arthur."

"Good." His cup was empty. He picked up the wineskin and took a long drink from it. "I don't mean to roar at you. But this situation . . . it's so horrible. Who else do you suspect?"

"Well . . . Pellenore."

Arthur snorted derisively.

"I know how unlikely it is, but we can't afford to overlook any possibility, can we?"

"I suppose not. And who else?"

"Those are the most important suspects. Everyone else who left the hall that night seems to have come back fairly quickly. It's unlikely any of them did the murder. Oh, and it might be useful for you to write Morgan, Mark and Guenevere to let them know I'll be visiting them on your business."

"Draft the letters. I'll sign them and send them."

"You'll have them by morning."

"They may be suspicious. Especially Guenevere. The notion I want to honor her on her birthday will put her on her guard at once. You'll never get her to talk. And Morgan won't be any easier."

"I plan to be subtle. You're a warrior. You wouldn't understand. Besides, it's primarily Lancelot and Mordred I plan to cross-examine. Neither of them is exactly . . . well, you know."

For a moment Arthur fell silent. When he spoke again he avoided looking at Merlin. "You know me. I'm not a thinker. I like to believe I'm an able administrator, a competent general, an honorable man—but I don't think a great deal. But Merlin," he turned his head to face him, "I honestly can't think of anything that's getting better."

"Middle-age weariness, that's all. When you reach a certain age, nothing in the world looks good anymore."

"No, that's not what I mean. I remember what it was like when I first became king. When I first conquered all of England. You knew me then, you were there. I had such hopes. Such dreams for the kind of land I wanted to build." He picked up the wineskin and poured more. "I'm so afraid this isn't it."

"Nothing human is perfect, Arthur."

"I'm not talking about perfection. I'm talking about simple peace. Find the killer for me, Merlin. Find him. And while you're at it, find my crystal skull and its shrine. And Excalibur. I feel naked without it."

On the way back to his tower, Merlin encountered Pellenore. The man was galloping as usual along a winding corridor, astride an imaginary horse, shouting, "Giddyup, boy! Faster! Faster!"

Merlin stepped back into a recess, hoping the mad fallen king wouldn't see him. And for a moment it seemed that he wouldn't. He came careering along, directly toward Merlin, and seemed about to keep going. But then he pulled up his steed and stared straight at him. "Have you seen them?"

"Your dragons?" He was not in a mood to humor the man. "No, Pellenore, I haven't seen them, no more than anyone else has."

"See how cunning they are? They need to be rooted out and killed."

"Of course." He stepped out of his recess and started to walk away. "Pellenore, I wish I didn't find you so alarming."

He ignored this. "I was a king, you know. I deserve a bit of respect. I never get it."

"No, I suppose you don't. You're not a king any longer, after all. Arthur is the one."

"For now."

Merlin looked around. "There are people who would consider a statement like that treasonous. There have been murders. You might want to be a bit more discreet."

"The beasts kill everyone they can. You've seen it. First Arthur's squires. Next . . ." He looked away from Merlin and smiled shyly. "I'm the only one who understands. If they kill Arthur, I'll be king again."

"Naturally. And that would be so good for all of us." But it occurred to Merlin this was an opening not to be missed. He switched seamlessly to a friendly tone. "Why don't you come walking with me for a while? We never talk."

"Well, all right, for a few minutes at least. But I have dragons to hunt."

"Yes, of course."

He took Pellenorc by the arm, and they ambled along the hall together. "What do you know about the death of the squires?"

"What squires?"

Knowing it was probably pointless, Merlin said, "Ganelin and Borolet. You've only just mentioned them."

"They were killed by a beast."

"Did you see it? Were you there?"

"It isn't just dragons, you know. There are griffins, manticores, ogres. A malevolent gnome lives directly underneath Camelot. And there is a sphinx. She sharpens her claws on the castle's stones. She is vicious. Arthur must beware."

Merlin smiled, wondering if someday madness might take him himself. Certainly most of the knights thought him . . . eccentric. "I'll be sure to tell him when I see him."

"Don't humor me, Merlin. I'm only mad in one direction."

What on earth could he mean? Or was this simply more madness? "Suppose the one who killed the twins is a human monster, not the kind you're hunting?"

"Do you know the answer to the riddle of the sphinx, Merlin? What walks on four legs in youth, on two in maturity and on three in old age? Answer: man. We humans are the worst, monstrous or not."

"I never knew you had such a dark view of humanity."

"I'm a deposed king. First there were flatterers and hypocrites at court. Now there are all the ones who pretend pity and compassion. Who could see humanity more clearly?"

Mad in only one direction. Indeed. "I've never gotten to know you, Pellenore. I think I'd like to."

"Be careful. The dragons devour everyone who gets near me."

"Should I wear armor?"

"Should Arthur?"

"There have been times, now and then, Pellenore, when people have suggested you're not as unhinged as most of us like to imagine. I've had that thought myself. I wish I knew."

"The ogres plant those thoughts. I'm mad as a rabbit in March. What do you know about Rome?"

"Rome?" He wished the old man's conversation was easier to follow. "It is the capital of Italy. But not the glorious place it once was. The Goths have overrun it and destroyed most of what was beautiful. Pellenore, you're a classicist, like me."

"I'm not anything like you, and you are not like me. People distrust you, Merlin. If you go around saying things like that, it will only get worse. Most people find knowledge suspect. People think you're in league with the dark powers. They merely think me insane."

"Perhaps I should chase a few beasts myself."

"Perhaps you should. Good-bye."

He whipped his imaginary horse and sped off down the hall.

Merlin watched him go, thinking that there must be some way of discovering exactly how addled the man was. And whether he was capable of murder. And, if he was, whether his mind was sound enough for him to be held accountable for it.

Certainly he seemed, in his peculiar way, to have a sensible, coherent view of the world. It simply didn't correspond to anyone else's. Is that what madness is?

He felt hungry and went to the refectory. There wasn't normally much activity there except at mealtimes, but he thought he should be able to scrape up a snack. The place was empty except for Nimue, who was eating a large bowl of soup and a small loaf of bread. She smiled and waved at him.

"Colin. I didn't think I'd find anyone here but the kitchen servants, if them. It isn't lunchtime."

"You'd be lucky to find them. There are so many little pantries and hidey-holes. It took me ten minutes to find someone to heat up my soup." She ate. "What did Arthur say?"

"About . . . ?"

"Don't be foxy. I know you were going to talk to him about Ganelin's chart. And about the status of the investigation." Some soup dribbled down her chin; not having a napkin, she wiped it with her sleeve. "Such as it is. If you catch sight of one of the maids or the kitchen boys, flag her or him down for me, will you?"

Merlin sat beside her and tore a piece of her bread for himself. "He wants us to go ahead with it."

"Us?"

"Us. You're to assist me. And Brit is to work with us."

"The three of us. If we were all women, we'd be like the Fates, closing in on a guilty man."

"You've been reading Greek tragedy. You're learning."

"I have to please a stern old teacher."

He laughed. "This bread is dry. Don't they have anything fresher? And I think Greffys may be joining our little party, too."

"Greffys? You're joking. Even for a squire, he's . . . well, you know."

"Yes, I know. But we're going to need someone who's on good terms with the cooks and valets and maids and so on, and that pretty much means one of the squires."

"I know some of the servants. And I think Brit does, too."

"It's not the same thing. The squires are half servants themselves. But believe me, if we don't need Greffys, I certainly won't use him."

"I mean, not to speak ill of the dead, but Ganelin wasn't exactly an intellectual. But he was Aristotle compared to Greffys."

"He's a boy, Colin."

"So am I." She sneered sarcastically.

"I think we're definitely going to be traveling. Give some thought to what you want to take."

"To Corfe, to corner Guenevere?"

He nodded. "Or Lancelot, or whichever one of her minions looks to be guilty."

"Do I have to go to Morgan's realm, too? I'd rather not."

"I hadn't thought of it, but it probably wouldn't be a good idea to take you there. No sense taking the chance someone might recognize you."

"Thanks." She was plainly relieved. "When do we get started?"

"First thing tomorrow, if Brit is free then. Or now, if you'd rather." He unrolled the chart on the dining table. "I keep looking for a pattern in this."

"Maybe there is none."

"That would be our luck. One thing stands out, though. The crosses, Xs and stars are all on one side of the Great Hall."

"If it is the Great Hall, Merlin. I mean, I know it looks

like it, but I knew Ganelin better than you did. That could just as easily be a diagram of some damn fool sports thing he was thinking about."

"That's exactly what we need. A positive attitude."

She shrugged. "I'm only trying to be helpful."

He focused on the chart. "But these triangles—they're spread out all around. See?"

She studied it. "You're right. On both sides of the hall and in every corridor."

"Only one creature goes gadding about the castle that way. I think the triangles must represent Pellenore."

Her soup was getting cold. She picked up her bowl and drank it off. "That makes sense. As much sense as anything about Pellenore can. I'm still hungry."

"You're a growing boy." He smiled a sweetly sardonic smile. "I just ran into Pellenore in the hall, on my way here. We had the oddest exchange. His lunacy has always struck me as lightweight. But he was saying the strangest things. He's smarter than I ever thought, and better educated, and even more perceptive, in his way."

"So how do we verify that the triangles are his? I mean, a crazy old man . . . And he's been here for a thousand years, hasn't he? Who would remember him from before?"

"I knew him then, slightly. But he went mad almost at once after Arthur defeated him and took everything away from him. There was never much chance to decide what I thought of him before—before he—" He made a twisting gesture.

"It's all ancient history to me. Where were his lands?"

Merlin looked surprised. "You don't know? They were here." He pointed downward, emphatically. "Camelot was his castle, and the shires around it were his domain."

Nimue whistled. "I had no idea."

"No one your age ever understands anyone older. The world began when you were born, didn't it?"

"Don't be condescending, Merlin. But then, there must still be—"

"Exactly what I was thinking. There must still be people here who served in his household. People who knew him then and know him now and understand what happened to his mind."

"Were any of Arthur's knights his?"

He wrinkled his brow. "I've never followed the knights' dongs all that closely. It's possible. Brit will know, or Arthur will. But there must be someone here."

"Who knows him now? Who does he confide in?"

"Heaven knows." He took the last of the bread and bit into it. "The dragons, I suppose."

"I'm still hungry. Where are the bloody servants?"

"Off in those pantries you mentioned, sleeping."

"Damn. I want more soup."

"Do we need servants for that? There's a fire in the hearth. I could use some, too."

And so the next morning Britomart met the two of them in Merlin's study. She was half-asleep and kept yawning then excusing herself.

"Bad night, Brit?" Nimue was full of energy. "You should be wide awake and ready for work, like me."

"Be quiet. If there's anything worse than a morning person, it's a self-righteous morning person."

Merlin got between then and recapped for Brit what they had deduced about Ganelin's chart. "If we can match our four suspects to the four kinds of symbols . . ." He smiled and let the thought finish itself.

Brit yawned again, more widely than before, and picked up the map and inspected it closely. "If this really is a diagram of the castle, then . . ." She wrinkled her brow. "Let's see. This is the Great Hall, at the center. And this shows only part of the rest of the castle. It leaves off ten yards or so in any direction. But . . ." She looked around, as if something she saw might correspond to something Ganelin had sketched. "The servants' quarters, the storerooms and the stables are off to the right of the hall. There are triangles in every hallway."

"Very Pellenore-like, wouldn't you say?"

She nodded. "Or at least, not very Mordred-like or Lancelot-like. Do you have any food around here? I need something to wake me up."

"Sorry. I can send a page to the refectory for you, if you like."

"No." She was becoming absorbed with the chart. "I'll cope till I can get there myself. And on the other side of the hall are the corridors leading to Arthur's tower and yours, the rooms where the knights live and the refectory. Crosses, Xs, stars." She looked up at him. "They radiate from the Great Hall. It might almost be possible to connect them into direct lines."

Merlin looked over her shoulder. "That's true for the crosses and Xs. The stars seem to wander a bit."

She traced them with a fingertip. "Who could have been wandering about like that? And why? It seems so aimless."

There was a tapping at the window. Merlin's raven Roc was there. He opened the window to let him in, and the bird flew onto his shoulder. Merlin reached up and stroked its head. "I think we can only get so far using the chart alone. There are other ways to proceed. If we can start eliminating the suspects, one by one, then the one left must be the killer.

If the chart backs up what we suspect, that's one more level of certainty."

"Makes sense, I suppose." Brit yawned still again.

"You suppose?"

"I've never been involved in anything like this before."

"None of us has, Brit."

Nimue shivered in the cold air from the window. She got up and pulled it shut. "I think we all agree that Pellenore is the most unlikely suspect, don't we? So he should be the easiest to eliminate."

"Exactly." Merlin rubbed his hands together like a man about to cut into a succulent steak. "What do you remember about Pellenore from the time when Arthur defeated him, Brit?"

"It's been years. More than a decade."

"I know. Try and remember. I was busy trying to get the country functional again, or I'd remember myself. I'd like to find some people who knew Pellenore then. And some who are close to him now, if there are any."

She concentrated. "I don't remember a lot. But after the battle, a lot of his knights defected to Guenevere or headed to the Continent to go off on their own quests or whatever. A good knight can find service at just about any court in Europe." She wrinkled her nose. "Why some of us are still here . . ."

"Hmm. It sounds vaguely ominous. But are any of them still here?"

"I think most of them are dead, or gone."

"His servants, then? Did any of them stay with him?"

She shook her head as if she was trying to clear it. "I don't think so. Why would anyone stay with a losing king? There's no advancement in that."

The raven fluttered its wings and squawked, and he

reached up to quiet it. "Damn. I wonder if Arthur remembers anyone."

"It can't hurt to ask."

And Arthur did.

There was one knight in particular, he recalled, named Byrrhus. He had been among the oldest of Pellenore's company, and he had signed on to Arthur's service after the climactic battle. But he had retired and left Camelot soon after that. "He sends me odd notes now and then. Half of them make no sense at all. But he's alive. Can you imagine it? A knight moving into a quiet, peaceful existence still alive and with all his limbs and both eyes intact."

Britomart didn't like the sound of that and said so.

Merlin enjoyed her discomfort. "Face facts, Brit. You've chosen a dangerous line of work." He turned to Arthur. "I don't suppose you know where he retired to?"

He rubbed his chin. "Londinium, I think. Or London, as the residents call it now. Yes, I'm sure of it. I remember he had opened an inn. It was called . . . let me think . . . it was called Nero's Nose or something of the sort."

"Fine." Merlin rubbed his hands together like an eager child smelling cake. "Then to London we go."

"Are you serious?" Brit sounded extremely unhappy. "Have you ever been there? It's the dreariest town in England. It only flourished when the Romans made it their headquarters. Once we drove them out of the country . . ."

"We're not going for a holiday, Brit. We have a job to do."

"Suppose he's dead? Or senile?"

"We'll know that soon enough."

• • •

London was a small, sleepy town on the banks of the
Thames River. It consisted of a few score houses, a shaky
wooden bridge spanning the river and a few decrepit shrines
to the Roman gods, some of them still in use. The place was
dominated by the ruins of a Roman garrison where children
played at being soldiers.

When Merlin, Brit and Nimue arrived there after half a
day's travel, it was raining. Brit got a bright red cloak out of
her luggage and wrapped herself in it. Merlin told her it
made her look like a fallen woman.

"Be quiet."

The river ran swift and muddy. Overlooking everything
were the remains of a Roman fort built of large, dark stones.
The long outer wall was dotted with watchtowers. Despite
the rain there were children playing atop them. But only the
front wall was intact; as they moved past, they could see
that the others had huge gaps in them.

They stopped on the hill overlooking the town and took
it all in, and Brit voiced her disdain for the place again.
"Look at it. What a dump. There isn't even a decent pub,
just a few inns where you can buy gritty beer and sour
wine."

"You know this place. And not just casually." Nimue's
tone was accusatory. "Why haven't you said so?"

"There are some things I don't like to remember."

Merlin was suspicious, too. "Where are you from originally, Brit?"

She frowned and gestured at the place before them.
"From that."

"Oh."

They spurred their horses. None of them could wait to
find an inn with a good fire and to dry off. To their surprise,

the streets were paved with large stones. "The Romans," Brit said with a snort.

"I've heard about Roman roads crisscrossing all of Europe." Nimue had a touch of awe in her voice. "Paved like this and still in use. What wonders they must have accomplished. They say that Rome will last forever. If it was all like this, I can believe it."

"Arthur is right." There was genuine sadness in Merlin's voice. "Nothing in the world is getting better."

"You both spend too much time reading books." Brit was not disguising how unhappy she was to be there. "Where are the Romans now? Where is Cleopatra? Where is Augustus?"

"They left us this." Nimue gestured at the fort and the stones beneath their horses' hooves. "What will we leave? Beer mugs."

"Arthur is holding the country together, Merlin." Brit's tone was oddly vehement. "That's more than the Romans were ever able to do. On the far side of town there are temples to their gods. Mars, Venus, Hephaestus, Vesta. Mostly ruins now, but when I was a girl a few crackpots still prayed in them. A lot of good it's done them."

Just at the outskirts of the town, Merlin asked a passerby carrying a sack of something for directions to Nero's Nose.

The man was baffled. "I've never heard of such a thing."

"It's an inn. Possibly run by an old knight."

"Oh, you mean Caesar's Bones, then."

"Yes, I suppose I do."

"It's right on the main street." He pointed vaguely in the direction he'd come from. "Right in the middle of town. You'll see it. And they'll be glad you've come. Not many people do."

There was not much traffic in London's streets. A number of buildings were made from the same dark stone as the abandoned fort. It occurred to Nimue that they had been built with stones from its damaged walls. A few others were made of limestone. But most were wooden, and ramshackle.

Such people as there were in the streets tended to keep their eyes lowered; no one seemed at all social. Brit muttered, "You see what I mean? The people here . . . they don't seem to have personalities. Or minds."

"You're too harsh, Brit." Merlin, oddly, seemed to be enjoying it. "People who know how to mind their own business, and who don't feel the need to prattle every little thing that occurs to them—that's a breath of fresh air."

"Ask another one for directions and see how fresh you find them."

"There's no need. Look, here is Caesar's Bones now."

The inn was small and unprepossessing. One tiny window, streaked with mud or something like it, looked out onto the street. A sign with a crudely painted skeleton and a Roman eagle announced the inn's name, a dim recollection of the defeat and expulsion of the Romans centuries before. The three travelers looked at one another, not certain what to expect, and dismounted.

There was no hitching post, so they tethered their horses to a stunted bush nearby. "Nothing here grows well. This is not a healthy place."

"You grew well, Brit." Nimue couldn't resist pricking her mood.

"Be quiet, 'Colin.' " She said the name lightly but pointedly, to remind Nimue that she knew something, or thought she did.

Merlin pushed open the door of the inn and they stepped

inside. As they'd been hoping, a large fire burned energetically in the hearth. They made straight for it and pulled up a table and chairs.

A thin, wizened old man emerged from a back room. "Good afternoon." He didn't sound as if he meant it. And he certainly did not look as if he might ever have been a knight.

"Afternoon." Merlin smiled at the man. "We've been on the road all day. We need wine and some nice hot beef."

"You'll get beer and rabbit. No one here eats beef."

Oh. "Uh . . . fine. I'm sure it's excellent fare."

"It's the best you'll find in London."

Brit snapped, "Is that saying much?"

The man ignored her. "Beer and rabbit for three, then. Will there be anything else?"

"A bit of information, if you please." Merlin was working at cordiality, hoping it would offset Brit's rudeness. "Would you be Byrrhus, by chance?"

"I would not."

"Is he on the premises?"

"No."

He was not to be put off. "But this is his inn, isn't it? People talk about Caesar's Bones all over the country."

The man gave out a short, derisive laugh. "They don't, and there's no use saying they do." Without another word he turned and went back to the rear of the building.

The three of them fell silent, not at all certain how to react. Finally Brit said, "And the man on the road said they'd be happy to see us."

"They'll be happy enough to see our money, when the time comes."

The publican came back with three large goblets of beer. He scowled at them and said, "Drink hearty."

"Uh, thank you."

He turned and left again.

Merlin looked himself up and down. "Maybe we look like we carry some disease."

"We do." Brit smelled her beer and pushed the goblet away. "It's called civilization. It's complete anathema here."

Nimue sipped her beer and made a sour face. "This is awful."

"The meat will be worse."

"I can see why you don't like to tell anyone this is where you're from."

Brit put on a wide smile. "We all have things we want to hide, don't we, Colin?"

Nimue froze, uncertain how to react. Merlin made a show of drinking his beer then wiping his lips with a broad gesture. "It's not the worst I've ever had."

"At least Morgan hasn't had a chance to poison it." Brit was not drinking, quite pointedly.

"Oh?" Nimue grimaced at her. "You haven't tasted it."

The owner came back with three plates of meat and bread. "Here you are."

"I don't believe," Merlin smiled as wide a smile as he could manage, "we caught your name."

"Robert." The man frowned.

"Well, Robert, we are from Camelot. I am Merlin, this is Britomart, one of the king's premiere knights, and this young man is my apprentice, Colin."

He stared at them. "Yes?"

Undaunted, Merlin pressed on. "We are on a mission from King Arthur, looking for a man named Byrrhus. He used to be a knight in the king's service, and we're told he used to own this inn."

"Will you be needing rooms?"

He looked to his companions. "For tonight, yes. One for Colin and me, and one for Britomart."

"Two rooms, then."

Brit laughed at him. "Yes, you've got it."

"And we'd appreciate some assistance." Merlin took out his purse and made a show of the gold coins in it.

Robert's eyes widened. Suddenly he was the most gracious host. "Anything you need, sir."

"Well, as I told you, we're looking for Byrrhus. Do you know where we can find him? Or do you know someone who might?"

Robert hadn't taken his eyes off the purse. "He's mad. He went mad years ago. He lives in the ruins of the old Roman temple on the hill."

"Which one? Where?"

He pointed vaguely. "Follow that road out of town. The hill's steep; you'll know it. Ruins on top."

Merlin handed him a coin. "I hope that's enough for our rooms and your trouble."

"More than enough, sir. Will there be anything else?"

"Not now, thank you. You have stables?"

"Yes, sir, out back. Eat well, sir."

They ate. No one bothered to comment on how bad the food was; it would have been belaboring the obvious. When they were finished, Merlin went off to find Robert and tell him they'd be back by nightfall. Then they departed in hopes of meeting the man they'd come to see.

It was raining more heavily. Their poor horses were miserable. They mounted and set off slowly. "Which way, Brit?"

She pointed, and they began to move.

The streets were quite empty now, so there was no one for Brit to make snide comments about. She seemed unhappy about it. Close to the edge of town the buildings thinned out and the road started to rise. Quite abruptly, the rain stopped, and ahead of them up the hill, through a light mist, they could see a cluster of old, ruined buildings. Rows of columns fronted them; one of them still had part of a dome standing atop it.

It took a few minutes to reach them; the horses had trouble getting their footing on the muddy grade. Finally, they were at the center of what must have been a sizable sacred precinct in its day. Ten temples of various sizes, built in various styles, loomed around them. The smallest of them wasn't much more than a shrine; the largest would have made a secure little fortress. Rainwater dripped from what was left of the roofs. Toppled statues, most of them missing arms, heads or both, littered the ground.

"Well." Merlin dismounted, looked around and rubbed his hands together. "At least everything will dry out now. Where do you suppose we'll find him?"

They stared at one another and shrugged. Brit said, "I think that one over there is the temple of Mars. That might be the logical place."

For want of a better suggestion they went and looked. Three Ionic columns stood, supporting nothing at all. A fragment of the pediment lay in the mud; carved into it was the name of the god. The walls and roof were mostly gone. An altar where a statue of the god must have stood once was covered with dead leaves and twigs. Nimue had a thought. "Those limestone buildings in town—this is where they got the stone."

"Should we have let it go to waste?" Brit sounded defensive.

"We? I didn't think you identified with these people."

Merlin interrupted the little spat before it could escalate. "Let's separate and check the other temples."

They did so. Most of the others were in even worse shape than that first one. Merlin and Nimue found it dispiriting; Brit was businesslike.

Finally, Nimue stepped into what seemed to be the largest and best preserved of them. There was no indication which god it had been sacred to. It was no cleaner than the others. But under a part of the roof that was still intact a fire was burning.

"Hello?" She raised her voice so much it sounded like a girl's; she quickly lowered it and repeated, "Hello? Is anyone here? Byrrhus?"

Seemingly from nowhere came on old man's voice. "Who are you? And how did you know my name?" It thundered through the ruins.

"I'm Colin, apprentice to Merlin, King Arthur's chief advisor." She ran back to the entrance and shouted, "Someone's here!"

In a moment Brit and Merlin joined her.

Merlin looked inside. "Where is he?"

"I heard his voice, but he's hiding somewhere."

Brit crossed the floor to where the fire was burning. "Byrrhus? Byrrhus, it's me, Britomart."

Startled, Merlin caught her by the shoulder. "You know him?"

"Knew him. When I was a girl. Where do you think I got the idea I could be a knight?"

"Why the devil didn't you say so?"

She whispered, "He was half-crazy even then. I don't know if he'll remember me."

"He remembers you." The oldest man Nimue had ever

seen stepped out from behind the altar stone. His hair was grey as steel; his face was severely wrinkled; his body was that of an athlete grown old. "You were a tomboy and a brat."

"Byrrhus!" Suddenly excited, Brit ran and threw her arms around him. "You're still alive!"

"More or less, yes. Get your hands off me. Knights should be more dignified."

"Our innkeeper told us you'd gone completely insane."

"By his lights, I suppose I am. I prefer living in the temple of Venus among squirrels and mice to keeping company with other human beings."

Merlin stepped forward. "Your view of humanity is so sensible. I am Merlin. This is Colin."

"I was about to roast some beef. Would you like some? And some wine?"

"We've just eaten some foul rabbit at Caesar's Bones." Brit hadn't stopped smiling. It was the first real emotion Merlin had ever seen in her. "None of us ate very much. And a cup of wine would take the taste away wonderfully."

Nimue banked the fire high with twigs and branches, and Byrrhus cooked meat for them. Merlin and Nimue stayed mostly silent, letting Byrrhus and Brit reminisce about old times.

"The stories you used to tell me about serving at Pellenore's court." She was uncommonly wistful. "Nothing in the world could have been more romantic."

"Poor old Pellenore. Is he still alive?"

"Yes." She hesitated. "And he's quite insane."

Byrrhus narrowed his eyes. "So are foxes."

Nimue asked him why he preferred to live in the temple's ruins. "I mean, the town isn't much, but at least the houses must be warm and dry."

"Warm and dry and full of people. I've had enough of them. At first I thought it was just court life I'd had my fill of, so I came back here. But everyplace is as foul as court. Bickering, arguing, lying, cheating ... the court is the world in small. A sane man can stand only so much."

When the meat was finished roasting on its spit, they ate, and it was delicious. Byrrhus poured large cups of red wine. At one point a squirrel scampered in and went directly to Byrrhus. He stroked its head and it nestled beside him, quite improbably. But when Nimue reached out to pet it, it ran off in alarm. "You have the taint of human society," Byrrhus said.

After Byrrhus and Brit had had time to reminisce, Merlin turned the conversation to Pellenore. "None of us knew him back in his good days. What was he like?"

"He was a good king. He believed in justice and fairness and equality. He built a court based on them, and it was quite wonderful till Arthur came along and destroyed it."

"But—but—" Nimue couldn't grasp this. "But Arthur is dedicated to those same ideals. We all know it. Camelot is the best place to be."

"Then why didn't he simply join himself to Pellenore? Why squash him?"

There was no answer. Merlin interjected, "Was he mad back then, too? You should see him now, galloping about Camelot, chasing phantoms."

Byrrhus bit pointedly into a cut of beef. "There are monsters at Camelot. And they are real."

"Nonsense. Arthur is a good king." Merlin was testy.

"Pellenore ..." Byrrhus lapsed into silence for a moment. Then he seemed to find himself. "Losing his lands and his castle—losing everything he had worked so patiently to build—devastated him. That was what unhinged him, if anything really did. He used to talk about killing Arthur and reclaiming it all. He promised that some day he would."

Merlin exchanged glances with Brit, then with Nimue. "Did you believe him capable of it, Byrrhus? Really capable of it?"

"He lost his bearings, moral, intellectual, political, social . . . It was so sad to watch." He looked from one of them to the next. "I don't know what he was capable of. And I didn't want to know. That is why I left."

None of this was what Merlin wanted to hear. In the space of a brief, odd conversation Pellenore went from being an unlikely suspect to a likely one. "What precisely unhinged him? Was it the loss of his lands or the fact that he became a mere vassal of the king?"

"Does it make a difference? None of you is drinking your wine."

"We had some terrible beer at the inn. The wine wouldn't go well with it." Nimue was not at all certain what to believe about Pellenore now. "You know what they say—never mix the grape and the grain."

From nowhere a strong gust of wind blew through the temple. "The gods." Byrrhus smiled. "They don't like me living in their houses and desecrating them with cook fires. I use the temple of Mercury for a privy. Someday they'll take their revenge on me."

Brit got to her feet. "You seem to be surviving them well enough."

"They'll get me someday. There's a boy in the village who is a werewolf. They'll send him for me."

Like Brit, Merlin and Nimue stood. They thanked him for his hospitality and made excuses about having to go. Brit hugged him and told him, "You're as strong as Stonehenge. No mere werewolf could hurt you. Be well, Byrrhus."

A few minutes later they were on their horses and heading back down to London. None of them said much.

But later, by the fire at the inn with more of Robert's bad beer, they went over their encounter.

"I don't see any room to doubt that he's mad." Merlin sounded glum. "We didn't learn a thing that's helpful."

"I don't know." Brit swirled the beer in her cup. "Just because he prefers rodents to human beings . . . I mean, who wouldn't?"

"And belief in Mars and Mercury? He's quite daft, Brit."

"Byrrhus seemed the most wonderful man possible when I was a girl. Now . . . But does that mean everything he said must be mad?" Brit avoided looking at Merlin, not wanting to see the answer in his eyes.

Nimue pushed her cup away. "I mean, yes, he believes the Roman gods hate him. But does that necessarily mean what he says about Pellenore is nonsense, too?"

"No. I think . . ." Merlin suddenly seemed lost in thought. "I think we have to believe that, at least provisionally. Pellenore is a more viable suspect than any of us believed."

"Slightly more viable, anyway." Brit sipped her beer, made a sour face and put it aside. "Even if he wanted to kill Arthur however many years ago, does that necessarily mean he still does? And how does that translate into killing his squires?"

"If he's mad it might." Nimue avoided looking at her.

Merlin stood. "I'm spent. Let's get to sleep. There's no way to answer these questions. All we know for certain is that we'll have to watch Pellenore carefully from now on."

"Arthur won't like it."

"Arthur can't very well tell us who to watch, can he?"

They said their good nights and went to their respective rooms.

There was a large, lively fire in the one Merlin and Nimue were to share. She told him to take the bed; she'd be happy curled up by the hearth. Just before he nodded off, she asked him, "Merlin?"

"Hm?"

"What if Arthur won't go along with us?"

"I'm not sure what you mean."

"Well, suppose we learn who did the killings—I mean really learn, beyond any reasonable doubt—and he won't believe us?"

He sat up in the bed and stared at her. "You have no faith in the king's wisdom and justice?"

"He's already expressed skepticism about all of our suspects."

"I can't think about that now. I'm too tired. Tomorrow. We'll have plenty of time to talk it through on the road to Corfe and Guenevere."

FIVE

THE SPIDER'S HOUSE

The next morning there was brilliant sunlight. The three of them had more of Robert's bad food for breakfast. Britomart wondered aloud whether their meal actually included Caesar's bones. Merlin settled with Robert and made certain of the directions to Corfe.

Robert's stable had a leaky roof. The horses were wet and irritable. Brit and Nimue spent some time drying them with cloths and currying them before they set off. While they were at it, Merlin wandered off on his own.

The town was more awake today. People came and went, on this bit of business or that. He tried to engage a few people in conversation, but they were unpleasantly taciturn. What was Londinium's chief industry? The ground did not seen right for farming. The river might provide transport for trade, but there wasn't much traffic on it. He wondered why England was so full of mysteries.

When he got back to the inn, Brit and Nimue had saddled

and loaded the horses and were waiting for him. They set off on the same road they'd used the day before, the one past the old sacred precinct. In the sunlight the temples appeared even gloomier. There was no sign of Byrrhus.

The packhorses were carrying supplies Robert had procured for them. Brit complained about it. "So we eat still more of that man's dry meat and sour beer. Why not just dine at the next swamp we come to?"

By noon the sky began to cloud up again, and it gave her still more to complain about. "English winters. I'd love to know who first decided this island was a good place to live."

"For once I agree with you, Brit." Merlin had been nodding off in the saddle. "Humanity should confine itself to the warm, pleasant parts of the earth."

"How many of those are there?"

"There are enough. I've seen them. North Africa, that's the place."

"Whatever brought you back to England, then?"

"Don't ask."

She looked back the way they'd come. "One thing's for certain. Londinium is dying and will die. Twenty years from now it will be deserted."

"Good."

The road south to the coast was better than the one they'd taken to Londinium. Wider, smoother. And there was more traffic. Despite his antisocial nature, Merlin was happy to see more people. If nothing else, it indicated healthier weather. They came to a town called Greenwich and found an inn called the Tusk and Claw where the food was delicious. The landlord and his wife were plump and cordial;

she told her guests they'd bought the place from an old Italian who had originally called it the Tuscan Law. Brit immediately ordered more supplies there and dumped in the river the ones they'd bought from Robert.

Nimue watched her, amused. "You shouldn't do that. The Thames is dirty enough already. That beer might kill the fish."

"The fish can fend for themselves. I never want to taste anything that foul again."

Merlin stretched out on the riverbank and chimed in, "Wait till we get to Corfe. Have you ever had French cooking?"

"Will we be staying at the castle, then?" Brit seemed surprised. "I took it for granted we'd be quartered with the soldiers there."

"If we're invited, we should definitely stay with Guenevere, don't you think? After all, we're going there to pry into her affairs. And Lancelot's."

Nimue listened to the exchange. "I've never been to Corfe. I don't think I knew there was a garrison there."

"A fine one. It's one of our most important ports." Brit was in her element. "We could hardly leave it unguarded."

"It doesn't make sense that Guenevere would have settled there, then. I mean, why would she want to be where Arthur's men could keep an eye on her?"

"It's never made sense to anyone, Colin. I mean, it is one of the best ports in England, so if the French wanted to invade, it would make a logical landing place for them. But the landing force would have to be enormous to overcome our men. Leodegrance doesn't have anywhere near that many men."

"Leode—who?"

"Guenevere's father," Merlin explained.

"Oh. But—but I still don't understand why Guenevere chose to live at Corfe Castle of all the places in England."

Merlin and Britomart looked at one another and shrugged. He said, "I've often wondered if Guenevere is as crafty as she likes to think."

Brit finished her dumping, they took a short walk around the town to help digest their food, and then full and satisfied, they resumed their journey to the south coast. The horses settled into a comfortable pace, and the three travelers settled into a comfortable silence. There were still plenty of other people on the road.

"We should have Arthur designate this a king's highway or something." Nimue was enjoying the trip. "And that inn, the Tusk and Claw—he should buy all his provisions there. It's better food than I ever tasted at Camelot."

Merlin enjoyed her enthusiasm. "Maybe we can simply kidnap the cook."

"I'm serious, Merlin."

"You don't find the name of the place ominous?"

"Never mind."

At dinnertime they stopped to eat in Bournemouth then moved on. They reached the coast road to Corfe just at twilight.

A long, sloping grade went down to the ocean, where the town sat. One ship was anchored in the harbor. Merlin was surprised; he said there was normally more traffic.

Above the town, secure between two hills, was the castle. It was large and dark, more enormous than any building Nimue had seen. Brit told her it had originally been a Roman fortress. "This is one of the best natural ports in the country. No one could miss its strategic importance."

It was not at all a typical castle. There was no curtain wall surrounding it, and not even a moat. To all appearances it was quite open and vulnerable. But on closer inspection its unusual design became evident. There was a central keep, octagonal in shape, rising some eighty feet. From it, eight wings extended. And each of them was topped with heavy fortifications. Anyone trying to attack the castle would have met with a rain of arrows from several directions.

"And the Romans built all this?"

"No, I think they only built the central keep."

Merlin told her, "The castle goes back centuries. Some people think it must be the oldest in England. It's so ancient no one remembers who added all those arms. But they certainly date from before the rise of modern castle construction."

"Arms? Is that a formal architectural term, Merlin?" Brit asked.

He smiled. "No, but arms they are. Eight of them. The townspeople whose lives are dominated by it call it the Spider's House. I've never been certain whether that refers to the castle itself or to its chief occupant."

Clouds had built up steadily all afternoon. At least the temperature had remained on the mild side; there wouldn't be snow. But a stiff wind roiled the Atlantic; huge waves were breaking all around. The ship in Corfe's harbor rocked wildly.

The town was smaller than Nimue expected, but it was full of people, all of them evidently busy. And prosperous. A good harbor draws trade, and trade draws wealth. There

were even women who were brazenly open about being
streetwalkers.

The roar of the waves was clearly audible from every
spot they passed. They found a little inn and had some
spiced wine. Then Brit led them to the garrison and identified them to one of the guards on duty. Another one went off
to find the commander. The three of them waited just inside
the walls.

"You're one of Arthur's military commanders, Brit."
Merlin was annoyed to be kept waiting. "Don't they know
you?"

"I haven't been here in years. But the commandant is an
old friend."

A moment later a man wearing chain mail for no apparent reason came and greeted them. He and Brit embraced
warmly, and she introduced him to Merlin as Captain John
Dalley, the garrison commander. He shook their hands vigorously and led them through the courtyard and Common
Room to his office, where they had more wine.

"I thought someone from Camelot might come, once
word of that ship spread. But how did you manage to get
here so fast?"

"What about the ship?" He had caught Brit off guard.

"Didn't you get a look at it? It's French." He lowered his
voice and looked around conspiratorially. "Guenevere's father."

"Leodegrance, here? Why haven't you notified the
king?"

"The ship put in late this afternoon. You should have
seen all the fanfare and fuss when she turned out to welcome him. I was just drafting a letter to Camelot now."

"I see. Do you have any idea what he's doing here?"

Dalley shrugged. "It could be anything from visiting his

daughter to planning a war to welcoming a new addition to the family tree."

Merlin spoke up. "Guenevere is pregnant?"

"Not that I know of. I was only speculating. But she bellies with Lancelot often enough."

"Has she . . . how shall I say? Has she been behaving herself lately?"

"As much as she ever does. She's always trying to recruit my men away from Arthur's service."

"You must get that letter to Arthur right away. And we'll be drafting one, too. You can send it along with yours."

"Is something wrong?" He obviously suspected they might be there to check on him.

"No, John." Brit was reassuring. "We're doing some . . . er . . . fact-finding for him. We just want to apprise him of our progress."

Relief showed. "I see."

"You have room to quarter us?"

"Yes, of course." He turned to Nimue. "And you—why is a fine young man like you not in the military? Aren't you training to be a knight?"

"No, sir. Just a humble scholar."

"Oh." He didn't try to hide his distaste. "Let me have someone prepare quarters for you. It will be a few minutes, I'm afraid."

"That's perfectly fine, John." Brit smiled. "I'm sure Merlin and Colin would like to see the town. When should we be back?"

"I wouldn't stay out too late. This is a port town. It can be rough after dark. And it's full of French sailors, which makes it even worse than usual."

"Oh. Well, we'll be careful. And I'll wear my sword."

"Even so. You have no idea what they can get up to."

They thanked him again, promised not to stay out too late and left the fort.

Nimue was spent from the day's travel. "Why are we going out? I'm tired."

"I want to get a look at that ship," Brit said.

Merlin added, "And if we keep our eyes and ears open, we may get some hint what's afoot. Leodegrance shouldn't have come without notifying Arthur."

"Maybe it really is just a family visit," Nimue said.

"Don't be foolish. These are politicians. They never do anything for simple reasons," Merlin said.

"Should Captain Dalley have let them land?" Brit asked.

"How, exactly, could he have stopped them? No, he's doing the right thing, writing to Arthur. Diplomacy is the king's province."

They walked along the widest street in town, heading for the harbor. No one paid them much notice. But Nimue kept studying everyone she saw. "The people here—they're all plump."

"It's a prosperous town," Merlin told her.

"If the French actually were to invade, how much help could they be?"

"Not much," said Brit, who clearly didn't want to think about it.

The wind from the Atlantic was getting stronger; occasional gusts were so strong the three of them had to lean into the wind to keep their balance. Merlin's hat blew off and Nimue ran to fetch it. Overhead the clouds were thick and black; there was one brighter spot in them, all that could be seen of the moon.

The waterfront was lined with little taverns, most of them crowded. Yellow lanterns hung outside them; a long row of them provided the sole illumination. Cats scurried along the road, avoiding everything human. A dog dashed out of an alley and chased one of them, but it was faster. At one of the taverns people were singing a particularly obscene song about the French king.

"Why are all harbor towns alike?" Merlin asked no one in particular.

"I've never been in one before." Nimue was taking it all in quite eagerly.

But Brit paused and said, "All places are alike. Every earth is fit for burial. There's the French ship up ahead. Let's go and see what we can see."

The ship was called the *Vienne*. It was riding high in the water, which struck Brit as odd. "We'll have to ask Dalley if they unloaded any supplies. If not—let's get closer. I want to see if there are soldiers."

But before they could approach any nearer, there was a flurry of activity behind them. A man in armor with a plumed helmet led a dozen soldiers directly up to them.

"You are Merlin, the king's counselor? And Britomart?"

"We are." Brit took charge; she kept her hand on the hilt of her sword. "And this is Colin, Merlin's assistant."

"You are to come with me."

"I beg your pardon? We are here on the king's business."

"Queen Guenevere requests your presence." He was not smiling. "You will come."

Merlin spoke up. "How did the queen know we are here?"

"You may ask her that. Let us go."

"Are we being taken prisoner? King Arthur will hardly be pleased. There isn't a warlord in England who hasn't felt his wrath. I hardly think he'd hesitate to invade Corfe."

The man with the plume stepped closer to Merlin. "Queen Guenevere requests your presence at Corfe Castle. You are to be her guests."

"Whether we like it or not?"

Brit stepped pointedly between them. "Captain Dalley of the king's garrison is expecting us back. You'd best let us send him word where we'll be."

Plume man smiled. "I'm sure you'll be able to write him a note from the castle. The queen is nothing if not a gracious hostess."

Brit looked around. They were plainly outnumbered, and she knew she was the only one with real fighting experience. Resigned, she said, "Very well, then. Let's go."

Plume showed his relief. He gave the order, and his men formed two columns, one on each side of their "guests," and they headed off toward the hills and the castle.

People in the street looked more than slightly alarmed at the little parade; they crossed to the far side, all the while pretending not to have noticed. But at one corner a pair of soldiers from the garrison were negotiating with a pair of women. When they saw Merlin, Colin and Brit leaving under escort by Guenevere's soldiers, their eyes widened and they left off what they were doing to head back to Captain Dalley.

The party proceeded to the edge of Corfe and began to ascend the hill to the castle. It loomed ahead of them, black and enormous, looking indeed like a huge spider. Nimue noticed that two of the "arms" that were visible were crumbling and apparently deserted. Guenevere must not be as prosperous or secure as she liked to pretend. But the rest of the Spider's House was lit brightly with dozens of torches.

On either side of it to the east and west were hills. She asked Merlin what they were called.

"East Hill and West Hill."

"Oh."

"This is a port, not a university."

They reached the castle and proceeded to the main gate, between two of the arms. Guards were posted, and a dozen torches burned brightly there. Plume exchanged a few words with the sentries then turned to Brit. "You will please follow me." Since they didn't have much choice, they did so. Six of the soldiers stayed at the gate; the rest moved on.

The interior of the castle was made of that same dark stone. Torches burned every six feet along the hallways. They smoked and sputtered; the place smelled of bitter fumes and ash. At least the corridor was straight; the place's plan was much simpler and more straightforward than Camelot. Nimue commented on it.

"Simpler?" Merlin seemed surprised at the observation. "The whole place is monotonously rectilinear. I suppose that must be desirable for some people."

At the end of the hallway-arm there was an abrupt change to a lighter stone, medium grey instead of dark grey. They had reached the keep, the oldest part of the castle.

Plume had not spoken a word as he and his men ushered them along. Now he said, "Her Majesty is in the throne room. Protocol is to be observed."

"What is the protocol for a prisoner?" Merlin sounded more amused than anything else.

"As I told you, you are guests, not prisoners."

"Of course."

The keep was more convoluted than the outer parts of the castle. Corridors wound; steps ascended and descended. After a few yards they came to a large doorway. Plume stopped and turned to face them. "Go in."

"Go in?" Merlin seemed surprised. "You and your guards aren't coming?"

"Go in." His face was stone.

Again not having a choice, they went in.

The room was octagonal, smaller than the Great Hall at Camelot. Dozens more torches burned, lighting it brilliantly. But there was no circulation; the stench of smoke was almost overpowering.

A dozen people stood around the room, talking, reading official-looking papers or merely contemplating the queen's serene majesty. It was late, after dark, an odd time for court business to be conducted.

But Guenevere was there, seated in majesty on a gilded throne, much larger than Arthur's fairly plain one. The throne was elevated above floor level; she looked down on her subjects. Next to it was a second, smaller one, presumably for Lancelot, but it was empty. There was no sign of Leodegrance either. She looked to the door as they entered and put on a diplomatic smile. Her ape rested at her feet and looked up lazily.

"Merlin. Britomart." Her Majesty was all cordiality. "And who is this young man? We recall seeing him at Camelot, but he was never introduced to us. And events were so hectic there." She added this last in a tone so sweet it dripped with sarcasm.

"This is my student and assistant, Colin."

"I see. We welcome you, Colin. As we do your older companions."

Merlin and Brit exchanged glances. She was playing with them. How long before the boom was lowered?

"We trust you traveled well and happily?"

Merlin had had enough. "What do you mean 'we,' Guenevere? You and your ape?"

"Is it possible you do not comprehend the royal plural?"

Brit took a step forward. "Why have we been brought here?"

Guenevere was all innocence. "Did not my men tell you? I wish you to be my guests."

"They told us, all right—at the point of a sword. An odd kind of hospitality."

"Oh, dear." She feigned dismay. "You have mistaken our intentions."

"Then why don't you tell us what they are?" Merlin was growing annoyed with her.

"But still, you must admit it is, shall we say, irregular, for you to have intruded on my domain in this way."

So she was going to play that game.

"I am under the impression," he said firmly, "that England is Arthur's domain. And even so, he did write you to inform you we'd be coming—and on his business."

"England may be Arthur's. Corfe is mine."

"Captain Dalley and his men might not see it that way."

"Irrelevant." She brushed it aside. "What is this business my husband has sent you here to conduct?" Another sweet smile. "Does he want a divorce?"

"You know perfectly well that if the king wishes to set his consort aside, he hardly needs permission. Especially since she never consorts with him." Merlin looked around the hall at the various courtiers and functionaries. "The present matter is, I must tell you, quite confidential."

She stiffened slightly. "I see."

"A long day's travel has tired us, Guenevere. We'll talk business with you in the morning. I believe Captain Dalley is expecting us at the garrison. If you don't mind, we'll be going."

Her manner changed as she realized they weren't about

to be intimidated. "Weren't you told, Merlin? I want you to be my guests."

"Is there room in the dungeon for all of us?"

She sighed in an exaggerated way. "You shouldn't be so suspicious. I want to know what Arthur wants. You, presumably, want to tell me."

"'Me,' Guenevere? Shouldn't that be 'us'? Or has the royal plural suddenly become obsolete?"

"I thought yours was a diplomatic mission, Merlin. Instead of diplomacy I find directness verging on rudeness."

"Yes, you're right." His manner dripped with irony. "We should never have had you abducted at sword point."

Unexpectedly, she laughed. "You will stay here at the castle. You may write to the garrison commander and tell him you are doing so. Rooms are being prepared for you. But I'm afraid they won't be ready for a few minutes. We have another guest who is leaving tonight."

"You mean your father."

"My father, King Leodegrance, is in residence here, yes. But he is not the one I mean."

"Who, then?"

"That is no concern of yours. You may use my library to write your note to the garrison. One of my men will take it. Your rooms will be ready shortly thereafter."

"Fine."

Guenevere stood regally and left the throne room. Merlin, Brit and Nimue found themselves alone, ignored by everyone else there. Brit looked around at them suspiciously. "Well, at least we're not to be tortured."

"Yet." Nimue was quite out of her depth.

"Relax, Colin. Guenevere is an ambitious harridan, but she must know she could never survive a war with Arthur. Once she became aware the garrison knows we're here, there wasn't much chance she'd do anything to risk that," Brit stated.

A boy in his mid-teens entered the room and approached them. "I am Petronus. People call me Pete. Will you come with me, please? I'll show you where there's paper and ink." He spoke English with a French accent.

"Might we stop at our rooms first? I'd like to rest for a few moments." Merlin wanted to try and catch a glimpse of the mysterious other guest.

"The queen's instructions were to take you to the library."

"But I—"

"Please, sir. Besides, it's in the same wing as your rooms. You won't have far to go."

There seemed no point arguing. If their rooms really were close to the library, they might get a look at the mystery visitor.

The boy led them out of the throne room and into another arm of the castle. More dark stone; more torches. Nimue coughed. "Do people ever get used to the stench here?"

The boy ignored this and kept walking.

A few moments later they reached the queen's library. An armed guard was there, presumably to watch them. The room was lit with candles, refreshingly, and not torches. There were fewer books than in Merlin's study at Camelot.

Just as they were going in, Brit glanced down the hall to see if she could tell where their rooms were. And there, in apparently heated discussion with Lancelot and Leodegrance, was Mark of Cornwall. As soon as he realized she'd seen him, he stepped into a doorway.

So two of the suspects were together in the same place, under mysterious circumstances.

Merlin wrote his note to Dalley. He asked that Colin be

allowed to deliver it, and to his surprise, it was permitted. Nimue, accompanied by four armed guards, left for the garrison.

"I never thought they'd allow that." Brit was surprised, not unpleasantly. "Maybe she means it. Are we guests, not prisoners?"

"I doubt if even Guenevere knows. Once she understood that our presence here was known to Arthur's soldiers . . . It will take her a while to decide what to do with us."

Before they could say more, Petronus showed up with two other boys, and Merlin and Brit were ushered to a suite of rooms farther down the corridor. Torches burned and smoked everywhere.

Petronus asked if there was anything they needed.

"Yes. Some candles. These torches give off such a stench," Merlin said.

The boys looked at one another, and Petronus said, "I guess we've gotten used to it."

"And their light makes too much glare for comfort."

"Candles are in short supply, sir. But I'll see if I can find some."

"Thank you."

The boys left.

Brit sat in an upholstered chair. "Did you see him?"

"See who?"

"Guenevere's guest."

"No. For heaven's sake, who is it?"

She told him. And he froze. "This was supposed to be simple. Eliminate the wrong suspects and one will be left. But now Pellenore is more actively under suspicion than before. And this. How much more complicated is this going to get?"

Brit grinned. "And how much more ominous? What can he be doing here?"

"I can think of a dozen possibilities, all of them alarming. Arthur can't possibly know."

"I've always hated politics, Merlin. This is why. War is so clean and simple. Mass slaughter. Bloodletting on a major scale. What could be more pleasant?"

"I'm afraid war and politics get mixed up. Mark is a military leader *and* a king, remember? I'll take the bedroom over there. Is that all right?"

She shrugged. "It doesn't matter. So. Guenevere is nearly out of candles. What do we make of that?"

"Money must be tight. Which means she's not interfering with the revenues from the port—at least not yet. I suppose that's a sign of loyalty, or what passes for it with her."

Petronus was back. He presented, ostentatiously, two candles. "One for each bedroom." His tone suggested this was a real luxury.

"Thank you, Petronus."

"Please, sir, call me Pete."

"Pete, then. When is breakfast?"

"Daybreak, sir."

"Fine. You'll come and show us to the refectory?"

"Gladly, sir."

"Excellent. Good night, then."

"Good night. Uh . . . sir?" The boy plainly had something on his mind.

"Yes, Pete?"

"You come from King Arthur's court, don't you? From Camelot?"

Brit told him, "Yes, we do."

"Everyone says it's the most wonderful place in the world. Will you tell me about it?"

They exchanged glances. The boy might be useful. Brit assured him they'd do so if they had time and the opportunity arose. He thanked them effusively, promised to see them in the morning and left.

Merlin chuckled. "Well, I think Colin can work on him while you and I fry the bigger fish."

She stood and stretched. "It's like war after all. When you see an opening, you exploit it."

"Politics," he said in a mock-confidential whisper, "is precisely the same."

Next morning the sun was blindingly bright and the air had a tinge of warmth. After weeks of premature winter it seemed odd. Merlin's room looked out over the town and the harbor. He stood watching them and turning over events in his mind. Nimue was still asleep next to the fire.

Petronus knocked and came in. "Good morning. I hope you slept well."

Merlin held a finger to his lips and pointed at Nimue, still deep in slumber. "Let's go to the next room," he whispered to Petronus. "Colin always takes a long time to wake up in the morning."

Brit was up, dressed and seemingly full of energy. The three of them stood at the window of their suite's parlor, watching the French ship bob in gentle waves. Another vessel, a small frigate, had docked during the night.

"You promised to tell me about Camelot," the boy prompted.

"So we did." Merlin didn't want him there. "After breakfast, all right?"

"Yes, sir." He was mildly disappointed; it showed.

A few moments later Nimue joined them, yawning deeply. Petronus, smiling, evidently happy for their company, led them out of their wing and to the refectory. Even in bright daylight the halls were dark; torches burned and smoked.

The room was long and rectangular. Several dozen people ate sausages, eggs and bread. There was a mix of French and native English accents. Portions were small. Merlin noted it; the queen was having money trouble, perhaps enough for her to enter a plot against Arthur. Even if she didn't become sole monarch, an alliance with a successful usurper would be to her benefit.

Guenevere and Lancelot were at the head table. Once again there was no sign of her father. She smiled when she saw the three of them and pointed to seats at another table to the left of her. They sat, and servants brought them food.

Before they were finished, the queen and her man stood and crossed to them. Guenevere was evidently quite curious about what Arthur had in mind. Lancelot renewed his acquaintance with Brit and suggested they get together and exchange military gossip.

Nimue excused herself from the table and found Petronus at another table in a corner of the hall. Merlin had told her about the boy and suggested she learn what she could from him. "My master says you want to hear about Camelot."

His face brightened. "Yes! Please." He looked around self-consciously, but no one was paying any attention to them.

"Why don't we go off somewhere we can be alone and I'll tell you all about it." She gestured toward the door. "And you can tell me all about Corfe. I've never been here before, you know."

The day continued to be sunny; the air warmed up to an autumn-like temperature. Guenevere's knights exercised and drilled in the courtyard on the north side of the castle. At mid-morning, Brit decided to join four of them who were wrestling and had sarcastically invited this woman knight to participate. Twenty minutes later she had beaten them all. After that, the others gave her more respect but avoided challenging her. She decided to run laps around the yard.

Lancelot had begged off spending time with her, claiming there was some business he had to attend to. But not long after she beat the quartet of wrestlers, he joined her. "Hello, again."

Brit was out of breath from her run. "You said you'd be tied up all morning."

"Luck was with me."

"With *us*." She smiled as cordially as she could manage. Merlin had briefed her on how to act with him—and on what she should try to find out.

"I'm afraid I'm not much of a minister. But I'm Guenevere's chief knight and therefore her chief advisor, so I get dragged into all kinds of discussions I can't contribute a thing to."

She mopped her brow with a towel. "What was this one?"

"Finance." He made a sour face. "I'm only good at spending money."

"How much money can it take to run Corfe Castle?"

He looked around, then lowered his voice slightly. "It

isn't just the castle itself. This is a royal household. There is a certain dignity to be upheld. It is not always easy."

She was going to comment on the meager food portions but decided it might be wiser not to. "Arthur gives her a certain allowance, doesn't he? Or rather, the nation does. I mean, she is a member of the royal family."

"Arthur cannot always be relied on to send it when he should." Again he looked around; no one was paying them much attention. "I miss France. Part of me would like to go back there to live."

"Being a queen's—" she groped for a neutral word, "advisor can't be a terribly hard life. Especially when the queen is so completely separated from the rest of England."

"Be careful what you say." His tone was hushed and urgent. "You'd be amazed how many ears she has. Even for me."

"She doesn't trust you? I thought the two of you were . . ." She let the sentence hang unfinished.

"We are." He said it a bit too quickly to be convincing. "I love her, and she loves me. Isn't that the way it's supposed to be?"

She was supposed to love her husband, but it seemed wise not to say so. "You know, I'm still hungry. Breakfast was . . . frugal, wasn't it?"

He moved very close to her and spoke softly. "I know a good inn in town. Let me take you there for your noonday meal."

"Why, Lancelot, I'd love that."

"And in the meantime, would you like to . . . wrestle?" His tone made clear that he was not talking about exercise.

"Uh . . . no thank you. I'm spent." She forced herself to smile. "But lunch would be lovely."

"Oh." He sounded part puzzled, part disappointed. He

looked up at the sun. "Two hours. Meet me here, not inside."

"Of course."

Looking around suspiciously, he joined a group of knights who were fencing on the opposite side of the courtyard.

Brit couldn't help smiling. So there was trouble in Corfe, and it wasn't just financial. And Lancelot wasn't exactly being discreet. With luck, this would be easier than she'd expected.

"So Arthur has a proposition for me?"

Guenevere sat in serene majesty at a large wooden table in the library. Once again, Merlin wondered at the relatively few books there. He decided to play with her for a while.

"I went for a walk on the roof earlier this morning. And imagine my surprise—there are ravens living here. They're almost as tame as the ones I take care of at Camelot. It makes me feel quite at home."

"The townspeople say they've always been here. But I've never found them very friendly."

"One of them came right up to me."

She was growing testy, which pleased him. "So what does my husband have on his mind? Is he planning to send me the money he promised?"

"I'm afraid I don't mix in financial affairs, Guenevere. But I'll ask him, if you like. Are you certain you remember the due date correctly?"

"Quite certain. Merlin, are you going to tell me what you're doing here?"

"Why, I came for the view. Corfe has the loveliest harbor in England."

"View, be damned. You said you've brought some kind of scheme from Arthur. I want to know what it is."

He clucked his tongue. "Really, Guenevere, you haven't got the hang of diplomacy at all."

"Nothing connected with Arthur is diplomatic. He is trying to starve me out of the country. I've had to ask my father for a loan."

So that was what he was doing at Corfe—if she was being truthful. "How is your father? I don't believe I've seen him."

"He is not feeling well. He has gout, and moreover, ocean travel never agrees with him."

"What a pity. But was that him we saw chatting with Lancelot and Mark last night?"

She glared and refused to rise to it. "What does my husband want? What new plan has he hatched for making me miserable?"

He had strung her out long enough. He leaned back in his chair and turned expansive. "A reconciliation."

"A—? Are you trying to be funny?"

"I assure you I'm perfectly serious. You have an important birthday next autumn, I believe."

"I turn forty, yes." Her eyes narrowed.

"Arthur would like to make it a national holiday."

For a moment she didn't seem to know how to react. Then suddenly she burst into laughter. "Of all the grotesque jokes. I've only just turned thirty-nine, and he ignored the occasion completely. Really, Merlin."

"I'm perfectly serious. And so is he."

"Why would he want to celebrate my birthday? Is it so important to him to announce to the whole country how much younger he is than his wife?"

"I can't vouch for his motives. But he wants to invite

people from every court in Europe. It would boost England's image internationally. But of course it would require your cooperation."

She pretended to brush a gnat off her sleeve.

"Guenevere, did you hear me?"

"I did." She examined her fingernails. "And I am properly impressed at Arthur's cheek. Was this thing your idea?"

"The king has more than enough ideas of his own."

She took a deep breath. "So Arthur needs me. And is willing to admit it."

"For this, at least. What do you say?"

"I'll have to think. And I'll have to consult with my own counselors. And my father. It's so fortunate he's here just now."

"And will you ask Mark?"

"Mark is gone."

Trying to sound casual he asked, "What did he want here?"

"Foolishness."

"Of what sort?"

"Is it possible Arthur does not know what his military commander gets up to?" She grinned like a predatory wolf in a children's story. "You may tell Arthur I'll consider his scheme. But I will need time."

"We'll have to start planning soon, you know. The invitations will have to go out by early spring. Arthur would like an answer as soon as possible." He looked at her, wearing a mask of innocence. "Now, if you can."

She stood. "I cannot. You may tell him I'll take it under consideration. No more."

"That is your final word?"

"For now, yes it is."

"Very well, then. I'll tell him. But he won't be happy."

She walked to the door then turned and grinned at him again. "If I don't agree to go along with this—will it hurt him?"

"I expect so. And all of England—including you. You must understand, his ambitions are not for himself but for the country."

"Yes. Of course they are. But does he really want the crowned heads of Europe to see what bumpkins inhabit this island?"

"That is not a proper sentiment for a queen of England."

"No, I suppose it isn't." Her grin grew even wider. "Nevertheless . . ."

"Needless to say, the main festivities would be held here at Corfe. That means an influx of money. Impressing the rest of Europe would require that we put on the best face possible."

She tried not to let her reaction show, but her eyes flashed for a second. "Precisely how great an influx?"

"That is open to negotiation."

"Negotiating with Arthur. He would enjoy placing me in a position where that would be necessary."

"From what I've seen, Guenevere, it may be necessary already."

She flashed a politician's smile. "When will you be leaving?"

"Tomorrow, I imagine." Quickly, he added, "With Your Majesty's permission, that is."

"The sooner, Merlin darling, the better."

"I'm hungry. Can we get something to eat?"

Nimue and Pete ambled about the castle's perimeter. Merlin had coached her in ways to draw the boy out, as he

had Brit. Petronus seemed to enjoy talking; she expected it
to be easy.

"I think the refectory's closed." He sounded slightly
abashed by the fact.

"Really? At Camelot we eat all the time." Quickly she
added, "Eat and exercise. No one wants to grow fat."

"Is the food good there?" He was a boy in his mid-teens;
that much was quite clear.

"It's quite wonderful. Succulent beef, aromatic breads of
all kinds, the most wonderful honey cakes . . ." She grinned
invitingly. "All the time."

"Colin, I don't much like it here."

"Really?" She feigned surprise. "I've always thought
Guenevere's court must be wonderful."

"She's a tyrant. Or as much of one as she can be with no
money. There's nothing here, nothing interesting. And no
room for advancement. My mother is an old friend of hers.
She thought sending me here would ensure my future. Instead . . ." He looked away from her, apparently embarrassed.

"I didn't get the sense you're so ambitious, Petronus."

"Is worrying about my future ambition, then?"

"No, of course not."

"I'd . . . I've thought about leaving here. More than
once." He still avoided looking at her. "I want to go to
Camelot, Colin. That's where the future lies."

She pretended this was unexpected. Slowly, deliberately,
she said, "I'll talk to Merlin about it."

"Will he take me?"

"I think he might be persuaded. But . . . but you say
there's nothing here. Surely that can't be true. We saw King
Leodegrance last night. And King Mark of Cornwall was
here. There must be room for an enterprising young man."

"Leodegrance is Guenevere's father. She's borrowing money from him."

"Things are that bad?"

He nodded.

"And what about Mark of Cornwall? He's not in the business of lending money."

"I don't know. Whatever he wanted, he didn't get it. There were arguments. He left angry and disappointed, I think. At least that's the gossip."

"Interesting." She changed the topic. "Maybe we can walk down to the town and get something to eat there."

"It's getting late. I have duties. Polishing Lancelot's armor." He sounded embarrassed.

"You work under Lancelot? Are you his squire? I didn't know."

"Mm-hmm. I don't like him. He doesn't like me. He's supposed to be training me for knighthood, but he uses me as a servant, nothing more. He likes to look good for his women, so I have to keep his armor gleaming."

"Women? I thought he and the queen . . ."

"Yes. She thinks so, too. But he is unfaithful to her every chance he gets. Will you talk to Merlin for me?"

She assured him she would, and he went off to do his polishing.

The sunny day brought a great many people out in Corfe. The streets were crowded, and everyone seemed to be in a pleasant mood. This might be the last sweet day before winter settled in, and winter on the coast was harsh.

Brit and Lancelot strolled the streets, chatting idly. He kept trying to take her hand. She kept pulling away. It was annoying him, and he let it show.

But Brit refused to acknowledge his amorous interests. "It just struck me—the streets here aren't paved."

He frowned. "Should they be?"

"I had the impression the Romans paved roads wherever they went. Even a dreary backwater like London has streets paved with stone."

"The Romans? That might as well have been a thousand years ago."

The harbor opened up before them. Leodegrance's ship and the frigate they'd seen earlier had been joined by another, from the looks of it North African, possibly Moroccan. Brit commented on the wide, lively trade that flourished in Corfe. "All Europe must come here, sooner or later."

"Who knows. Are you hungry?"

"Famished."

"Good. There's a first-rate inn just up ahead."

They went inside and found the place crowded with patrons. But the owner recognized Lancelot and found them a table at once. He ordered wine, beef and vegetables for them.

"I hope you like wine, Britomart."

"I'm from Camelot. We drink it like water."

"Good. And afterward . . ." He looked straight into her eyes. "I'd like to get to know you better."

"I thought we were already doing that."

A server brought large cups of wine. They drank quickly and Brit asked for more.

"You know what I mean. I'd like to get to know you . . . intimately." For an instant he sounded like a shy schoolboy.

"Why, Lancelot, I thought you were the queen's . . . what would be the word? Consort?"

"Choose the word you like. We are devoted to each other.

But I grew up on a French farm. The example of the rooster is not lost on me."

She put on a shocked expression and ordered a third round of wine. It was beginning to show on him, though it was not on her.

"So you mean to tell me you cheat on Guenevere?"

"What the queen doesn't know won't hurt the knight."

"But . . . well, I mean, she is the queen. She does have the power. Crossing her might . . . well, you know."

"She trusts me."

"Women can be such fools. But you seem to have her fooled, all right. I watched you the night of that ceremony at Camelot. You looked at her so adoringly."

"And then I snuck off."

"You don't mean to tell me you . . . then? I mean, who did you find?"

He shrugged as if to wonder if it made a difference. "Some little girl in the kitchen."

"You're joking. So." She made her voice hard. "You value me at the same price as a kitchen servant."

He was really feeling the drink, and it showed. "I never said that."

"You did. Fortunately, I value myself higher than that."

He sulked. "I didn't mean it that way."

"No, of course not. Men never do."

"This wine is strong. Aren't you feeling it?"

She smiled sweetly. "I'm not one of King Arthur's knights for nothing. The only one I know who can outdrink me," she told him pointedly, "is Mark of Cornwall."

"A fool. Why he came here with his damn fool scheme—"

She leaned back casually and put a leg over the edge of the table. "What scheme is that?"

Suddenly, he seemed to realize what was going on. He narrowed his eyes and peered at her. "When are you going back to Camelot?"

"That's up to Merlin."

"Go soon. Women should never be knights."

With that, he got up and stomped out of the inn. A moment later the server came with food for two. Brit ate hers happily, then tucked into his. She was stuck paying for it, but it had been well worth it.

"So. What do we know?"

It was well after dark. Merlin, Nimue and Brit sat by a huge fire in the Common Room at the garrison, drinking mulled wine. After the day's events, Merlin decided he'd feel more comfortable there. And there was the fact that their horses and luggage were there; they'd be able to make a quicker start in the morning. Besides, he was still not certain where they stood with Guenevere. So just after sunset they made their way to one of the ruined wings of her castle and slipped unobtrusively out and down to the town.

Dalley was relieved to see them. "When you didn't come back last night I was concerned, even with that note you sent."

He went off to arrange for sleeping quarters for them—the usual room for Merlin and Colin and a second one for Britomart. They relaxed and took stock of the situation at Corfe.

"First, we know that Guenevere needs money and blames Arthur for it, rightly or wrongly. The situation is so bad, people are leaving her service, or want to." Merlin ticked off the points on his fingers. "Second, Lancelot claims he was, er, becoming acquainted with a kitchen girl when Borolet was killed. So we need to question the cook staff when we get back. And third, Mark is up to something. No one will say what."

"Maybe Arthur sent him for some reason." Nimue was out of her depth and knew it.

"It's possible, Colin, but I don't think so. Arthur knew we were coming here. If he was sending Mark, too, he'd have mentioned it."

Brit looked thoughtful. "That makes sense, but—"

"But?"

"We all know Mark. He's always been solid and dependable. Why would he be acting like this?"

At that moment Dalley rejoined them. "Your quarters are ready."

"Excellent. It's been a long, tiring day." Merlin started to stand up.

"But before you retire, there's someone at the gate who wants to see you."

"Who, for heaven's sake?"

"Shall I show him in?"

"I suppose so, but—"

"I'll be right back."

The three of them looked at each other. Brit said, "If this is another 'invitation' to the castle, I don't want to go."

"No, Brit, we're safer here."

"And better fed." Nimue laughed.

A moment later Dalley was back. Just behind him was Petronus; he looked anxious. "Hello. I hope you don't mind my coming here."

"England is a free country, Petronus." Merlin tried not to sound too stern. "What can we do for you?"

"I . . . I want to come with you. I told Colin today."

"Yes, he told me. I'm afraid we weren't sure how seriously to take it."

"You left suddenly. They're angry about it." He was only wearing light clothing; evidently he had left in some haste. He moved closer to the fire.

"I'm not at all certain we can simply . . . take you, Pete. Things are tense enough. We don't want to cause an incident, even a minor one."

He looked from one of them to the next. "Please. *Please*. I hate it here. I want to serve King Arthur at Camelot."

Merlin sighed deeply then gestured to his two colleagues to join him off in a corner. "What do we do?"

Brit argued for taking him with them. "Guenevere can hardly grow much angrier at Arthur. Besides, he's only a boy. How much harm can his defection do?"

They huddled for another few moments. Petronus stood very near the fire, trying, without much success, to hear what they were saying; it was a cold night and he wasn't dressed for it. Finally, they rejoined him, and Merlin told him that, yes, he could accompany them to Camelot. "But this is very unusual. You are pledged to Guenevere's service. You must give us your word you'll obey orders and not make any trouble."

"You have my word, sir."

Dalley spoke up. "I'm afraid the compound is full. We don't have another room to spare."

Petronus offered to sleep next to the fire in the Common Room. "It's only for one night, after all."

After another brief huddle Dalley decided that would be all right. Relief showed in the boy's face.

Soon it was time for everyone to retire for the night. Dalley showed them to their rooms, which were down a hallway off the Common Room; Petronus stayed behind. A moment later Brit came back, carrying her red cloak. "Here. You'll need this."

"Thank you. I'm freezing."

"Couldn't you have gotten a cloak before you left?"

"I left on impulse. I was afraid I'd only have that one chance."

She wrinkled her nose. "Are you an experienced squire, then?"

"As experienced at Lancelot has let me be."

"I don't have a squire. We'll talk tomorrow, all right? Sleep well."

"Good night, Britomart."

He waited till he heard their doors close then lay down beside the hearth and wrapped himself in the cloak.

"Murder! Murder!"

It was the middle of the night. Someone sounded the alarm. Groggily, the three travelers climbed into their clothes and went to the Common Room. Petronus lay beside the fireplace soaked in blood.

Merlin rushed to him. "He's not dead. I think the wounds aren't deep."

But the boy was bleeding heavily. Merlin tore strips of cloth off his own robe and made bandages to staunch the blood.

Dalley rushed in and saw what was happening. "By all the gods! Is he all right?"

"I think so." Merlin looked up at him. "Do we know what happened? Who did this?"

"Both of the sentries at the gate have been killed. Run through."

"No!" Brit got down beside Merlin and stroked the boy's hair. Softly, she asked him, "Did you see who did this?"

"No. I was asleep. I felt a stabbing pain in my side and then . . . I don't know."

"I heard a scream," Dalley explained. "I came running. A man in a dark cloak was over him, sword raised, about to hack him. When he saw me he turned and ran."

"You didn't see his face?" Merlin worked to maintain his composure.

"No. It was too dark. Shadows from the fire—"

"It's all right. I think the boy will be fine."

"That's more than can be said for my sentries. I can see, perhaps, one of them being taken by surprise. But both? It makes no sense."

Everyone fell silent except Petronus, who groaned softly.

Then with a start Brit exclaimed, "He was wearing my cloak! This was meant for me!"

SIX

THE LAND OF WOULD-BE WITCHES

Petronus's wounds turned out not to be too serious; they were more bloody than dangerous. But he was badly shaken, too much so to ride a horse. Captain Dalley arranged for a carriage to transport the four of them back to Camelot, and an armed escort to ensure their safety.

Merlin was grateful. "At my age, riding a horse is not fun. My back is still aching from the journey down here."

Brit oversaw preparations for the trip; Merlin spent time alone, thinking over the events they'd witnessed. Nimue suspected he knew who the killer was, or had a strong suspicion; but when she asked, he put her off. "It's too early. There is still no proof."

They traveled swiftly and were careful to avoid London and Caesar's Bones. Thankfully, there was no more rain or snow, and they made good time. The party arrived at Camelot two nights later; it was nearly midnight and most of the residents were already asleep. They installed Petronus

in an unused room in Merlin's tower, and Nimue offered to
check on him periodically. There were candles to light the
room. "No smoke. No awful smell. It's good to be home,"
she said.

Arthur was not happy. It was the next morning; he paced his
study, trying a new sword. "This is no good. It doesn't have
the right heft or the right balance. I want Excalibur back."
Arthur glared at Merlin then struck at the stone windowsill
with his sword. The blade broke neatly in half. "I've tried
three of these. None is as good as Excalibur. I want you to
find it for me."

"That means finding the killer. You know we're doing
what we can. But we have to be realistic. Excalibur may
well have been melted down by now. Or shipped to the
mainland and sold on the international market. The same
for the stone and the shrine."

Arthur listened to Merlin's account of the events at Corfe
and frowned ever more deeply. Merlin laid it all out, coolly,
dispassionately. Ganelin's chart was on the table in front of
him.

"Our villain would have killed again, Arthur, and the victim would have been Britomart this time."

"And this boy, this—what is his name?"

"Petronus."

"Petronus. How is he?

A slight smile crossed Merlin's lips. "His wounds
weren't terribly deep, despite all the blood. Nothing vital
was pierced. But it was quite traumatic for him. He can't
understand why someone would attack him so viciously."

Arthur slashed the air with the broken sword. "He
doesn't know about the murders, then?"

"No. It was . . . awkward. I suppose that would be the word. He thinks Camelot is a peaceful, harmonious court. He'll be over it in a few weeks, possibly less."

"Splendid. The boy is lucky you were there to tend him."

"As I said, it looked worse than it actually was. I'm planning to have Colin take care of him while Brit and I are off in the lake country."

"Well, we have that to be thankful for, at least. There's been enough death." For once, Arthur was not drinking. Merlin wondered whether it was a good sign or a bad one. "Colin isn't going with you?"

Merlin shook his head.

It puzzled Arthur, but he let it pass. "There's no possibility Petronus was really the intended victim? He was defecting from Guenevere's court and Lancelot's service, after all."

"It's always a possibility, of course. But he was wrapped in Brit's cloak."

The king paced some more. Then abruptly, he stopped and declared, "Lancelot. It must have been Lancelot."

"What makes you so certain?"

"The boy was his squire. He'd have seen his defection as a personal affront. And you said he had left the Great Hall the night Borolet was killed."

"That is perfectly possible, of course. And do you think the queen put him up to it?"

"Damn." It was perfectly obvious to Merlin the king did not really want to think about any of this. "There's no way of knowing, is there?"

Calmly, Merlin told him, "We'll know in time. Patience and reason are our allies."

Arthur tossed what was left of the sword into a corner and walked to the window. "You know what I want."

"Yes."

"Then do it."

"Do we have your permission to investigate Mark?"

Arthur sighed; Merlin had never heard him sound quite so weary. "Do what you have to."

"You didn't send him to Corfe, then." It was a statement, not a question.

"No. Of course not. Go to Cornwall and see what you can find out."

"Arthur, you're going to have to do something about him. Until and unless we can demonstrate clearly that his presence at Corfe was innocent—that he was there looking to gain access to the harbor for his tin shipments or some such—it would be a mistake to keep him in charge of the army."

Arthur paused. "Do you think I don't know that? Do you think it isn't the first thing that occurred to me?"

"Then do it. Come up with some pretext and start easing him out of power."

He eyed a wineskin on a corner table then seemed to think better of it. "But how? If he is a traitor, I hardly want to put him on his guard before we act. And if he isn't, I don't want him to suspect we think he might be."

"Oh, the problems of being king." Merlin smiled at him. "You wanted this, remember?"

"It wasn't supposed to be so complicated."

"Everything human is. Especially when subtlety is required."

"Don't be so smug." He seemed to be groping for something less highly charged to talk about. "You've been training Colin in medical treatment?"

"Some. Happily, not much real knowledge is required

here. It's mostly a matter of bandaging the boy's wounds and keeping him off his feet till they heal. Of course, keeping a boy that age in bed for several weeks will be an interesting challenge, but I think Colin will be up to it."

"Several weeks? For minor wounds?"

"I'm not completely sure we can trust him. He is from Guenevere's court, after all. His defection could be a convenient fiction to cover spying."

Arthur moved next to him and looked at the chart. "And this thing. Have you made any progress deciphering it?"

"Well . . ." Merlin was suddenly in his element; he put on his best teacher manner. "These crosses seem to be heading roughly in the direction of the refectory. If we can establish that Lancelot was there with one of the girls, then we've eliminated the first set of symbols and the first suspect. And I'm more and more certain the triangles represent Pellenore. They ramble all over the castle."

"But if Lancelot didn't kill Borolet and Ganelin, it doesn't make sense that he'd attack Brit."

"You said it yourself. The attack may have been unrelated to the earlier killings. It may have been about Petronus. Or maybe Lancelot realized Brit had gotten him drunk and talkative in a way he didn't like. He confessed to constant infidelity to Guenevere. And of course Guenevere herself may have been behind the attack, if she suspected Britomart was seducing her man."

"Or her man was the seducer. You think too much, Merlin."

"There's no such thing as thinking too much. It's what makes me useful to you."

Arthur resumed his pacing. "Go to Cornwall. Find out why Mark was there."

"First, Morgan, I think. She and that wizened weasel of a son of hers will be easier to eliminate."

He narrowed his eyes. "You think Mark is the villain."

"I think there's a good chance of it. But I've been wrong before."

"I can't imagine such a thing."

"Don't be sarcastic, Arthur. You must understand what that means. We have a terrible problem. He's the military commander. A good many of the knights will be loyal to him. Removing him—arresting him—will be tricky. You need hard, absolutely irrefutable proof."

"Find it. Whether it's Mark we're after or not, find it. Do whatever you want. Go to Byzantium and investigate the emperor if you must. But find me the killer." He glared around the room. "And get me my sword back. And the Stone of Bran."

Merlin stopped at the door. "Oh, and about that school for the squires and pages?"

"Later, Merlin."

The mood throughout Camelot was subdued. Brit, Nimue and Merlin were all determined not to let out word that they were on the trail of the twins' murderer. The official story was that they were simply running some errands for the king. But people knew better, or at least suspected. Maintaining an official silence was becoming difficult. And there was a certain amount of tension: who was suspected? Even the servants were on edge.

Merlin made his way back to his tower, stopping to chat with various people, nearly all of whom tried to find out why he'd gone to Corfe, what he'd found there and why he'd come back with one of the squires from Guene-vere's court. He fielded all the questions quite tactfully, so that no one realized how evasive he'd been till after he'd moved on.

He found Nimue in Petronus's room, checking ban-dages. He said good morning to her then asked, "How are you feeling this morning, Pete?"

The boy was smiling. "I'm at Camelot. I'm to be Brito-mart's squire. How could I not be happy?"

"Believe me, it could happen. Are your wounds giving you much discomfort?"

"They itch."

"That's a good sign. It means they're healing, and quickly."

"Good. Can I go out and exercise with the other squires?" He shifted his weight in the bed.

"You are to remain in bed and in this room until I give you permission to do otherwise. We want you well and healthy. Do you understand?"

"But I feel fine."

"You're to do as you're told. We have one rebel to deal with; we don't need another."

"Rebel?"

Merlin had let himself forget that the boy knew nothing about the Stone of Bran and the murders, and that he'd de-cided not to tell him yet. Nimue covered his slip. "I'll tell you about it later, Pete, all right?"

Merlin asked her to join him in his study, and they climbed the spiral stairs together.

"I'll prepare a calmative potion for you. Put it in his food or his drink and it will make him less restless."

She laughed. "And easier to control?"

"To the extent boys that age can be controlled at all, yes. And I'll prepare a salve to help his wounds heal. Have you had a chance to talk with Greffys?"

"Just for a moment or two. I don't think he's found out much."

"He hasn't been talking to the servants?"

She nodded. "He has, but he's out of his depth."

"Then it's just as well you're staying behind. Have him introduce you to the more talkative among them and see what you can learn. But remember, be discreet. Be indirect. We don't want to put anyone on his or her guard."

"I know what to do."

"I want to move quickly. Brit and I will leave to visit Morgan tomorrow morning. If you can find the girl who was with Lancelot, or at least someone who knows definitely that he *was* with a girl, we will have eliminated one suspect, at least."

"If. Do you think there is such a girl?"

"I think Lancelot is probably too dim to have invented a story like that. What would be the point?"

"Male boasting. Never underestimate the power of the male ego."

"See if you can find out, one way or the other."

"But Merlin . . . why would a girl from the kitchen . . . ?"

"Don't be naïve, Nimue. Knights, lords and kings have their way with women of the lower ranks. Remember Anna? It is called privilege. If there is something you should never underestimate, it is the vulnerability of women."

"Vulnerability? There might be another name for it. But I'm more grateful than ever to be disguised as Colin."

He smiled. "I'm glad you are, too. You are the most apt pupil I could want."

"Why, thank you, Merlin." She blushed.

"Didn't you know I think so?"

"You've never bothered to say it before. Men."

He crossed to his table and found a sheet of paper. "Here. I want you to try and find the chemicals on this list for me. You should be able to locate them in the armory, I think. Tell the armorers they're for me."

She took the list and read it, puzzled. "Acids?"

"I'm no swordsman. And this is getting dangerous. We can't count on our villain mistaking someone else for one of us a second time. I'll be in the stables, at the blacksmith's forge. I have some glass-blowing to do."

Arthur wanted Merlin and Brit to take an armed escort. He told them so at dinner in the refectory. Merlin insisted that would only attract attention. "We'll be safer traveling on our own."

"Nonsense. You're both ministers of the state. And you're much too valuable to put yourselves at risk. Suppose someone comes at you with a sword? Look at what happened to Petronus. You're an able man, Merlin, but you aren't much good in a fight."

Brit bristled at this. "And I, of course, am completely useless."

"Britomart, we are dealing with a cunning villain here. Possibly a mad one. I won't have you vulnerable when it is avoidable. You will travel by carriage, not by horse, and you will have an escort of soldiers. I'll have Accolon lead them. This is not debatable." He turned and walked away from them.

And so the next morning a carriage and driver were provided, along with a detachment of six men on horseback, including Accolon. Brit and Merlin stepped inside their conveyance unhappily, and with a lurch it began to move. The horses' hooves clattered loudly on the courtyard stones.

Brit felt her skill as a knight was in question. "I've beaten most of the knights here in single combat." She sulked. "Including Arthur himself. He knows I can take care of myself."

"You mustn't take this personally, Brit. He's underestimating me, too. But it is a matter of public policy. If we bring Mark down, you will be the country's top military officer. If I were advising the king, I'd tell him to do exactly as he's doing."

"How, exactly, is he underestimating you?" She asked the question with a sneer in her voice.

"He is assuming the only way to defend oneself is though main force."

"Isn't it? Merlin, you're well into middle age. And you've never been an athlete. How could you possibly defend yourself from an attacker?"

He smiled, reached into his pocket and produced a handful of small glass globes. Each of them contained some clear fluid. "With these."

"With marbles? Merlin, you're not serious."

"These are made from very thin, very fragile glass. And inside each of them is a quantity of aqua regia."

"Acid? You mean to fight off an insane killer with marbles full of acid?"

"Aqua regia is not simply acid—it is the strongest acid known to science. It can dissolve gold. If someone comes at me with sword drawn, it will stop him, believe me."

"You're making a fairly big assumption. Suppose he attacks from a distance? With spears or arrows?"

"No defense is perfect, Brit."

"I'll say." She smirked. "Why don't you leave your safety in my hands?"

"Yours, or the soldiers accompanying us?"

"Be quiet."

Their party moved through the moors, not far from the hamlet where Anna had lived. The sky turned dark, and streamers of mist snaked through the air. Trees were stunted and twisted. One of the soldiers in their escort produced a flute and began playing mournful melodies. For a time, the soldiers talked among themselves; then they grew more subdued. At one point an enormous owl swooped down at the carriage as if it might be prey for the bird. One of the soldiers swiped at it with his sword, but it was too quick and too agile.

"I don't like this," Brit complained. "This is like a landscape out of a nightmare."

"Yet you're certain your sword will be effective here."

"Stop bickering, Merlin. I'm serious."

"Have you never traveled through this part of England before?"

"No, of course not. I'm a military commander, and Morgan doesn't have much of an army."

"What kind of landscape did you expect?" he asked in a mock-serious tone. "We are visiting the realm of the witches."

The flutist's music echoed eerily through the fog. When the party stopped to rest Brit asked him about his instrument. "It has the strangest sound, like nothing I've ever heard."

The man held his flute out to her. "Here you are, my lady. There aren't many like it left."

She took it. It was the color of faded ivory, and it had unusual heft. "What is this made of?"

"Bone, my lady. This was carved from the thighbone of some ancient enemy defeated in battle. My father willed it to me."

"Human bone?"

He nodded. "That is why it sounds so mournful. It has felt everything human."

Gingerly, she gave it back to him. "Try and play something livelier, will you?"

"The instrument dictates the music, not the musician."

"Nevertheless, try and play something that might lift our spirits out of this terrible place."

"Yes, ma'am."

The party traveled on. In time the swamps gave way to little lakes, then to larger ones. But the sky remained dark and the fog never lifted, not even momentarily. They came to a small village that actually had an inn, and Merlin decided they would spend the night there.

Accolon disagreed with this. "I think we should try and make it to Morgan's castle tonight. We're being followed."

Merlin looked down the road behind them. There was no one in sight. "Are you certain?"

"Quite certain. They've been there since just after we left Camelot."

Merlin let out a long, deep sigh. "I'm so weary of this. But we need rest, Accolon. We'll stop here tonight."

"Yes, sir."

The innkeeper, happy to have nine paying guests, went out of his way to make them feel comfortable. Supper was surprisingly large; wine flowed freely; beds were ample and soft and warm, and there were cheerful fires in each room.

Brit was not happy as she ate her meal. "This tastes like fog."

Merlin was amused by her discomfort. "You have eaten fog, then?"

"We've been eating it all day. This meat has the same foul taste as the air we've been breathing. It has polluted everything."

"And Morgan has breathed it all her life. Perhaps that accounts for her personality and behavior."

"Do you really think there's a chance she's behind the murders? I thought you had decided someone else was the culprit."

"Don't underestimate Morgan, Brit. She has a notorious chest of poisons, and she uses them as instruments of policy in her little queendom. She sits in that hideous castle of hers and casts her spells and charms, and chants her invocations to all her imaginary gods. Then when they fail she resorts to poison or a knife in the dark. And people wonder why I prefer reason and logic to superstition and belief."

"You're no one to talk, Merlin. Everyone knows you rigged some kind of trick with that sword of Arthur's—"

"Excalibur."

"Yes. Everyone knows you set up some sort of ruse with it to convince people he was destined to be king. So much for logic and reason."

"What could be more reasonable than using people's gullibility to one's own advantage? Or to the advantage of one's king?"

"Then why convict Morgan of these crimes? Political

murder is one thing. Rulers have been doing that since the first people crawled out of caves. But viciously hacking two boys to death—that's another thing entirely. From what you say, it doesn't sound like her style at all."

"Morgan is as murderous as any queen in history. She takes handsome young men as lovers, and—"

"A queen's right."

"And she keeps dogs. Large, evil things, white with red ears. When she is finished with her lovers, she kills them and feeds them to the dogs."

"That's horrible." Brit's eyes widened. "And Arthur wanted to bring civilization to England. He hasn't been able to civilize his own sister. But . . ."

"Yes?"

"If she wanted to murder at Camelot, wouldn't she have used poison, then? That seems more in character, from what you've said. A broadsword is not subtle enough."

"That is what I keep thinking. And hoping."

"You want Mark to be guilty, then?"

"No, of course not. Don't be glib. If I've ever been wrong about anything, I wish it were this. But I'm afraid I'm not."

They slept and had a good, hearty breakfast the next morning. Then they set off through the dark, fog-shrouded world as they had the previous day. The mist was even thicker; at times it was difficult to see the road. Accolon and most of his men had drunk too much the night before; they were plainly hungover.

Then at length Morgan's castle reared up ahead of them through the fog. A massive, black, rambling place, even darker and more ominous than Guenevere's castle at Corfe. Lights flickered faintly in the windows.

"How can anyone live in a place like this?"

"Perhaps she chose it because it suited her, Brit."

"Did she choose it? Or did she inherit it?"

"Point taken. This has been the home of the witch queens for centuries. It is not what you would expect the seat of women's government to be like, is it?"

"Be quiet, Merlin."

"In Rome you may see the ruins of the house where the college of Vestal Virgins resided. It is the foulest, ugliest building in the city. There is something about women living together, monastically . . ."

"Shut up."

"The Vestals were infamous for using poison to further their interests, too."

"Please, Merlin, this is not something I want to discuss."

They came to a place where sentries had been posted. The captain of the escort explained that Merlin was here on the king's business, and after a thorough search, they were permitted to move on. As the castle drew near, it looked more and more ominous, more and more a place of death.

Petronus was feeling restless. And he was bristling at having to obey Colin.

"I'm fine, Colin. Let me get up, and show me the castle."

"Merlin's orders were for you to remain in bed till you're completely healed."

"I am. I feel fine."

"Let me see your wounds."

Reluctantly, he submitted to an examination. And his wounds had in fact healed, for the most part. But Nimue expressed doubt about whether it would be wise for him to leave his bed. "Merlin knows more about healing and medicine than any man in England. You should do as he instructed."

"Please, Colin. We can have some fun together."

A moment later Greffys knocked and came in. "Colin, I've been looking for you."

Nimue introduced the two squires. They seemed to bond almost at once. But Greffys had business on his mind. "I've been getting to know the servants. Some boys say they remember Lancelot in the scullery that night. Arthur said I should tell either Merlin or Britomart."

"You can tell me. You know I'm Merlin's apprentice."

"That's what Arthur told me to do."

Petronus listened to their exchange, puzzled. He asked what was going on, and Nimue finally gave him a brief account of the murders and the theft of the Stone of Bran and Excalibur. "That's why we were at Corfe—investigating whether Guenevere might be behind it all."

"And is she?"

"I don't know. I don't think so. I don't think Merlin thinks so."

He put the pieces together. "But then—whoever attacked me—"

"Exactly. But we don't know who it was. Or why."

"So I'm involved in this. I mean, without knowing a thing about it, I've become involved. I want to see the man who attacked me brought to justice."

"With Merlin hunting him, you will. I'm sure of it."

Greffys became impatient listening to them. "These boys I've found, we ought to talk to them now. They don't much trust anyone above their social station."

"Then let's go."

"And I think they know the girl Lancelot was with."

Petronus got to his feet; he was slightly unsteady. "I'm coming, too."

Nimue decided she did not have the energy or will to argue with him; he would be on his feet soon enough, one way or another. "All right. Let's hurry."

They made their way through the castle to the Great Hall and beyond it to the kitchen. Two boys were waiting there, seated at one of the tables. They weren't much older than Greffys, and they looked nervous.

The taller of them stood and looked suspiciously at the three of them. "Who are they?" he asked Greffys.

Greffys introduced them. "Colin here is Merlin's apprentice."

"An apprentice wizard." The boy didn't try to hide his distaste. "Poring over books and memorizing spells while we scrape the floors and tables clean."

"And this is Petronus, Britomart's squire." He introduced the kitchen boys as Dennis, the one who had questioned him, and Tom.

Dennis, scowling, said, "You told me there'd only be one."

"Petronus here was attacked by the same one who killed Borolet and Ganelin."

"Really?"

Petronus nodded. "I want to find him."

Nimue decided it was time to take charge. "Greffys tells us you saw Lancelot here that night, Dennis."

The boy nodded. "He had a girl. All the knights come here when they have girls, or when they're looking for one." He looked around and lowered his voice. "To do it in the pantries, where no one can see."

"Was he here long?"

"Long enough." Dennis leered.

"And she was with him the whole time?"

He nodded.

"Who is she?"

"Gretchen. Tom's sister." Dennis sounded smug.

"We'll want to talk to her."

"No one's supposed to know." Tom sounded betrayed. "She'll be mad at me if she knows I told anyone."

"This is important, Tom. I can promise you each . . ." She pretended to be doing a sum in her head. "I can promise you each a gold coin when Merlin gets back."

"A gold coin!" Dennis couldn't hide his excitement.

"Just persuade Gretchen to talk to us about that night." Weakly, she added, "There will be a coin in it for her, too."

Merlin and Britomart were installed in rooms in Morgan's castle. It seemed to Brit their welcome was rather grudging. Merlin was sanguine. "We did come uninvited, after all."

"Courtesy to strangers and travelers is the hallmark of civilization, Merlin. Especially travelers on the king's business. She did have a letter from him."

"Civilization is a comfortable lie, Brit."

The women at Morgan's court all dressed, like her, in billowing black robes with enormous sleeves. Brit tried to force herself not to think of them as witches, but they so self-consciously assumed that image, it wasn't easy. They all seemed to work at being cold, aloof and distant.

Alone with Merlin, she commented on it. "It's so strange. They don't even make noise when they walk or move."

"That takes years of practice."

"And how much practice does it take to be rude? You'd

think at least a few of them might show signs of friendliness now and then."

"They are struggling to preserve a matriarchal society that is fast being eclipsed. Not just here, not just by Arthur, but all across Europe. In most places it is dead already. I imagine they must consider friendliness a luxury."

"Some society. Dull clothes and bad manners."

"Morgan's kind of government has always rested on superstitious flummery. 'We rule because the Goddess says we ought to.' And how could anyone know the purported Goddess wants Morgan to rule? Because Morgan says so. It has only been a matter of time before a society like that began to come unraveled. All Arthur has done is hurry the process."

Suddenly, Morgan herself appeared in the doorway. "What my brother has done," she intoned grandly, "is slaughter thousands of innocent people in his bid for power. He has destroyed a culture so subtle and complex he has never even bothered to try to understand it. And he has sent the two of you here to help the process along."

"You see hidden motives everywhere, Morgan." Merlin made himself smile. "But life at court does that to everyone. Arthur has some specific requests for the ceremonies at Midwinter Court, and he asked me to come discuss them with you."

"Since when does Arthur concern himself with the niceties of ritual?"

"I should think you'd be happy he's doing it at all."

"Better late than never, Merlin?" she japed. "The gods and goddesses he has slighted so pointedly may not see things that way."

"And they will choose to express that through you, of course."

"Of course. I am their priestess. And they have been . . . dislodged from their proper place."

"We expect to have recovered the Stone of Bran by Midwinter. Surely that must be a sign of their favor."

"Nonsense. Merlin, what are you doing here? What do you really want?"

He sighed an exaggerated sigh. "We are here for the reasons I've stated. It isn't necessary to look for intrigue everywhere, Morgan. That suggests a particularly morbid view of humanity."

"I see things as they are. You will come to my chambers tomorrow after breakfast, and we shall discuss court ritual."

"Fine."

Brit spoke up. "Is there any chance of a late meal? We spent all day on the road."

"I'll send someone to the kitchen to see."

"Thank you."

Morgan turned grandly in the doorway, letting her robes swirl with an intentional flourish. "Till noon, then. Be prompt." And she swept off down the hall.

It was late at night. Camelot's halls were all but deserted. Torches cast stark shadows on the stones. Nimue, Greffys and Petronus made their way to the refectory.

At the entrance, Tom and Dennis were waiting for them. "Hello," Dennis said. "She's waiting. She wants her gold coin up front, before she'll talk."

"Doesn't she trust us?"

"Do you really want me to answer that?"

Nimue walked past him into the kitchen and looked around. There were rough-hewn benches in a room made of rough-hewn stones. In one corner, by a large cook fire, stood a young woman apparently in her late teens. Her hair was long and dark, and she wore it in braids. She was dressed in a ragged floor-length skirt of brown homespun or some similar material and a very low-cut top. Her feet were bare.

"Good evening." Nimue remembered to smile. "You are Gretchen?"

The girl smiled and tossed her hair coquettishly. "Yes. And you are . . . ?"

"Colin. I am Merlin's apprentice and assistant."

"The sorcerer's apprentice. Like the old story."

"Merlin is not a—" She decided there was no point starting an argument about something so irrelevant. "Dennis and Tom say you have something to tell me."

"Dennis and Tom," she said with emphasis, "tell me you have some gold for me."

"When Merlin returns, you will be amply rewarded."

"Then when Merlin returns, I'll tell you what I know." She heaved her bosom and looked at Colin quite pointedly. "I've seen you around the castle. You're an attractive boy— man."

"Thank you."

"Do you want to get acquainted?" Sensing she was on shaky ground with him, she added, "Free?"

"No thank you."

"All the knights want me."

"And most of them have her." Tom laughed. "Lancelot wasn't the first."

She swiped at him angrily, but he pulled away, laughing at her.

Nimue jumped on the opening he'd given her. "You were with Lancelot?"

"Well." She pouted. "I guess you could say that."

Tom tapped Nimue's shoulder and pointed. "They did it

in that little pantry over there. Everybody calls it 'Gretchen's Bedroom.'"

Nimue refused to be distracted. "And this was on the night of the ceremony with the Stone of Bran? The night Borolet was killed?"

Gretchen reached out and touched Nimue's arm. "You're strong for a scholar."

"Answer my question, please." She decided to take a softer tone and play up to the girl. "Please."

"Yes, that was the night. Meet me here later, all right? No one will know."

"You're certain it was Lancelot? And it was on that night?"

"Yes, it was him. Tall, blond, with the nicest muscles. And really dumb. He gave me twice what I would have asked for."

Petronus laughed and said, "No wonder Guenevere is hard up for money."

"He kept asking me to keep our little affair a secret. Said his girlfriend would get nasty if she even suspected. But I figured he was making that up, to keep me quiet. They all say that. Even the king."

"Arthur—?!"

"Yes, good, noble King Arthur. He tells me no one understands him, same as they all do. But he's never given me a thing, the bastard. Not one royal farthing for poor little Gretchen."

A couple of other kitchen servants walked in, talking. Nimue watched them, made mildly uncomfortable by their presence. Lowering her voice, she asked, "Is there anything else you can tell me, Gretchen? Anything about Lancelot, I mean."

"He talked to me in French. When his passion peaked, he spoke French."

"About that night—how and where did you meet him?"

"Why don't you and I discuss that privately?"

"Really, Gretchen, that is not what I'm after."

"All men are after that. What kind of man are you?"

"A scholar, unraveling a mystery."

She shrugged. "Call it what you like. It always comes to the same thing with men."

"And with women. You want your money. Merlin will pay you."

She moved beside Nimue and rubbed against her. "I'd rather get it from you, Colin."

"I'm afraid I can't give you what you want."

"Then leave me alone. Send Merlin to me. With coin."

Swaying her hips, she walked off into the corridor that led to "Gretchen's Bedroom."

Nimue looked at Greffys. "Well. That is that, it seems."

"You should come back to her. She's worth it. Believe me."

"A boy your age, Greffys? Spending good money for women? That doesn't seem right."

"How old were you the first time, Colin?"

"Old enough. And there was no cash exchanged. But never mind." She wanted to change the subject.

Petronus said, "Then the girl must have been homely."

"I shouldn't have let you out of your sickbed, Petronus. Behave yourself or I'll order you back to it. Let's go."

As they left the kitchen, Gretchen watched from the dark corridor, wishing Colin was friendlier.

• • •

The next morning, after breakfast, Merlin met privately
with Morgan.

"You said Arthur has some specific requests for the Midwinter ceremonies. As if he knew a thing about ritual and
tradition. What does he want?"

"Well, I'm not certain you'll like it."

"Go ahead. I can only imagine the worst. And Arthur
isn't *that* imaginative."

He bristled at this but resolved to go on. "He wants
prayers to the gods."

"Naturally. What else?"

"And not the goddesses."

"Oh." She stiffened slightly. "The Morrigan, the great
Goddess of Death, has always ruled here. It would not be
wise to ignore her."

"I believe he knows you were named for her. Nevertheless . . ."

"And Danu, her daughter. We are Tuatha du Danu, the
People of Danu. Has Arthur forgotten?"

"Arthur is quite keenly aware of how effective religious
myth is as propaganda. That is precisely why he wants male
deities, not female ones."

Morgan narrowed her eyes. "I've known Arthur all my
life. He isn't that thoughtful. This is your idea."

"Arthur authorized it."

"I shall pray to England's traditional deities. That is not
subject to further discussion."

"I see. That is your final answer?"

She nodded.

Merlin rose to go. "That settles it, then. I'll carry that
news to the king."

"Do so."

"Trust me, Morgan, I will."

"And then?"

"He will have to consider whether to have you officiate."

She forced a smile. "Who else would have that privilege?"

"There are other priests. Thank you for clarifying your position, Morgan."

"I am the high priestess of England, chosen of the gods. Remind Arthur of that. To permit anyone else to officiate at a holiday as important as Midwinter would cause a scandal, to say the least."

"Of course. I'll be certain to tell him." He decided to take a shot in the dark. "Oh—by the way?"

"Yes?"

"What was Mark doing here?"

She showed no reaction. "You know about that?"

So he had been there, as he had been at Corfe. "It is not easy to keep intelligence from Arthur, Morgan. You should know that."

"Or from you?"

"If you like."

"Mark wants to be king. You must know that, or suspect. Arthur is a fool to keep him in a position of power."

"And he wants you to . . . to do what, exactly?" He smiled a politician's smile.

"If you are so adept at gaining intelligence, you shouldn't have to ask. Good day, Merlin. Have a nice journey back to Camelot." Suddenly she narrowed her eyes. "Where is that woman you came with?"

"Britomart? I imagine she's exercising with your knights."

"I hope so. Good day, Merlin."

• • •

Brit had agreed to look for Mordred while Merlin kept the boy's mother occupied. She found him in the library, reading a book.

"Knowledge, at the court of Morgan le Fay, Mordred? Surely superstition is the thing. Or religion—assuming there's any difference. I'd be careful. You may be setting a dangerous precedent."

"It's only one of Caesar's war commentaries."

"You're a warrior, then?"

"No, a historian." His guard was up; his tone revealed it.

"Oh. I see."

"Court life doesn't really suit me. I've always wanted to go to Alexandria, to see the great library there."

"Merlin's been there. Did you know that? In fact he lived there for a while."

"Really? I'll have to ask him about it."

"I'm sure he'll be happy to tell you all about it." In a confidential tone, she added, "He likes to talk."

"So does Mother. There are times when I'd give my entire inheritance for a bit of peace."

"Tell me, is she really a witch?"

"She really thinks she is," he whispered. "Doesn't that come to the same thing?"

"Why hasn't she married you off yet? You are the royal heir, after all."

"I was betrothed for a time. But I'm not really interested in women. I think the girl understood that. She ran off."

"Just between us, I'm not really interested in men." Her tone was confidential, but she was smiling.

Suddenly Mordred seemed to relax. "Marriage . . . it seems so unnatural to me."

"To me, too."

"I always felt sorry for the poor girl."

"You have a reputation for being disagreeable."

Suddenly he put his guard up. "I imagine I am, to most people. I want to be left alone with my books, not bothered with ritual and protocol and backstabbing plots and all the other rubbish that fills Mother's world." He sniffled and wiped his nose on his sleeve. "And Uncle Arthur's. And yours, for that matter."

But she saw the opening she wanted. "Yet everyone says you and Lancelot were off whoring together the night of that ceremony at Camelot."

"When that boy was killed?" He seemed to find it odd. "No, I left the Great Hall that night, looking for the privy. And I got lost—Camelot is such a bewildering place. But I did see Lancelot. He said he was going to the kitchen and asked me if I wanted to join him with the girls there."

"You didn't, though?"

"I needed the privy." He sounded mildly embarrassed; then suddenly his tone shifted. "What madman architected Camelot? Even for a castle it's quite impossible. I mean, no one in his senses would choose to live in a castle. They're all unbearable. But Camelot—!" He wrinkled his nose, as if that gesture said what needed to be said. "Uncle Arthur must be insane to live there. They say he took the place from mad old Pellenore. That says it all, doesn't it?"

"I imagine so." Brit decided that, against all probability, she could learn to like Mordred. Or at least she wanted to. He wiped his nose on his sleeve again, and she remembered who and what he was.

And he seemed to remember to put his guard up. "You aren't married. Women should be."

"So should princes."

"Not scholar-princes." His tone was defensive but hushed. "I swear, someday I'll run away to Alexandria."

"You really should talk to Merlin. I think the two of you might get along, if either of you would give the other a chance."

"Merlin is my mother's enemy. And the enemy of religion, or superstition as he calls it. You too." His habitual suspicion was returning.

"Is it so awful to think human affairs should be governed by reason?"

"Human beings aren't reasonable creatures. That is why we need the gods. We are capable of reason, but how often do we make our decisions based on it?" He leaned back in his chair and assumed an air of nonchalance. "No, it's to be Alexandria for me. They say the library's walls are lined with books thicker than the stone they're built of."

"I imagine so." She stood to go. Mordred's moods shifted so quickly she didn't think she'd learn anything else useful from him. "Well, I'm going to get some exercise. Would you like to join me?"

"No thank you."

"Until later, then."

"Have a good day, Britomart." He smiled at her. "Go and bother someone else for whatever it is you want to know."

There was dense fog the next morning. Merlin suggested delaying their return to Camelot. But Brit for some reason was anxious to leave. "The roads are marked. And we have our escort; they'll find the way."

No one saw the party off. Morgan claimed to be occupied with court business, and there was no sign at all of

Mordred. So the carriage and its escort set off through the thickest fog any of them could remember. The sound of the horses' hooves was deadened by it; the entire world was quiet. Accolon and his men talked in muted voices.

Merlin started another of his panegyrics on life in sunny Egypt, and Brit lapsed into daydreams; she had heard him rhapsodize about Alexandria often enough. But he kept up, and she decided to voice her annoyance. "Don't the Egyptians live among the corpses of their ancestors?"

"They do not forget their past, if that is what you mean."

"It sounds perfectly morbid. And they believe in magic. You should have picked up a few pointers while you were there."

"I saw enough charlatans taking in the gullible to have a fair idea how it is done. Is that what you mean?"

"It's no fun trying to needle you, Merlin. What did you learn from Morgan? Anything useful?"

"She told me Mark had been there. But I couldn't get her to say why."

"Mordred admitted he'd left the Great Hall on the night of the first murder. He says he got lost in the halls."

"I suppose that is plausible. Camelot is a bewildering castle."

"And he says he met Lancelot, who was on his way to the kitchen for some illicit lovemaking."

"We'll have to see if we can find anyone who saw him."

"Did you know Mordred was betrothed once? He says the girl ran away."

"Imagine."

"I asked around and got a good idea when she left. Where did Colin come from, Merlin?"

"Don't pry, Britomart."

They came to a place where the ground was soaked and the fog was even more dense than it had been everywhere else. Accolon looked into the carriage and told them they'd be slowing down.

"Not too much, please." Merlin said he wanted to make Camelot by sunset tomorrow, if possible.

"We'll do our best. But the ground is treacherous."

"We're anxious to get back to Camelot, Accolon."

"Yes, sir. But—"

"But what?"

"We are being followed again."

"Splendid."

A moment later the sounds of scuffling came from outside the carriage. Swords clanged; voices were raised. Accolon shouted orders.

Merlin and Brit looked out to see they were surrounded by a dozen or more armored soldiers. Brit drew her sword and jumped out to join the fight. She, Accolon and their men fought bravely and managed to disable three of the attackers. Slowly, patiently, Merlin stepped outside onto the soft, damp ground and reached into his pocket. When one of the attackers came at Merlin with sword drawn, he produced one of his glass globes and smashed it into the man's face. The man screamed, covering his face with his hands, and stumbled off into the fog. But his sword had pierced Merlin's thigh, and some of the acid had burned his hand.

Unruffled by the commotion around him, Merlin walked around the carriage, tossing more globes in the faces of the attacking knights. One by one they screamed, covered their faces and lurched off into the mist. Soon the skirmish was over. One of Accolon's men was badly wounded; the rest were all right except for minor cuts.

Britomart was quite all right. Out of breath, she joined Merlin. "I'll never scoff at your little marbles again."

"Science and reason defeat brute force every time, Brit." He bent down and washed his burning hand in a puddle.

"Nonsense. It worked for you this time. But if there had been more of them . . ."

"There weren't."

"There might easily have been. We were lucky."

"You and the others fought bravely, Brit. Bravely and skillfully. We all won this fight. Now let us get moving again before more attackers appear."

"There won't be any more. We've beaten them. And they have no way of knowing how many acid globes we have."

"A good deterrent, then."

"But we'll have to be watchful until we reach home."

Slowly, Accolon restored order. The wounded soldier rode in the carriage with Merlin; Brit rode his horse. And despite the fog and the unsteady ground, the party made good time. There were no more attacks.

They arrived at Camelot late the next night. The next morning, well rested, they met in Merlin's study. He was walking on a cane and seemed unconcerned about it, and the acid burns on his right hand were bandaged. Nimue asked what had happened, and Brit explained.

"Will you be all right, Merlin? I wouldn't like to see you walking on that stick all the time. Will your hand be scarred?"

"At my age, what difference does it make?"

"That's an absurd attitude to take."

Brit couldn't resist adding, "So much for a life based on reason."

But Merlin ignored them and unrolled Ganelin's chart. "Now. Let's put this together with what we've learned and see if we can't make sense of it."

SEVEN

TIN, WINE AND SILVER

"Now let us see. We think these triangles, which wander aimlessly all about the castle, represent Pellenore. Does that assumption make sense to both of you?"

Brit and Nimue nodded.

"Good. Then there are these stars, which also drift around but only on one side of the Great Hall. I surmise those stand for Mordred, right?"

Again, they indicated their agreement.

"And there are the crosses. If we were to connect them in a continuous line, we'd find them heading in a somewhat roundabout way for the refectory. Those may very well be Lancelot. That leaves our Mr. X. The Xs go in a more or less direct way toward Arthur's tower, where the killing took place. And our most probable guess for his identity is Mark of Cornwall."

"But Merlin," Nimue said, "the key word in what you said is guess. Arthur wants proof. He'll never agree to convict anyone based on guesswork with nothing concrete to back it up. Suppose the crosses are Mordred and the stars Lancelot? How can we prove it one way or the other?"

"We have statements from the suspects themselves. And we have what the servants saw, or in Gretchen's case, more than simply *saw*."

Nimue smiled at this.

"But there must be more of them. Ganelin would not have marked this chart without some basis. There must be more servants we have not identified yet who saw one or more of our suspects that night. I intend to find those servants. Ganelin found them; I will, too."

"But—" Something was bothering Brit and it showed. "We are still simply assuming Mark is the fourth suspect. We don't know. No one saw him, that we know of. Suppose it's someone else? Or suppose that trail of Xs goes somewhere other than to Arthur's tower? The chart doesn't extend that far. And suppose Mark really is Mr. X as you call him. Just because a servant saw him in the corridor is hardly proof he committed murder."

"Well, someone saw him—or rather someone saw someone—because the chart is marked. Whether it was Mark . . . well, that seems likely to me. But that is what I want the two of you to discover." He sat back in his chair. Nimue had never seen him quite so stern; it was clear his wounded leg and hand were causing him pain. "In Cornwall."

Brit registered alarm. "You want us to go to Mark's territory? After the attack we suffered?"

"Arthur is sending official word to Mark that you will be visiting him, to discuss some military maneuvers for next spring. And you will have a larger escort than the one we had. He won't dare harm you."

"If he is the villain." Brit said this emphatically.

"He is."

"How can you sound so confident?"

"Because, Brit, of the attack on you, or on Petronus, at the garrison in Corfe. The guards were killed. They would never have let Lancelot get that close to them. Or anyone else, for that matter. *Except Mark.* They would have recognized him as the commander of the army, and they would have let him approach, never expecting him to strike them."

"Good point."

Nimue studied the chart, looking doubtful. "But still, we'll be terribly vulnerable."

"You have the advantage of knowledge. Mark doesn't know that we know."

"He must suspect, at least, or why follow and attack us?"

"He knows we know he's up to something. He can't possibly know we think he is the murderer. And as I've said before, the very fact that the man we suspect is also the head of the king's armed forces makes for a very delicate situation. How can we know what kind of loyalty he has among the other commanders, and among the troops? I can't tell you how deeply I hope I'm wrong about this. But everything I know suggests Mark is the one."

"I can find out about the other commanders." Brit was looking increasingly unhappy. "I can make some discreet inquiries, among knights I know I can trust."

"When you get back from Cornwall. And remember, you mustn't do anything to force Mark's hand. Be subtle, be indirect and pick up whatever you can learn. Use all the guile you have."

"Guile isn't much good against armed swordsmen, Merlin."

"No, but it is priceless against blunt stupidity."

"Why do I not find that comforting?"

"Arthur will provide a large enough escort to keep you safe. Discover what you can."

Looking unhappy, or at least severely dubious, Nimue and Brit rose to go. Just as they were leaving, Merlin said, "And Colin? Use *all* the guile you have."

"Uh . . . yes, Merlin."

Nimue followed Brit down the stairs, past the spot where she'd found Ganelin. Suddenly Brit turned on her. "What did he mean by that?"

"I—I don't know."

"Who are you? Where did you come from?"

"I don't know what you mean. My name is Colin. You know that."

"There has been talk about a young woman who fled from Morgan's court. Mordred's betrothed. She disappeared about the time you came here."

"N—no."

Merlin appeared at the top of the staircase. "Come back here, both of you."

Slowly, sullenly, they climbed back to his study.

He closed the door behind them and leaned against it, wincing from the pain in his leg. "Now, Brit, what exactly are you suggesting?"

"Someone from Morgan's court may be here in Camelot. And there have been murders. Can you not guess what I'm thinking?"

"Colin was with me in the Great Hall when Borolet was killed."

"Are you certain? You yourself just said that he's full of guile."

He sighed sadly and looked at Nimue. "Tell her."

"But I—"

"Tell her!"

And so Nimue confessed to Brit that she was not really Colin, not really a boy at all.

"So you see, Brit," Merlin added when she was done, "I've known all along. I've encouraged Nimue to carry on this masquerade."

Brit looked doubtful. "What have you known? How can you know what loyalty she feels to Morgan le Fay?"

"There is no doubt in my mind. Colin—Nimue is loyal to Arthur and Camelot and everything it represents. I've heard her complain about Morgan's superstitious nonsense often enough. And no one sane could want to marry a horror like Mordred."

Brit was unconvinced but kept quiet.

"We can't start fighting among ourselves, Brit. We have to trust each other. This kind of squabbling is the worst thing we can do."

"I suppose you're right."

"I am and you know it. Time is short. Midwinter is approaching fast, and it is more important than ever. It may be the last chance we have to lure Mark here unsuspecting."

"But without proof—"

"I can provide proof. I've commented recently about using people's superstitions against them. And Mark is as gullible as anyone. That will be his undoing. But we need him to come here, unsuspecting and without his guard up. Ensuring that will be your job. When you get to Cornwall, comfort him, flatter him, make him believe his position is secure."

"Merlin, I want to know what you're up to. What are you planning?"

"In time, Brit. Go to Cornwall. Everything depends on

the two of you getting Mark to lower his guard." Softly, he added, "Please. We are too far into this investigation to let it come apart now."

And so the next morning Merlin saw Brit and Nimue off to Cornwall. Their carriage was larger and heavier—and better protected—than the one they'd used on their visit to Morgan, and a detachment of sixteen armed soldiers escorted them.

Just before they left, Nimue took Merlin aside. "I'm afraid, Merlin. She doesn't trust me. And how sure are you that she isn't loyal to Mark?"

"Brit is one of my oldest, closest friends here. I'm as sure of her as I can be of anyone."

"Mark is one of Arthur's oldest friends, remember? And Britomart thinks I'm working for Morgan."

"I've noticed the tension between the two of you before. I was never certain what caused it. But it will pass. Get to know her. You'll like her and she'll like you."

Uncertain, unhappy, she got into the carriage with Brit, and the column left Camelot.

Then Merlin headed to the castle library, where one of the copyists was working on something for him. "Good morning. Is it ready?"

"Nearly, sir." The copyist was a slender young man in his late twenties. "It's simple enough."

"Fine."

"Are you certain you don't want any illuminations or enhancements? It's so plain." He wrinkled his nose. "Unattractive. I can do better work than this."

"Just a plain, straightforward copy of the chart, please, with no crosses, triangles and such."

"Yes, sir. It will be ready in an hour or so."

"Fine. Bring it to me then, will you? I'll be in my tower."

Next he went to Arthur's tower and found Greffys. "I should be ready this afternoon. You've explained to the servants what I want?"

"Yes, Merlin. But—"

"But what?"

"They're suspicious."

"Who wouldn't be? But they must understand that we're investigating the murders. And they must understand that they themselves are not under suspicion. Tell them that. Reassure them. I'll do the same when I talk to them."

"Yes, Merlin. I thought you wanted the investigation kept secret."

"The time for that is past. I think we should be ready to begin by mid-afternoon. Bring the first of them then."

"Yes, sir."

"And Greffys?"

The boy had turned to go; he paused in the doorway. "Yes?"

"You've done a fine job so far."

The squire beamed. "Thank you!"

And so at mid-afternoon Greffys brought the first of the servants to Merlin's study. She was one of the kitchen girls, a buxom redhead in her early twenties. And she was plainly nervous.

"Good afternoon." Merlin smiled in a way he hoped was fatherly and reassuring. "You are Alice?"

"Yes, sir."

"Has Greffys, here, explained why I want to talk to you?"

"Yes, sir."

"Good. You understand, my only interest is in the information you might be able to provide. No one thinks you've done anything out of line."

"Yes, sir."

"Excellent."

"Yes, sir."

"Uh . . . yes."

"Yes, sir."

"Do you remember the night of the ceremony for the Stone of Bran?"

"Yes, sir."

"The night Borolet was killed?"

"Yes, sir."

"Can you say anything besides 'yes, sir'?"

"Yes, sir."

He sighed. "You recall that night, then?"

"Yes, sir."

"Where were you?"

"Sir?"

"When we all gathered in the Great Hall, where were you?"

"In the kitchen, sir, making honey cakes."

"As I remember it, the supply of those ran out early."

"Yes, sir. They didn't tell us there would be so many people. I—"

"That's all right, Alice. When you were finished with your duties, where did you go?"

"I—I had to go to the loo, sir."

"And did you see anyone on your way there?"

"Yes, sir."

"Who?"

"I saw Morgan le Fay's son."

"Mordred? Where did you see him?" He unrolled the

copy of Ganelin's chart. "Here. You see—this is the Great Hall and all the corridors that lead from it. Can you show me where you were when you saw Mordred?"

"Yes, sir." She squinted at the chart; she seemed to be working to remember. Then she extended her index finger and pointed. "Here."

"Did he say anything to you?"

"He asked me how to get to the—to the privy."

"I see."

"So I gave him directions and he went off—in the wrong direction. He was so lost. He was so cute."

"I don't believe I've heard anyone else describe him that way. Did you see anyone else in the hall?"

"No, sir."

"I see. Fine. Thank you very much, Alice."

She stood, made a shy curtsy, turned and left.

Merlin got out the original chart. The spot where she'd painted was almost exactly where Ganelin had marked one of his little stars. It looked as if Merlin's guess had been right. Each ★ represented a place where someone had seen Mordred.

The carriage and its escort made good time on the journey to Cornwall. The weather was sunny and dry and the roads were good. They stopped at Winchester for a midday meal. Brit said she knew the town and one particular inn where the food was always good. Accolon, who was again in charge of the escort, posted soldiers outside the inn.

Nimue and Brit had not talked much in the carriage. Their mutual distrust was obvious and getting worse. Brit in particular conversed in monosyllables, and only when it was necessary. Nimue tried making chat about the weather, the countryside, anything she could think of to try to break the ice, but to no avail.

Over lunch she decided she'd had enough. "Do you really think this sullen silence is going to help us do what we have to?"

Brit took a bite of her roast beef almost aggressively. "I don't know. But I can't think of any reason why I should trust you, *Colin*." She said the name with emphatic contempt.

"Merlin trusts me. Isn't that what matters? He told you himself he's the one who has encouraged me to continue this pretense."

"I've been suspicious of you from the outset. From the day you arrived at Camelot."

"What did you suspect me of? No crimes had been committed then."

"No, but I find it impossible to trust someone whose identity is such a complete mystery."

"You know who I am."

"And if I've been suspicious, don't you think other people must be? Your involvement in this investigation puts us all at risk."

"I don't see how."

"Never mind." Unhappy, Brit called to the innkeeper for more meat. A few minutes later they were back on the road.

Greffys brought more and more of the servants to Merlin for interrogation. And one session after another went much like the first one had gone. Some of the servants were talkative and cooperative; some were silent or nearly so, sullen and distrustful.

They had been in the hallways for various reasons—hunger, restlessness, nature's call. Some of them had seen one or more of the suspects; most had not. But one fact emerged clearly from the first several interviews—none of them had seen anyone in the halls who might make a plausible suspect except the suspects who were already known to him. Mordred, Pellenore, Lancelot. So far he had found no one who'd seen Mark.

Then one of the stable boys claimed to have seen him. As before, Merlin showed him the copy of the chart and asked him to indicate where. The boy pointed precisely to a spot where Ganelin had marked an X on the original. "You're certain of this? It was King Mark of Cornwall that you saw?"

"Yes, sir. I know him. I've groomed his horse for him."

"And this is the spot?"

"Yes, sir."

"And you told Ganelin about this? He questioned you?" The boy nodded.

"Very well. Thank you. You may go."

"Uh . . . sir?"

"Yes?"

"Ganelin told me my information was valuable."

"And so it is."

"He said you'd give me a farthing."

"Oh." Scowling, Merlin found his pocketbook, got out a coin and gave it to the boy. "Thank you again."

"Anytime, sir." Beaming, he left.

So Mark was the X. There seemed less and less room to doubt it.

But Greffys was puzzled by it all. "Excuse me, sir, but I thought King Mark was a friend of King Arthur."

"The Hebrews have a holy book called Micah, Greffys.

One of the things it says is 'A man's enemies are the men of his own house.'"

"But—but didn't Arthur come to power with Mark's help?"

"That would be a politic way of putting it. As a young man Arthur became determined to unify England. Until then it was a patchwork of tribes and confederations, all of them at each other's throats all the time. Arthur realized that England would never progress—would never advance to par with the rest of Europe—until some kind of unity could be imposed."

The boy seemed bewildered by this.

"Look, Greffys, there is power here. We have the population and—thanks to the Cornish tin and wine—the economic clout to stand shoulder to shoulder with any country on the Continent. We are only beginning to see the benefits that come from a unified nation, but they are real, and they will grow."

Greffys narrowed his eyes. "And Arthur realized all this? Or was it you?"

"I had traveled widely, yes. I think perhaps I was the one who opened Arthur's eyes to the possibilities."

"You are the real power behind the throne."

"Nonsense. Arthur had the military genius to make unity happen. I'm hopeless at such things."

"Even so. You make policy for the nation."

"Balderdash. But Arthur had a long struggle ahead of him. Warlords being warlords, they fought him. Sometimes viciously. Mark was one of the most savage. Do you know his history?"

"No, sir."

"His father, King Felix of Cornwall, died under mysterious circumstances. His heir was Mark's elder brother, Bouduin. Mark killed him and took the throne."

"That is terrible, sir. How could Arthur ever trust a man like that?"

"That is politics. At any rate, that is politics as it has always been practiced. Mark entered into a treaty with an Irish warlord and married the man's daughter, Isolde, to seal it. But Isolde, who was much younger, fell in love with Mark's nephew, Prince Tristram. The two of them died, again under mysterious circumstances. So you see, Greffys, Mark's history is bloody enough to make him a good suspect for us." He paused, suddenly concerned. "Uh, you do understand that I'm telling you this in confidence, don't you? None of this is to be spread around."

"Yes, sir. But . . ."

"But what?"

"Well . . . what kind of a place have you sent Colin and Britomart into?"

The weather was as sunny as could be expected in an English winter, and warm—it might almost have been early spring, not December. Inns had delicious, ample food at reasonable prices; the wine they served was full-bodied and sweet. There was every sign they were approaching a prosperous region.

The landscape was mostly granite hills interrupted by farmland. There seemed an outsize number of crippled men on the roads—men missing limbs or walking on crutches.

Whole fields were covered with wooden trellises; Nimue had never seen anything like them and asked Brit what they were. There had not been much talk between them. But Nimue was determined to learn everything she could, even if it meant questioning someone she didn't much like.

"They're for grapevines. Mark's people have figured out how to cultivate them. It's the first time anyone's done it in England. I assume the wine we had at that last inn was made here."

"They always say vines can't grow in England."

"Look at the soil. It's black and rich, like the soil at Mount Vesuvius in Italy."

Nimue was puzzled. "There are no volcanoes here."

"Brilliant observation."

Then odd buildings began to appear here and there across the landscape. Again she asked Brit. "They're so tall and thin. What can they be for?"

"They house the equipment for the mines. Enormous air pumps powered by bellows, and huge wheels wound with cable to lower the miners down to the lower depths."

"It sounds dangerous."

"It is. There are accidents all the time. You've seen all the cripples on the road. Arthur pays the widows a bounty."

"Big of him."

"Cornwall is the most prosperous place in England, and the mines are what makes it so. Bronze can't be made without tin, and Cornwall produces the only tin in Europe. Arthur might well be bankrupt without it."

"I see."

Then in the distance, at the head of the Cornish peninsula, loomed Mark's castle. It was not especially large by the standards of castle architecture, and Mark had had the exterior whitewashed and the towers painted bright red and blue, very un-castle-like; it gleamed, even in the weak winter sunshine.

As the party approached it they came to another of the mine-head buildings at the side of the road. Nimue heard machinery creaking inside, and there was a smell of chemicals in the air. Men, covered in dirt, came and went. And there was a guard post, and a barrier blocking the road.

Amid some noise and confusion—roads in Arthur's England were not barricaded and travel was supposed to be free—the travelers came to a halt and Accolon exchanged words with one of the guards. Brit put her head out one of the windows and watched to try to make out what they were saying. There were at least a dozen guards on duty, more than seemed necessary or even reasonable. "Military men," she muttered to Nimue. "Security becomes an obsession."

Just as Nimue looked out, too, Accolon rode his horse up beside the carriage. "I'm afraid there's a problem."

"What problem could there be?"

"The say they didn't know we were coming."

"Even if that is true, what does it have to do with anything? This is a free nation; citizens are allowed to travel about unhampered by this kind of thing."

She stepped out of the carriage and strode ahead to the checkpoint. "I am Britomart, King Arthur's military advisor."

The guard in charge was a young blond man. He looked nervous. "Yes, ma'am, I recognize you from Camelot. Do you have orders from the king?"

"We do."

"May I see them?"

For a instant it occurred to her that the man almost certainly could not read, and she could have shown him anything. But why risk it? "Our orders are not in writing. But we are here on official business. The king wishes me to go over plans for spring maneuvers with Mark."

" 'We' ?"

"Myself, my assistant Colin and our escort."

He looked doubtful. "No one is permitted to cross into Cornwall without some legitimate reason, properly documented. I'll have to send to King Mark. Please wait." He conferred with one of his men, who mounted a horse and headed off toward the castle.

Brit scowled as pointedly as she could manage to show how unhappy she was then went back to the carriage, explained to Nimue what was happening and settled in to wait. "Listen, Colin. I don't like the look of this. Blocked roads, a lot of guards where a few would suffice . . . It makes me suspect Merlin may be right about Mark. At the very least, this makes it more certain than ever that he's up to something he shouldn't be. We're both going to have to be alert."

"Merlin gave me some of his acid globes before I left."

"Fine. But that isn't what I mean. Keep your eyes and ears open. We must learn what's going on here."

"Merlin gave me some very specific instructions."

"That's good. We may have to rely on one another."

"And our guards?" She was pleased that Brit seemed to be opening up to her but somewhat alarmed at the circumstances.

"I'm guessing Mark will put them up in barracks, with his men, while we're quartered in the castle. Stay alert and cautious, Colin."

"You too. Do you . . . do you think we can actually pull this off?"

"If we can pry Mark away from his wine and wenches, we can."

"Don't hope for that too hard. His women and his drink are what we're counting on."

"We're crazy. This will be dangerous. If Mark even suspects . . ."

"Yes?"

"We could end up with our heads on poles."

Nimue fingered the acid globes in her pocket and hoped everything would go smoothly.

More than two hours passed. Brit, Nimue and their soldiers were bored. Some of the soldiers played dice to pass the time. Nimue ambled about, talking to Mark's men. None of them was friendly or communicative. But she noticed that one of them had a badly scarred face—scarred by acid.

Then the rider returned and conferred hastily with his commander, who then approached the carriage. "King Mark says you are welcome to join him at his castle. But he requests that you leave your weapons here."

Brit registered shock. "I am one of the king's ministers. Surely Mark isn't suggesting I abandon all security."

"King Mark—" he said the word *king* with special emphasis— "guarantees your safety while you are in his domain."

"Excuse me for saying so, but that isn't the issue."

"Nevertheless, if you wish to remain in Cornwall, you are to surrender your weapons."

Brit conferred hastily with Accolon and the most experienced of his men. None of them was happy with Mark's demand, but Brit had a job to do, so there seemed little choice. Unhappily, they all surrendered their swords. The guards made a quick search of their things; happily, they didn't recognize the acid globes as dangerous. Then, late in the afternoon, led by a detachment of Mark's men, they headed to the castle.

Mark was waiting for them in the courtyard when they arrived. He was wearing animal skins; he might have been one of the barbarians who sacked Rome. And he was half-drunk; he held a huge flagon of mead or wine or some other intoxicant. He wasn't wearing a sword, which Nimue took as a positive sign. "Maybe swords are banned here completely."

"Don't be naïve."

Mark greeted them heartily and claimed he was especially happy to see his second-in-command. "And how is our beloved king?"

"He is fine, Mark, and he sends his regards. And a request. I'm afraid our visit is official; we have military matters to discuss."

"Tonight, after dinner." He let out a loud laugh, quite uncharacteristic of him; Brit assumed it was from whatever he was drinking. Then he ordered some servants to take them to their rooms and make them comfortable. "Supper is at seven. You'll hear the gong summoning everyone. I like big parties."

"No wonder Arthur likes you."

"Just ask anyone for directions to the dining hall. I'll see you then."

Brit's and Nimue's rooms were in different wings of the castle. After getting settled in, Nimue found her way to Brit's suite. No one she met along the way would talk to her in any but the most perfunctory way. "I'm nervous, Brit. The atmosphere here is so . . . so . . ."

"Yes, it is."

"Did you notice that soldier with the disfigured face? I think the scars are from acid. He was one of the ones who attacked you and Merlin."

"No, I hadn't noticed. I'm impressed. You may actually be as smart as Merlin always says you are."

She ignored this. "Let's find out what we need to and get out of here as soon as we can."

"It may take time."

A man appeared at the door and stepped in without knocking. He was short and squat, like Mark, with bright grey hair and an enormous mustache. "How are the roads to Camelot?"

"Who the devil are you?" Brit didn't try to hide her suspiciousness.

"I am Giovanni Pastorini, King Mark's metalsmith."

"The one who made the shrine for the Stone of Bran?" Nimue was impressed.

"Yes, exactly. King Mark has offered my services to Arthur to fashion a sword to replace the one that was stolen from him."

"I see." Brit put on a politician's smile. She was thinking she might get useful information out of him. "Well, the roads are fine, Giovanni. I may call you that, mayn't I? Unless the weather takes a bad turn, you should travel well. When do you leave? If we finish our business with Mark quickly, perhaps you might travel with us."

"I am leaving first thing tomorrow morning, I'm afraid."

"Ah. Well, we'll see you at dinner, then. We found some good inns on our way here. You'll want to know about them."

"I couldn't be more appreciative. Till dinner, then." And he left as quickly as he'd come.

Brit and Nimue looked at each other. Brit said, "It doesn't make sense to me that Mark has imported an Italian metalsmith."

"I remember Merlin saying the same thing."

Brit shrugged. "Well, it's his court. He can keep whatever retainers he wants, I suppose. And kings can be eccentric. There's a king over in France who keeps his own royal fish breeder."

"The more I see of royalty, the more Morgan's court seems typical to me."

"Let's not get carried away. There's a big difference between importing a metalworker and keeping a chest of poisons."

Mark, rather mysteriously, did not appear for supper that evening. Both Brit and Nimue noticed that Pastorini was absent, too. They made subtle inquiries, prying, probing, trying to find out something that might tell them what they needed to know. But everyone at Mark's court claimed—or feigned—ignorance.

Finally, Brit cornered the majordomo and asked whether she'd be able to meet with Mark the next morning. "On King Arthur's business," she added pointedly.

The majordomo promised her he'd make certain there was room in Mark's schedule for her and headed off to get some wine.

Mark's court was much like Arthur's. Knights drank too much; servant girls flirted with them. It was boisterous and colorful; Nimue said it came as a relief after Guenevere's and Morgan's courts. "It's alive."

"Yes, but with what? Have you noticed the way they all call Arthur simply 'Arthur' but refer to Mark as 'King Mark'?"

"Yes, I had. I found it odd. But Mark is the king here."

"It's one more thing to take into account."

Their night was empty. No one at the castle seemed to feel inclined to entertain these emissaries from the court at Camelot. Brit, uncharacteristically, got drunk. Nimue tried, without much success, to hide her disapproval.

"Don't scold me, Colin. This is the best wine I've had in years."

"Was I scolding?"

"You were, with your eyes."

"We're here on important business. And we may be in danger. I think we should be in our right senses."

"Drunk or sober I'm the equal of any man in Cornwall."

"Of course you are. But—"

"Go out and take a walk if you don't want to drink with me."

Nimue glared at her but decided a walk sounded like a good idea. "I'll see you later. Be careful."

"Be careful," Brit drunkenly mimicked her.

The air was cold and crisp outside. The quarter moon was brilliant in a clear western sky, and there seemed to be a million stars. The Atlantic was calm; gentle waves fell on the coastline. Nimue ambled about the perimeter of the castle, enjoying the evening. Soldiers on sentry duty made their rounds; she tried making conversation, but they ignored her.

Then she saw a cloaked figure leave the castle by a rear entrance and scuttle off into the night. Intrigued, she followed. He headed quickly down the road to the nearest mine head, the one with the barricades where their party had been stopped. She followed, working to keep up.

When the cloaked man reached the sentry post he identified himself: he was Pastorini. He exchanged words with the guard on duty. They were not near enough for her to make out much of what they were saying. But she heard one word clearly, and it struck her in a way that made it seem to ring through the night: *silver*.

Brit went to sleep early. First thing the next morning, Nimue told her what she had heard.

"It's quite possible." Brit yawned and stretched. "Cornwall is made up of granite mostly. Granite frequently has deposits of various metals. The first one they discovered here was copper. But it wasn't worth much; there's copper all over Europe. It was when they went down deeper that they found the tin, which is more precious than they ever imagined. There are zinc, lead and iron, too, though not much of them. And maybe silver as well." She wrinkled her nose. "Probably not a lot of that either, but . . ."

"So we have a motive for Mark—silver mines."

"Tin would be sufficient motive. But I'm still not convinced he's the one we're after. I only wish we knew why he'd been visiting Morgan and Guenevere."

"Let's go see if we can find out. It's time for breakfast."

The dining hall at Mark's castle was smaller than the one at Camelot. Tables were crowded together; servants bumped into one another a lot and spilled things. Brit and Nimue had seats near Mark's, who came staggering into the hall just behind them.

"Morning, Mark." Brit did not hide her disapproval. "You haven't been drinking this early in the day, have you?"

He sat down and called for food in large portions. Then he turned to her. "There's been an accident at one of the mines. The axle of the great wheel broke as the lift was lowering some men down to the lode. Fourteen were killed."

"Oh."

"It's always something."

"A crowned head never rests easily."

Suddenly he seemed to find it odd that she was there. "So what is this about Arthur wanting maneuvers?"

"In the spring. I suggested Salisbury Plain."

"Good suggestion. But why?" He caught a serving girl by her skirt and told her to bring him wine.

"Our spies in France have been picking up intelligence that Leodegrance may be planning an invasion. Arthur wants his forces at full readiness." She invented freely.

"Guenevere's father?" A thought hit him. "So that's why she wouldn't—" But he caught himself and broke off.

"Wouldn't what, Mark?"

"Nothing." He lapsed into a sulky silence. After a moment he asked her, "Do you have any ideas for these maneuvers?"

"One or two. Arthur wants me to go over them with you. And so . . ." She spread her arms wide as if to say, and so here I am.

"If the army will be drilling in spring, then—"

"Yes?"

He glared at her, his eyes full of suspicion. "Never mind."

"Really, Mark, you've had too much wine to discuss serious matters. Why don't you go sleep it off? We can talk about it later."

"Too much wine? There's no such thing. You sound like an old woman. No, it's worse than that—you sound like Merlin."

"Don't be rude, Mark."

"Why Arthur listens to that old busybody . . ."

"Merlin made him king."

"That's what they always say, but I don't believe it. Every time the man opens his mouth he spits dust."

She had finished her breakfast.

"We'll talk later, then."

"Fine." He turned his attention to his breakfast.

At Camelot, Merlin had located several more servants who remembered who and what they'd seen that night. Greffys had been enormously helpful to him. But there was still nothing indisputable, nothing that might hold up at a trial. One serving girl saw Mark in the hall that led to the king's tower. And another remembered Lancelot propositioning her. Two more had run into Mordred. And an unsurprising number remembered seeing Pellenore dashing about the castle on one of his weird quests.

It occurred to him that Petronus might know something useful. The boy had recovered quickly, but Merlin had insisted he return to his room, if not his bed, and remain there. He didn't want him drifting about the castle, prying into things that were none of his business; he had come from Guenevere's court, after all.

He found Petronus in bed and to appearances unhappy about it.

"Good morning, Pete. How are you feeling today?"

"Restless. I keep watching the other squires exercising down in the courtyard. Let me join them. Please."

"Soon, perhaps. There are some things I want to ask you about."

The boy sulked. "I don't know anything."

"Don't take that attitude."

"You think I'm too dull to know I'm healed. If I don't know that, what can I know?"

"Know that I can have you shipped back to Corfe."

"Oh." He pouted. "Please don't. I don't want to go back there. Britomart has promised I'll be a proper squire with her, not just a glorified valet."

"I wouldn't like to send you back, but if you are going to be uncooperative . . ." He spread his hands apart in a helpless gesture, as if to ask, what can I do?

"What do you want to know?" He asked it with all the ill grace of an adolescent boy who was not getting his way.

"I want to know what you remember about King Mark's visit to Corfe."

Petronus blinked; he seemed to be concentrating. "Which time?"

"He's been there more than once?!"

"Yes, at least five or six times in the last year, I think." He sat on the edge of his bed.

"Be certain. It is important."

He focused. "Yes, definitely at least five times, and maybe more."

"You're quite certain?"

"Yes. Of course."

"Do you know why?"

He shook his head. "He kept having private meetings with Queen Guenevere."

"And who else?"

"Lancelot. And her father came over from France the last two times."

"Would you be willing to testify to that? To the king, I mean?"

"Certainly. But—"

"Excellent. You've been more helpful than you know, Petronus."

"Thank you, sir. But I still don't understand."

"You may have helped me solve two horrible crimes."

Confusion showed in his face. "But—"

"We'll talk more. Now I'm off to see Arthur." He got up to go.

"Have you heard from Britomart at all?"

"No. But I'm sure she and Colin are fine."

"Are they friends? I mean, I . . . I . . . they seem to . . ."

"Yes?"

"I wouldn't want her to take Colin as her squire instead of me."

"I don't think you have to worry about that. Colin is not the man he seems."

"I don't understand."

"And that, Petronus, is just as well."

"May I leave this room now?"

Merlin hesitated.

"Please, sir. I can't stand being confined here."

Again Merlin said nothing.

"You haven't put me under guard. You haven't had to. I could have left anytime I wanted to, but I followed your orders. Doesn't that count for anything?"

"Listen to me, Petronus. Things are more complicated here than you understand. You'll be free soon enough, if everything works out."

"And if it doesn't?"

"It will. We both have to believe that."

Late that night, a strange woman moved through the halls of Mark's castle. She wore a clinging, diaphanous gown; her breasts were almost fully exposed by the low cut; and her bright blond hair was covered by a sheer veil. She walked lightly, almost like a spirit. A large candle illuminated her way through the half-lit corridors. No one who saw her paid her the least attention, despite all the security. She had gotten in, after all, so she must be there legitimately. Drafts in the castle made her gown flow and flutter. One startled serving-woman thought for a moment that she was seeing a ghost.

Slowly, she made her way through the castle till she came to Mark's quarters. A guard was on duty; his face, too, had been scarred by acid. He was used to young women being summoned to the king's bedroom late at night; they exchanged a few words, and without hesitation he let her go in.

The room was nearly dark; only one candle burned in the far corner; there were no drafts and it burned steadily. Mark was lying on his bed, more drunk than she'd seen him before. He was half-undressed and only half-conscious, it seemed, and he was muttering something barely audible. Nimue smiled. This was precisely the state she'd hoped he'd be in.

Groggily, he looked at her. "That candle is almost as large as my sword."

She smiled. "It doesn't weigh much."

"Who are you?"

"My name is Eleanor. You told me to come, remember?"

"I did?" He tried to focus on her, without much success. "You work in the kitchen."

Another smile. "That's right."

With a small struggle he sat up on the edge of the bed. "Come here and sit by me."

Lightly, with a little laugh, she did so. He put an arm around her. "Pretty girl."

"Handsome king." She hoped he was too drunk to notice the irony in her voice. Or to act on what were, quite clearly, his intentions.

He caught her by the shoulders and tried to kiss her. And she let him. He tore at one sleeve of her gown and kissed her naked shoulder. Patiently, she permitted it.

Then, gently, she moved a few inches away from him. "Everyone says you should be king."

Baffled, he looked around the room. "I am."

"King of England."

"Oh, that. That is being taken care of. It is only a matter of time. Come over here and let me feel your breasts."

She backed off another few inches. "You must hate Arthur for taking your rightful place."

"Arthur is a fool. And so are you, if you don't let me make love to you."

She resigned herself to being pawed and moved back beside him. He fondled her stomach. "Pretty girl."

"You said that already."

"Pretty!" He shouted it with force. "I want you."

"Here." She stood up. "Let me get you another cup of wine."

She crossed the room to a little table and poured it, and she added a sleeping powder Merlin had given her. Now she had to hope he would talk before it took effect. When she handed the cup back to him, he took it and drained it in one long drink. This pleased her, though she was careful not to let it show.

"Arthur." He said the name with contempt. "He's a better general than I am, but that's all. All this rubbish about peace and harmony in England—who could take any of it seriously?"

"Not me, sire."

"No. But he's king. My people work the mines and refine the ore. My people die. And all the profits go to Camelot. Next year our vineyards will turn a profit." He looked at the empty cup in his hand and held it out to her; she dutifully refilled it. "And all the damned money will go to Arthur. Arthur. Arthur. His army hangs over us, a constant threat. Did you know there are actually people who call him the Sun King? Because of his damned blond hair, I imagine. Blond hair is for women, like you. No real man is so fair. The king's mines. The king's wineries. I'm the king. I'll have them back soon enough. Come here and kiss me."

She did not resist, though she found it unpleasant.

"What will you do to Arthur? What are your plans?"

He blinked, plainly trying to clear his head. "Who are you? You don't work in the kitchen."

It was easy enough to deal with. She kissed him again and whispered, "You are a beautiful man and I love you."

And he forgot his suspicions and kissed her back. "Arthur—the wheels are turning. His days as king are numbered."

"You would commit treason?"

"To get back what is mine! The fool has actually sent someone here to tell me his military plans. I spent all afternoon with her."

"What is your plan, then?" She stood and backed across the room.

"Never you mind, pretty girl. What's your name? Why don't you take that dress off?"

"What will you do to Arthur?"

"Come here, damn it! I want you! You said you love me. And you have to do that. I'm the king." He staggered to his feet and tried to grab her, but she was too quick for him. He lost his balance and fell back onto the bed. Feebly, he tried to get up again, but it was no use; he would not walk again till morning, and even then he would feel the wine and the drug.

Nimue looked down on him and grinned. It had been easier than she'd hoped.

Gingerly, she left the room, smiled at the guard, told him to have a good night and made her way back to her own room. In moments she was out of her gown and back in Colin's male attire. It felt good. She had only worn the gown for an hour, but being back in male things felt wonderful. She stuffed the gown under the bed and went to sleep.

The next morning Nimue was wakened by loud pounding at her door. The room was cold; she had been sleeping under a pile of furs. Before she could get up to open the door, it burst open and Mark came stomping into the room. A half dozen guards waited behind him in the corridor. He raised his arm and pointed accusingly.

"You!"

She sat up groggily, alarmed.

"You! Colin! Where is that girl?"

"Excuse me, Your Majesty, but what girl? I'm afraid I don't know what you mean."

"There was a girl last night. She came to my room." He sounded more bewildered than ferocious. He held up his hand and rubbed his forehead. "Called herself Elaine or some such. I think she drugged me."

The guards outside had their swords drawn.

"A girl? What on earth could a girl do?"

"This one was treacherous. A scheming, lying—"

"But, Your Highness, what does this have to do with me?"

He stopped and took a deep breath. "She was seen. She was seen coming this way—toward this wing. Someone saw her at your door. You must have seen or heard her."

She thought quickly. The gown she'd worn was still hidden under the bed; if they searched the room— "A blond girl in a low-cut white dress?"

"Yes. Where is she, damn it?"

"I saw her pass. Late at night. She was running."

"Which way?"

She pointed down the hall that led to the castle's main entrance.

One of the guards leaned in. Nimue recognized him as the one who'd been on duty outside Mark's room the previous night. "As I told you, sir."

Mark turned and flared at him. "How could she have gotten out past the guards there?"

"They don't question people who are leaving, only the ones who are trying to get in."

Mark scowled. "She can't have gotten away."

"The question is, how did she get in to begin with?"

"Damn breach of security. She might have been anyone. She might have been an assassin. Let's question the guards at the main gate."

They turned to go. Then the guard turned back into the room and stared at Nimue. His eyes narrowed suspiciously; he seemed to be inspecting her carefully. She froze; she didn't even breathe. He peered at her.

He was about to say something when from down the hall came Mark's roar. "William! Come on!"

The guard shook his head, as if to say he didn't know

why he would suspect Colin. Then he turned and followed his king.

A few minutes later Britomart came to Nimue's room. Nimue told her what had happened and the things Mark had said the previous night.

"So. Merlin has been right. Arthur has been a fool to trust Mark, and I've been a fool to doubt Merlin's judgment."

"Why a fool, Brit? To all appearances Mark has been a loyal subject to Arthur."

"Yes, but . . . I should have known. Something should have told me."

"There's no way you could have."

"Then why do I feel so completely foolish? But . . ."

"Hm?"

"Even given that Mark is engaged in treason, that doesn't prove he killed the squires."

"It makes it that much more likely."

"Arthur wants proof. *Proof.*"

"If we can get him to arrest Mark for treason, and if there are no more murders . . ."

"That's not good enough. Arthur is no fool. Everyone plots to advance his own interests. If we arrest everyone who does that, who would be left?"

"Cheerful thought."

"There has to be a way to unmask Mark. But how?"

Nimue crawled out of bed. "Let's get going. I hope we can make Camelot by tonight. I want my own bed and a king who'll leave me alone."

Late that morning their party left Mark's castle and Cornwall. The weather had been good for their entire trip. Now clouds were building up on the western horizon, and the Atlantic looked restless. Waves began to pound both sides of the peninsula. There was a stiff wind.

Accolon and his men had enjoyed two days of leisure, but even they were happy to be returning home. Accolon said they were all made nervous by the air of secrecy and suspicion that pervaded Mark's castle.

Nimue had been careful to bring a supply of acid globes and kept them where she could reach them quickly if they were attacked. "It seems incredible to me that Mark is letting us get away."

Brit shrugged. "As far as he knows—or can imagine— the woman who was in his bedroom last night is the real spy and the real danger. She has nothing to do with us. Or let us hope that's what he thinks. You did an excellent job, by the way. I shudder to think what you had to do to get him to open up."

"Less than you'd think. He was drunk when I got there. Drugging his wine was simple."

"That's good. But . . ."

"Yes?"

"How far would you have gone, if you'd needed to?"

"I don't know. And I'm glad I didn't have to find out."

They traveled as quickly as the roads would permit, and they were home an hour after sunset. The night sky was black with clouds. Nimue hoped it wasn't an omen.

They went straight to Merlin's tower and told him what they'd learned. He seemed upset by the news. "It would be Mark."

"I thought you suspected him all along." Nimue was puzzled.

"I did. But a suspicion has turned into a near-certainty,

and with it all the awful possibilities have become more real."

Brit leaned back and put her feet up on the table. "Suppose we send soldiers to arrest him before he can do anything more?"

"Arthur won't wear it. We still need hard proof. Besides, the scenario we've assembled doesn't quite make sense to me. Mark is trying to provoke some kind of nationwide insurrection, that much seems clear. What on earth would murdering two boys gain him?"

Nimue was about to say something when they heard footsteps on the staircase outside; someone was running. A moment later there came a loud knock at the door. Merlin asked who it was.

"Greffys, sir. I have news."

"Come in."

Greffys opened the door and stepped into the room, out of breath and panting heavily.

"You need to start exercising more often, Greffys." Brit was amused at his entrance. "Climbing a few steps shouldn't wind you so."

He ignored her. "I have news, Merlin." There was urgency in his tone.

"What is it? For heaven's sake, Greffys, calm down."

Panting, he said, "We've found them."

"Them? What on earth do you mean?"

"The Stone of Bran and Excalibur. We've found them."

EIGHT

THE PHANTOM OF CAMELOT

"Found them where?" Merlin's voice was low; Nimue thought it was possible to hear skepticism in it.

"Come, sir, please. The king sent me to fetch you."

All of them got to their feet, Merlin more slowly than the others. Brit watched him, wondering if it was the effect of his age, his injuries or unhappiness at this wrinkle when he was so certain he had solved the killings. They followed Greffys down the spiral staircase and through Camelot. Merlin, still walking with his cane, lagged behind the others. Torches lit the halls starkly. It became apparent they were heading to the wing where the petty kings were quartered.

"Greffys, I want you to tell me where they were found. Where precisely are we going?" Merlin had never sounded more grave, or more concerned.

"To Pellenore's room, sir." The boy kept walking and picked up his pace slightly.

"Pellenore had them." It was a statement, not a question.

"Yes, sir."

"And were they being guarded by a dragon?"

Greffys looked back over his shoulder. "The king sent me for you, sir. He wants you there."

In another few moments they had reached Pellenore's quarters. Arthur was in the corridor outside, pacing, looking quite unhappy, talking to a young woman. Pellenore was a few feet away from him; he had pressed himself into an angle of the hallway, and the expression on his face said clearly that he was puzzled and alarmed. Four knights attended Arthur; one more, with sword drawn, stood over Pellenore.

"Merlin. Thank heaven you got here."

"What is it, Arthur? What is this about?"

"This is Alarica. She is one of the household staff." He turned to the young woman. "Tell him." Merlin recognized her. He had interviewed her among the other household staff, briefly; she had known nothing of interest.

"Well, sir, I was cleaning out King Pellenore's rooms, like I always do. With winter coming on and Midwinter Court almost here, I wanted to give them a more thorough cleaning-out than usual. As I was changing the bed linens, I felt something hard under the mattress. And there it was— Excalibur."

"Under the mattress?"

"Yes, sir. It made me suspicious, so I looked under the bed, and there was the silver box."

"It was just sitting there? Not wrapped or bagged or anything?"

"No, sir. Just sitting there. I could see how it gleamed and I knew it must be valuable. And of course I recognized Excalibur. So I went to the king's chambers and told him."

She looked around uncertainly. "I didn't think it would cause all this commotion, sir."

"No, of course not. Were these things there before now?"

"I couldn't say, sir. Like I told you, I was being extra careful."

Merlin turned and walked to where Pellenore was being held; he made himself smile. "Pellenore. Hello, Pellenore."

The old man was trembling. "Merlin." He took hold of Merlin's sleeve. "You know me. You know I didn't do this. The beasts—the beasts are behind this somehow. You understand. You know what the beasts are capable of. Tell them. Please, Merlin, tell them." There were tears at the corners of his eyes.

"Pellenore." Merlin made his voice soothing, hoping it would calm the man. "Pellenore, did you take these things? Did you kill the twins?"

"Those boys." He stammered it. "No! Merlin, it was the beasts. It must have been them. They thrive on human blood. Please, Merlin, tell the king."

"All right, all right, Pellenore. I believe you."

For some reason this seemed to fill the old king with even more terror. His eyes widened and he began to shake quite violently. "Tell him! Tell him, please!"

Arthur made a signal, and two of the knights led Pellenore away at sword point. "Put him in the dungeon," Arthur instructed them loudly. "Not the one where we kept the twins' bodies. That would be much too grotesque, even if it would be fitting."

Pellenore began shrieking and crying out irrational things about his dragons and griffins. The knights prodded him with their swords, and they all disappeared down the corridor and around a corner.

Alarica looked at Arthur; it was clear she didn't understand what she'd done, or what her find had caused. "I'm
sorry, sir. I don't mean to cause so much trouble."

"It's all right. You did the right thing. Go to the kitchen
and get some wine for yourself. That will calm you."

"Thank you, sir." Still clearly puzzled and unsure, the
woman left.

Arthur turned to Merlin. "Well, there you have it. We
have our killer."

"Are you certain, Arthur?"

"How else could he have come into possession of this
and the shrine?" He swung Excalibur a few times, plainly
enjoying its heft. "I won't need a new sword after all. I can
send Pastorini back to Cornwall where he belongs."

"Pastorini. Of course." Merlin seemed pleased. "That
explains it. May I see Excalibur, please?"

"What on earth for?" Arthur handed it to him.

"Would you say it is damaged at all, Arthur? Haft still
firmly attached? Blade straight and true?"

"Of course. Pellenore stole it, but why would he have
damaged it?"

"If he had slept on it every night for all these weeks,
would the blade still be straight? Wouldn't it be bent?"

"What are you saying?"

"Besides, Pellenore is daft, not stupid. Why would he or
anyone else sleep on a thing like this?"

"Get to the point, Merlin—if there is one."

"I'm telling you that I still don't believe Pellenore is our
culprit."

Arthur snorted derisively. "The stolen things were found
in his room. That is evidence enough for me. Frankly, it's a
relief to have it all over and done with."

"I can imagine."

"My boys can rest in peace now."

"Oh—so can we all."

"Good. I'm glad you understand that. Now don't go muddying the waters with a lot of claptrap about reason and logic. We have the killer, and it is the man I've suspected all along."

"Arthur, will you listen to me?"

"We should have realized he'd do something horrible sooner or later."

"Arthur!" He spoke loudly and firmly, then lowered his voice to a confidential whisper. "We have to talk about this. Mark is—"

"We can try him during Midwinter Court. It will be good for people to see my justice in action."

"Arthur, will you listen to me?"

The king sighed. "You would have to take the pleasure out of this moment. What is it?"

Merlin took him by the sleeve and led him to a corner out of earshot of the others. "Mark is up to something. We have evidence. Ni—Colin has heard him."

Impatiently, he asked, "Up to what?"

"Let us talk in the morning. I'll tell you about it then."

"Fine."

Very late that night, long after midnight, Merlin was sleepless. He knew he would not rest until the truth had been uncovered and justice done. Rising from his bed, he dressed and got a torch.

Holding the light aloft and leaning on his cane, he negotiated the steps awkwardly. The castle was empty. He could hear, now and then, the sounds of guards stirring in the corridors, just out of sight; otherwise the place might have

been quite empty of people. Torches in wall sconces burned
every dozen feet along his way. It occurred to him that with
both of his hands occupied, he would be an easy target for
any assassin who chose to strike—as they had struck him
before. Would Pastorini attempt such a thing? he wondered.
Had the metalsmith come alone or with soldiers? His footsteps and the tap-tap-tap of his cane echoed.

The corridor sloped downward. In a few moments he
was in the dark bowels of the castle, and his light was the
only one. Rats, snakes, other creatures less immediately
identifiable scuttled out of his way as he progressed. Any
one of them could have bitten him, but all he could think
was, *Poor Pellenore, reduced to these awful surroundings.*
And the deeper he went, the colder the air grew.

Ahead of him he saw the light from another torch—the
guard's light. The doors of unoccupied dungeons hung
open, the interiors gaping at him horribly. He moved more
quickly.

The single guard was sitting on a rough wooden stool,
nodding off. An empty wine bottle lay on the floor beside
him. Arthurian security. Twenty feet away, he cleared his
throat loudly to rouse the man.

The soldier stirred and looked around groggily. Merlin
recognized him as an old campaigner, one of Arthur's stal-
warts. He was in his fifties, too old for any kind of service
but this, now. Merlin groped to remember his name but
couldn't.

For a moment the man registered alarm; then he recognized who was coming. "Merlin, sir."

"Hello. I would say 'good evening' but that hardly seems
appropriate down here."

"No, sir. How long has it been since the king closed the

dungeons? I never thought I'd see service down here. You look well."

"You too. I wish I felt well."

"Age gets us all, doesn't it? A few months ago I felt a terrible spasm in my left arm. Since then it hasn't worked properly, not at all." Then he realized the oddness of the situation. "What are you doing here, sir?"

"I want to see the prisoner."

"No one is permitted, sir."

"Nevertheless, you know me. I am Arthur's chief advisor. Let me in."

Doubtfully, the man stood up and took the key from a loop at his waist. "You're sure you're permitted, sir?"

"Arthur won't mind."

The guard hesitated. "That isn't an answer."

"Yes it is. I'll take responsibility if there should be any awkward questions asked."

Plainly uncertain, the guard unlocked the door. The lock and the hinges were badly rusted from years of disuse; they creaked quite alarmingly. Merlin took his torch and went inside.

The room seemed smaller than a proper dungeon ought to be; it was not much more than a cell, really. The stone floor was covered with dirt; cobwebs filled the corners. Some living thing scurried away. The air was freezing. In the light from the torch, Merlin could see his breath.

Along one wall, a rough shelf was cut from the bedrock. Pellenore was curled up on it. But he was not asleep. Merlin saw the torchlight glint in his eyes.

"Hello, Pellenore."

"Merlin. Why have you come here?"

"Why, to visit. Why else?"

"Are you working with them?"

He didn't have to ask who Pellenore meant. "No, Pellenore. The beasts are all asleep."

"They're not. They've made themselves small. I can hear them scuttling around in the darkness."

"Mice. Rats, maybe."

"They are the beasts. And they are here. This is the very deepest heart of Camelot, and they have found me here."

Merlin crossed the cell and sat down on the edge of the stone shelf. "Enterprising beasts would find you anywhere, wouldn't they?"

The old man didn't like the sound of this. "Hold your torch toward me, will you please? I'm cold."

"It is icy here, isn't it? Camelot has an icy heart." He wedged the torch against the rock shelf and let it stand there.

"But hearts have veins and arteries, don't they? Besides, Camelot has an icy king now, too."

"Arthur is not a bad man, Pellenore. He is simply overwhelmed by having gotten what he wanted."

The old king rubbed his hands over the torch's flame. "This used to be mine, Merlin, you know that. The entire countryside. I was a good and fair king, or tried to be, and my people were happy, or seemed to be. The land was fruitful and prosperous. Then Arthur came and took it all away."

"He would not be much of a king without ambition."

"I had my lands, and then all I had was Camelot to rove around. And now I only have this cold little cell full of hungry little beasts."

"I'll have someone bring you a brazier of coals. No one wants you to freeze to death."

"Merlin, I miss the world. I want my world back." He began to cry, and his voice broke. "Nothing has turned out the way I wanted it to."

"The world never turns out the way anyone wants it to, Pellenore. When I was young and living in Alexandria, anything seemed possible. I believed that with enough knowledge, I could accomplish anything. When I saw the chance to make Arthur king here, I saw my opportunity. Human society, I believed, was perfectible." He sighed. "At least I try to avoid being too foolish about it all. There is nothing more insufferable than an old fool."

Pellenore inched closer to the fire. "Everyone thinks I'm a fool, don't they?"

"You have lost so much more than any of the rest of us have ever gained."

"Except Arthur. He will lose it, too. But don't bother to warn him. He is a bigger fool than I ever was."

Merlin started to agree—started to explain that Arthur was a big enough fool to be blind to evidence he himself had asked for. But what would have been the point? "I only came here to make sure you are all right. A social visit, no more—and just listen to the two of us. A pair of sad old dotards."

"All hearts have veins and arteries. Otherwise, what good would they be? Thank you for coming, Merlin. Goodbye."

Feeling as if he'd been dismissed, and finding it odd, Merlin stood to go. He felt a brief impulse to embrace Pellenore, but he resisted it. "I'll send those coals."

"Please don't bother. Why waste heat on rats?" Oddly, he smiled. "Or on dragons, or on old men, for that matter?"

The cold stone had made Merlin's bad leg ache even more. Limping and leaning heavily on his cane, he left.

Tomorrow he would have to try and make Arthur see the light of reason. He was not at all certain he didn't prefer the cold darkness and the odd conversation of a mad old man.

The morning was overcast, one of those bright grey winter days. A cold wave had struck, and there were flurries.

Merlin had not slept well. So much depended on his meeting with the king, and he wanted to be as prepared mentally as he could be. Nimue came to his rooms early and found him sitting by the fire. "Are you all right?"

"My leg is bothering me."

"It will heal. I mean all right about Pellenore's arrest."

He exhaled deeply. "No. Of course not. Pellenore is harmless and I know it perfectly well. Arthur should, too."

"He wants a simple answer and he has it. He wants things to be clear and neat and easily explained. He's human."

"Don't remind me." He looked at her. "If there were another race, other than the human race, I'd go join it."

"You're tired, that's all."

"Look at us. We have achieved such wonders. I have stood at the foot of the Pyramids, looking up in awe. I have beheld the Parthenon and wondered at its harmony and proportion. I have seen the grandeur of the Coliseum. Our race has achieved such magnificent things. And you tell me that being human means wanting things simple."

"For most of us it is."

He got to his feet wearily. "My leg is aching. I suppose it is the weather." He took a step, leaning heavily on his cane. "I have this to look forward to, for all the years remaining to me."

"I wish you'd say something optimistic."

"Optimistic meaning simple?"

"If you like, yes."

"I don't have time for this, Nimue. I have to go off and deal with the king. I hope he listens."

There were more than a hundred steps leading down to the ground floor; it seemed to Merlin that it took him forever to descend, even with Nimue's help. Then she went off to breakfast and he made the long walk to the king's tower. The halls were crowded, as they were each morning when the castle came awake. People came and went on their daily business; now and then one of them would jostle him, and his leg exploded with pain. Then there was the staircase leading up to Arthur's rooms.

Arthur was in a hearty mood. "Good morning, Merlin. Magnificent weather, isn't it? Cold always brings out the best in me. Remember all those battles we fought in winter?"

"Blood and snow. You fought them, I didn't."

"You're in your stern teacher mode."

"I suppose so. Or my melancholy one. Can I sit?"

"Of course."

"I've practiced medicine most of my life. You would think I would be able to do something to abate my own pain, wouldn't you?"

Arthur stared at him.

"Or maybe . . . Arthur, am I any good? Have people only said that I have helped them to humor me?"

"You're feeling somber. Getting old."

"Brilliant deduction."

"I've been wounded in battle more times than I can count. What's wrong?"

"Age, Arthur. Which, more and more, looks to me like

the essence of life. The candle burns brightest just before it
goes out."

"Nonsense. You're good for years."

"What a horrible thought. Is there no rest for me, then?"

"Not while I need you." He smiled, hoping it would help.
It didn't.

"Arthur, I believe Pellenore is innocent."

"You want to conduct his defense?"

"I'm a scholar, not a lawyer."

"That's the first nice thing you've said, Merlin."

He shifted his weight. "Mark is up to something. He's
been making secret visits—to Morgan, to Guenevere, probably to a lot of other minor rulers."

"Army business."

"You sent him, then?"

"No, of course not."

"Then . . . ?"

"Look, I've told you before. I've known Mark for years.
I trust him. He was one of my first allies."

"You mean one of your first conquests, Arthur. He's bitter. He resents that you've appropriated his mines and his
vineyards."

"He gets a portion of the profits. Surely that's fair."

"He doesn't think so. Can you have someone get me
some water please?" He took a tiny envelope of powdered
medicine out of his pocket. "A painkiller."

"It's that bad?" He sent a page for water.

"You need to ask? Did you know Mark has a silver
mine?"

"What?!"

"You heard me. They found silver in one of the tin deposits. I presume that is where Pastorini got the silver for
the shrine he made for you."

"Silver."

"Silver, yes."

The page returned with a ewer of water and poured a cup for Merlin, who stirred his powder into it and drank it at once.

When the boy was gone, Arthur asked, "You're certain about this? Silver?"

"He told Colin so himself."

Arthur narrowed his eyes suspiciously. "Why would he tell Colin a thing like that?"

He dodged the question. "And Colin overheard a conversation between two of the mine's guards as well."

"Silver." Arthur whistled. "I'll have to talk about it with him. He should be here for court in a couple of weeks."

"I'd wear armor."

"He is not the killer, Merlin. Whatever he's up to, it must be for the good of the country, secret mines and all. We have our villain, and he's in jail. That's that."

Merlin sighed. "I'll be going, then." He started to stand.

"Not yet. I told you—I need you."

Merlin sat again. "For what now?"

"I need your scholarship."

"*Amo, amas, amat. Veni, vidi, vici.*"

"Don't be impertinent, Merlin. I'm serious."

"Tell me."

"Well, now that we have the Stone of Bran back, I need you to do some serious research. The stone has power. I want you to learn how to unleash it—how to control it."

"And I suppose you want me to learn this in time for court?"

Arthur was pleased. "Exactly."

But Merlin wasn't, and he didn't try to hide it. "And if I can't? If after all it is only a piece of sculpted quartz?"

"It is the Stone of Bran, Merlin. If anyone can master it, you can. Go and do it. Consult with Morgan if you must; do anything you have to. But learn the secret."

Wearily, he stood. "Yes, Arthur, of course."

A young soldier rushed into the room. "King Arthur, sir."

"Walter." Arthur smiled an artificial smile. "Walter of Londinium. Do you two know each other?"

Merlin had seen the man about Camelot, but they had never actually met. Arthur introduced them. But Walter had something on his mind, something evidently urgent. "Sir, I just went to take King Pellenore his breakfast."

"Yes?"

"He's gone."

Arthur froze. Slowly, he said, "Repeat that."

"The cell is quite empty, sir."

"That isn't possible."

Suddenly Merlin burst out laughing. "Of course. He tried to tell me last night, but I was too tired or too slow to grasp it."

Arthur rounded on him. "You were with him last night?"

Merlin nodded, still laughing. "This castle used to be his, remember? He knows it better than you or I could, every hidden passage, every concealed corridor. He tried to tell me that, but I didn't hear him properly."

"What were you doing there?"

Merlin shrugged. "I went to see him. He's an old—no, *friend* would not quite be the word, but we have known each other a long time. That precious man. You all think him mad, and he's made fools of you."

Angry, seething, the king turned back to young Walter. "Find him. Search. There must be a way out of the dungeon. Discover it. But find me that man."

Walter saluted crisply and rushed off.

"It's no use, Arthur." Merlin's laughter was starting to abate. "Pellenore, crazy old Pellenore, has won. He's beaten you. Can't you see that? These old castles are riddled with hidden hallways and secret passages. Whatever madman planned this place must have included them in his plans. For Pellenore. He could live in them for months—maybe years—like a phantom. The mad old king has won."

"Go to your damned library, Merlin, and learn about the stone. Do something useful. And for God's sake, stop laughing at the rest of us all the time."

"I can't help it. Nothing is funnier than a human being with delusions of control."

"I am the King of England, damn it. I will not be the object of ridicule, not for you and certainly not for Pellenore. Go and do what I ordered you to do. Learn how to master the Stone of Bran."

Not hiding his amusement, Merlin stood to go. He realized with pleasure that his painkiller had started working already. "Yes, Arthur. Of course. All you have to do is order up miracles and you will get them."

"Get out of here, Merlin. I've never lost my temper with you before, but there is a first time for everything."

"Yes, Arthur. Of course."

"I want miracles."

"Yes, Arthur."

And so the hunt for Pellenore began. Teams of knights, squires and pages scoured Camelot, checking walls for hidden seams and secret hinges, to no avail. One team found a hidden door in the armory; other than that, the search turned up nothing.

Arthur himself oversaw the search of Pellenore's dun-

geon cell. "There must be a hidden passage. There must."
But none was found for the longest time. Then by chance
Arthur sat on the stone ledge, leaned back against the wall
and felt the stone shift slightly. No one could find a latch or
spring mechanism, but when main force was applied, the
stone swung back, revealing a long, dark—and perfectly
empty—corridor.

It was thirty feet long and ended in a blank stone wall.
More force was applied, but these stones proved unyield-
ing. Worse yet, there was no sign anyone had been there for
years; the floor was littered with dirt and debris and cobwebs hung undisturbed. There were no footprints, no hand-
prints, nothing.

Merlin couldn't resist observing that there might be
other passages as well, that this might not be the one Pellenore had used in his escape. Arthur fumed.

But over the following days, Pellenore was seen, or
rather evidence of his presence was seen. Food disappeared mysteriously from the kitchen. Blankets and clothing were taken from knights' rooms. A maid, tidying
Accolon's chambers, shrieked in terror and ran when a man
emerged from a wall there. He took a pillow and vanished
again. No one knew where the mad king would appear next,
and given his supposedly homicidal bent, everyone was on
edge.

"I want him found." Arthur addressed a gathering of his
officers and knights. "*I want him found*, do you all understand that? Midwinter Court will be happening soon. I'll be
sending out heralds to summon everyone. We can't very
well have Pellenore leaping out of walls, terrifying our visitors. Or worse yet, slaughtering them."

And so the hunt continued—and continued to be
fruitless.

• • •

Merlin watched it all, deeply entertained. "Wanting to isolate Pellenore and incapacitate him, Arthur has done the reverse."

Nimue was anxious, like everyone else in Camelot. "Has it occurred to you that he may be right? That Pellenore may actually have killed the twins? That whatever Mark is up to may be unconnected?"

"And I suppose you think the old man's dragons and griffins and whatnot are real?"

"No, of course not. But he thinks they're real. He could easily have killed the boys, for whatever mad reason, then convinced himself it was really his imaginary beasts who did it."

"Better still," Brit added, quite diverted by it all, "they may actually exist."

"Dragons that kill with swords? Of course." He snorted.

"I know you, Merlin." She scowled at him. "I know the way your mind works. You've never liked the military. You want Mark to be the murderer."

"I feel guilty about all of the wars I set Arthur on, yes. When I rigged the—when he pulled Excalibur from the stone, I expected him to become king peacefully. The idea was to use people's superstition against them, and for their own good. Instead there was nationwide warfare. Death and bloodshed on a vast scale. Do you really think I think framing Mark for the murders would atone for that? If you do know the way my mind works, you must know better than that."

"I know there's a murderer loose and we're all in danger. Wouldn't you say so, Colin?" Since their journey to Cornwall together, Brit and Nimue had found a measure of respect for one another; at least the active suspicion and hostility between them had abated.

"I don't know what to think," Nimue said. "I'm still new here. Merlin knows everyone so much better than I do. But—"

"But what?" Merlin was losing his patience.

"But—can we afford to take the chance?"

Suddenly, his face lit up with a broad smile. "Of course! That's it!"

It caught Brit off guard. "You know where he's hiding?"

"No. But I've suddenly realized how to flush the real killer out of secrecy."

"How?"

"Never you mind. I'll explain in good time. But it relates to what we've been talking about."

Brit frowned. "I can't stand you when you're smug and cryptic."

"I know, I know."

"Then stop it. Explain yourself."

"Not now. I have to find the king."

Merlin rushed through the castle as quickly as he could on his injured leg. Just as he reached the foot of Arthur's tower, he met Greffys. "Is he up there?"

"No. He's in the Great Hall with the heralds."

"Good. I only hope I can catch him in time."

Together they headed for the hall, Merlin limping behind the boy. People gaped as the two hurried along corridor after corridor. No one could remember seeing Merlin in such a hurry, wounded leg and all. His cane tapped the stones like a woodpecker.

They found Arthur sitting on a table in the Great Hall

with a plate of honey cakes in front of him. On the other side of the hall two dozen of his heralds had gathered and were waiting for him to finish his treat and address them.

"Merlin, Greffys, have one of these. The cooks are getting better."

"So am I, Arthur." Merlin beamed. "I've found it."

"Found what? What the devil are you talking about?"

Merlin looked around and lowered his voice. "The stone—I've found the key to unleashing its power."

The king gaped at him. "You're joking."

"No."

"Did Morgan tell you?"

"No, Arthur, I found it myself. I'm not called the greatest scholar in England for nothing, you know."

"What is it, then? Tell me."

"Not yet. I still have to track down some details. But I'm glad I've caught you before you sent the heralds out."

"You want this announced?"

"To everyone. I want the whole country to know the power the Stone of Bran has given us."

"This doesn't sound like you, Merlin. What power?"

"The power," he said slowly and carefully, "of life and death."

Arthur fell silent for a moment. "It is that powerful?"

Merlin nodded gravely, in his best "sage" manner.

"You're right. All England must know of this. This will make us the greatest power in Europe."

"If not in the entire world." Merlin was pleased at the way this was going. If Arthur believed his tale, then it seemed likely that most everyone would. "Have the heralds announce it. Tell them I shall demonstrate at Midwinter Court. Everyone in England will see the truth then."

"Excellent work, Merlin."

"And it might be wise to have military escorts accompany the heralds, at least the ones who are summoning Morgan, Guenevere and Mark. Just to make certain they accept your gracious invitation."

Arthur narrowed his eyes. "We know who did the murders, remember?"

"Yes, of course, Arthur. I simply want to make sure, that's all."

"You're up to something. But I'll do it."

"Oh, and something else occurred to me."

"Yes? What?"

"Have you given much thought to the entertainment for court?"

"No, I can't honestly say that I have. Why?"

"While the heralds are out, have them look for Samuel Gall's company of actors. They are the best in the country. Have them summoned here to perform for the assembled nobles."

Arthur bit into another cake. "I will. But it isn't like you to worry over performers. What's back of this?"

"Why, Arthur." He was all innocence. "I simply want your court to be memorable, that is all."

NINE

ILLUSIONS

It snowed for three days. The world was soft, white and frigid. On the second morning Merlin was in his tower reading, with Roc on his shoulder, when he heard a scratching at the window. The other two ravens, the ones that had been missing, were there, trying desperately to get inside.

He opened the shutter and let them in. They flew directly to the hearth, not too close, and warmed themselves. Then a moment later they flapped their wings and went to his shoulders and nuzzled him.

"I thought you were dead," he whispered. "But you've come back. Is that a sign?"

Roc, standing at the edge of the table, squawked shrilly as if to say, "The world does not send us signs."

Merlin named the other two birds Phoenix and Osiris, after two mythological figures who had conquered death. They began responding to their names almost at once.

• • •

By the third morning, Merlin was feeling restless. He headed to the stables and asked one of the grooms to prepare a horse cart for him.

Camelot was full of activity as the household staff decorated for Midwinter Court. Every available space was hung with holly and evergreen branches, to signify the triumph of life over death on this feast when the sun reached its lowest point and began to climb in the sky again. Hundreds— thousands—of candles were set about; the castle would be ablaze with light as, at least in theory, the heavens were. Singers and musicians and handbell ringers rehearsed, loudly, songs celebrating the season. And great stores of provisions were being brought in from surrounding farms and villages so that Arthur's guests would want for nothing.

Arthur circulated through the castle, overseeing it all and beaming at the work, and even helping to arrange the holly now and then. When he encountered Merlin he greeted him heartily. "They're doing a wonderful job, aren't they? I love holidays. The lights, the colors . . . and we're having plays. One of the heralds found your friend Samuel Gall."

"Fine, Arthur." He adopted his patient teacher manner.

Arthur blinked and gaped at him. "Do you mean to tell me you don't like the Midwinter feasting?"

"I do not mean to tell you anything at all about it. But since you ask . . ."

"Merlin, how on earth can you not enjoy this? The lights, the colors, the music . . . I've loved Midwinter since I was a boy."

"You are still a boy, Arthur, in more ways than you realize."

The king looked at him suspiciously. "Explain yourself, killjoy."

"I have never understood the concept of happiness by the calendar. 'Oh, goodness, it is such and such a date. That means I'm going to feel good and find life wonderful. Never mind that there are assassins on the loose.'"

"Go and have a drink, Merlin. You need it."

"As it happens, I'm heading to the kitchen, for some breakfast."

"Even that will help."

So Merlin left Arthur happily hanging holly and humming hymns to the newborn sun. In the refectory he encountered Petronus who, always anxious to make himself useful, offered to be his driver.

They finished eating and walked to the stable together. "But, sir, where are we going?"

"A great deal is going to happen here in the coming days, Petronus. I need to be alone, to think and to meditate, at least for a few hours. There is one place in the world where I have always been able to do that."

"And where is that, sir?"

"Stonehenge."

"But . . . but that is in Salisbury, sir."

"I know it. If the roads are passable we can get there in two hours or so. Let us hope. You may go to the local inn to keep warm while I spend contemplative time at the monument."

"But won't you be cold?"

"At my age cold is a constant. I need this time alone."

Petronus fell silent for a few moments. Then as they walked to the stable he said, "It sounds as if you are going there to pray, sir."

"Don't be preposterous. Stonehenge is a gift of the ancients, who could not possibly have envisioned the circumstances that take me there. It is a place of harmony and proportion, of intellectual peace. In a snowfall it is even more so. I need to experience that just now, before the guests arrive for court. There may be danger here; I need to think and prepare myself mentally for what I have to do."

"And what is that?"

"You will see soon enough."

"Yes, sir."

Just as they reached the stable, the doors flew wide open and two small donkey carts and a large horse-drawn carriage drove in. Merlin glared at them; people were arriving early, and he might not be able to get away after all.

Then he stopped to wonder who the conveyances belonged to. "Hold off for a moment, Pete."

He watched as the passengers began to alight. Recognizing the leader, he crossed the stable to him and threw his arms around him. "Samuel! I had no idea you would arrive early. I knew Arthur had invited you, but . . ."

Samuel was a man of Merlin's age, clean-shaven, fit. "The king summoned us. And performing at these courts is always a good source of income for us. If nothing else, other nobles will see us and want us to appear at their own courts. You know the artist's life."

More men descended from the carriage. Most of them were young; among them there was one boy, younger than Petronus, with bright red hair. They set about taking trunks and boxes off the carriage's roof. Samuel pointed to one after another and told Merlin their names. "Robert, Pierre, Wolf, Francis. And this boy with the flame-red hair is Watson, our leading lady. He plays tragic heroines so convincingly audiences are moved to tears. He will break hearts."

Petronus had been listening without saying anything. Finally, it made sense to him. "What play are you acting out?"

"Bringing to life." Samuel was emphatic. "We are the best in England. Artists, not common play-actors."

"I love plays."

"When we perform, young man, everyone loves plays." He turned back to Merlin. "The king has requested our *Fall of Troy*. Just wait till you see Watson, here, play Hecuba. You're in for a real treat, Merlin."

"I'm sure of it. But—"

"We've been making a hit in the provinces with the *Assassination of Julius Caesar*, but Arthur has forbidden us to play it here."

"Wise man."

"Is he nervous, then?"

"You haven't heard?" Merlin explained about the killing of the squires, the escape of Pellenore and the rest of it. "So you haven't come to a happy court. And a play about assassinating Caesar would hardly be the thing. But listen, I'm glad you're here. I'm going to be staging some theatrics of my own. Perhaps you can give me some instruction in stagecraft." He lowered his voice and looked around to make certain no one was eavesdropping. "To be specific, in conjuring. This has to be terribly effective. A great deal depends on it."

Mildly puzzled, Samuel told him, "I'll be happy to help in any way I can. But what on earth—?"

"I'll explain later, when we're alone. You remember where my rooms are?"

"Are you still living in that drafty tower?"

"Yes. Come in an hour or so." He looked at Petronus. "We won't be making our outing after all, I'm afraid. But thank you for offering to drive me."

J.M.C. BLAIR

Puzzled and disappointed, Petronus left. A moment later Merlin followed, leaving the actors to deal with their props and costumes.

Like almost everyone else, Nimue was getting into a holiday mood. She found Merlin in his study, preoccupied, sulking, stroking the head of one of his ravens and studying Ganelin's chart still another time. His fingertip traced the paths of symbols, and he seemed quite lost in thought. At the bottom of his breath he was muttering, "It must be. It must be."

"You work too hard, Merlin." She decided to try and cheer him up. "The snow won't stop falling. If I were still a kid I'd be riding my sled. Kids must be doing that all over the country."

"Go and join them, then."

"It's the best time of the year, Merlin, and the world has turned perfectly gorgeous. You should be happy."

"You know what I'm dealing with, Nimue. What *we* are dealing with. This may be our one last chance to flush out the killer."

"Even the king is cheerful."

"If he was less so, he would have taken my advice and had Mark arrested. Cheerfulness never accomplishes anything permanent."

"Really, Merlin, I know you're going to tell me I'm too young to understand, but I hope I never come to understand seeing the world that way. Look—your pets are back. Isn't that a good thing?"

"Yes, of course it is. They love me and I love them. But Nimue, optimism is not useful if it blinds us to the facts."

"We don't actually have facts, remember? Only symbols on a chart and conjecture about what they mean."

"Even so."

"Suppose it isn't Mark who's flushed out by this charade?"

"Then we will apprehend the culprit, imprison him—or her—and Mark will go back to his treasonous plot, whatever it is. He may bring Arthur down. He may bring the whole country down, for that matter. Does that really strike you as cause for optimism?"

"You're impossible."

"If you were a true scholar, you would know that nothing is impossible. I find myself thinking about Morgan. She wants her son to be king. If she had learned somehow that the twins were Arthur's sons, it would have given her more than enough motive to—I wish things weren't so complicated."

Greffys knocked and opened the door. "Excuse me, sir. Arthur wants you."

"Tell him I'll be there as soon as I can."

"He asks that you come now, sir. The queen is here."

"Guenevere?"

"And Lancelot."

"They would be the first to arrive. Tell him I'll be along shortly."

"Yes, sir. She, uh   the guards who brought her say her parents were with her at Corfe."

"Leodegrance and Leonilla? Splendid. There's nothing suspicious about that, is there?"

"I couldn't say, sir." He left.

Merlin turned back to Nimue. "I know you think me a worrisome old man, but—"

"Let's say overly anxious."

"Fine, anxious then."

"Overly."

"Please, Nimue, not now. I don't know what to expect over the next few days. When the killer realizes he is trapped—whoever he may be—he is apt to do almost anything. People will be hurt, possibly killed, and we have had more than enough of that already. And you and I will be in peril. Are you certain you want to do this?"

For the first time her mood turned serious. "Quite certain."

"He will lash out."

"Even so."

"I could get Greffys to do it. Or even one of the young actors. It isn't absolutely essential that Mark recognize you."

"There are actors? Are we going to have plays?" Her mood brightened again instantly.

"Yes. Apparently Troy is to fall again, within the walls of Camelot."

"I hadn't heard."

"Arthur loves plays. We get them every Midwinter, every May Day . . ."

"He's a good king."

"Let us go and attend Her Majesty and her lover."

In the courtyard, Arthur was greeting his wife and Lancelot when Merlin and Nimue arrived. Just as they stepped into the yard he was helping Guenevere down from her carriage. The soldiers he'd sent to escort her were milling about, evidently glad to be home.

"Merlin! Colin!" Arthur called to them heartily. "Look who's come to visit for the holiday!"

Guenevere scowled. "Is that what you call people who have come here under armed guard? Visitors?"

"Why, Guenevere, you make it sound as if you were brought under duress."

"I can't think what gave me that idea. Could it have been a detachment of your soldiers?"

"Oh dear. You have me wrong. I was only concerned about your safety. The countryside is fraught with marauders."

Lancelot stepped out of the carriage and leaped to the ground. "Our own soldiers could have protected us equally well, I should think."

Arthur ignored him. "But, Guenevere, you are my vassal—my wife. Your soldiers *are* mine."

"That is rubbish, Arthur, and you know it perfectly well."

He put on an enormous grin. "I'm told your parents are holed up in your castle at Corfe."

"Cannot a woman's parents visit her without you suspecting the worst?"

He played dumb. "Why, whatever do you mean? What is the worst?"

"They've come to visit me, that is all."

"There might possibly be people who would find their presence in England odd, not to say suspicious."

"Or wise." She smiled and nodded in Merlin's direction. "If you should decide to detain me, they would know at once."

"Guenevere, darling. What suspicious minds you all have."

"We have a great deal to be suspicious of."

The captain crossed to Arthur, whispered something in his ear then went back to his men. "My captain tells me he made certain the shades in your carriage were kept drawn. For your own protection of course—to make certain no one could suspect you both of conducting reconnaissance. I hope it wasn't a problem for you."

Guenevere was arch, distant. "Why should anyone want to inspect your snow?"

"Queens have been known to have sinister motives." He smiled even more widely than Guenevere. "But let me have you shown to your suite of rooms."

Lancelot reached around and rubbed his back in a quite pointed way. "Thank you. The journey over these dreadful English roads was agonizing."

"You will of course remain in your rooms unless you have permission to do otherwise." He was all heartiness.

Both of them froze. Slowly, venomously, Guenevere intoned, "That will not be agreeable, no."

"I'm afraid I must insist. Again, it is for your protection. There is an escaped killer, a madman, loose in the secret passages that riddle Camelot."

"Then your penal system is as defective as your highways," Lancelot snorted.

"Regrettably so. Still, I must insist you not go wandering about the castle. We wouldn't want to see either of you come to harm."

They bristled and protested, but Arthur was clearly within his rights. He had them escorted—"for their own protection"—to a suite in the drafty north tower of Camelot, which was the oldest part of the castle. It was cold and not in good repair, and it was seldom used except for storage.

Guenevere made a pro forma complaint, demanding that she and Lancelot be installed in her old quarters. But Arthur explained patiently that Merlin occupied those rooms now, and Guenevere couldn't possibly want to inconvenience him, could she? Then she demanded that they be moved to a warmer, more up-to-date part of the castle, but Arthur told her that his was likely to be the largest Midwinter Court in years; every bit of space in Camelot would be occupied. "You'll have more privacy there."

Steaming, seething with anger, Guenevere and her man settled into their apartments. As a parting shot she told her husband, "If Merlin really can resurrect the dead, perhaps you can have him start by reviving your monarchy."

Then Arthur and Merlin left, pleased at how plainly upset she was. "Come," Arthur whispered. "I want to talk."

Merlin followed the king to his tower. "You're in a good mood."

"My wife has come to visit. How could I not be?"

"As long as you have her securely under lock and key. Did you know before today that Leodegrance and Leonilla were in England?"

"No. I should never have let Guenevere settle at a port city. I know, I know, you warned me. I thought our marriage vows might count for something, however minimal. They're up to something."

Merlin feigned sorrow. "And no one's ever warned you."

"Don't be sarcastic, Merlin. Has it occurred to you that this insurrection—or whatever is being planned—may be their idea, not Mark's?"

"He appears to be going along with it cheerfully enough."

"Don't remind me." He sat down heavily and sighed. "You've been right about this all along. Learning the French king and his wife are here drives the point home. If there's anything a king shouldn't be, it's trusting."

"And your point?"

"Don't make this harder for me than it already is, Merlin. I've been naïve, maybe even foolish. I admit it. Now advise me."

"I advise you to arrest them. All of them. Send troops to Corfe and arrest Leodegrance and his wife. Until we can get to the bottom of this."

"On what charge?"

"Invent one. Make something up. Sedition. Conspiracy. Conduct unbecoming a Frenchman."

The king sighed even more deeply. "No. I don't think that's the answer. England has never known civil war. Doing that could certainly start one."

"The army is loyal to you."

"Stop toying with me, Merlin. You know how they respect Mark. And after all, I became king by defeating all of them. Besides, have you ever met Leonilla? She's a gorgon—worse even than her daughter. She could probably spew enough acid to melt the walls of any prison I have."

Merlin shifted his weight uncomfortably. It seemed a good moment for a politic lie. "I've been so focused on finding the murderer I haven't really given this much thought."

"Do it now, for God's sake."

"Suppose the murders and the plot are related, as I've been telling you all along?"

Arthur swallowed his pride. "Then you were right and I wasn't. Is that what you want to hear?"

"I am convinced that Mark killed the twins, or had them killed. I'd wager he did it himself."

"Why? What could he possibly have had against them?"

"He's been trying to foment this plot. But no one seems to want to go along. Guenevere because she's planning her own war, with her father's help. And Morgan—heaven only knows what Morgan is up to."

"Maybe she's loyal to me, or to our family."

"Don't be foolish, Arthur. She wants to be queen. She thinks it's her right."

"And so it is, I suppose. We have destroyed the old order. Birthing a new one should be easier than this." He looked at his advisor. "Shouldn't it?"

"If you say so, Your Majesty."

"Shut up."

Over the next two days the snow became heavier. Despite it, people came from all over England for Arthur's court. Knights, dukes, barons, earls and petty warlords made the trek. And all of them were abuzz with speculative gossip about Merlin's "miracle."

The Stone of Bran was legendary. And most of the educated class—of whom there were not many—took the old legends to be just that. The prospect of seeing a miracle, of the kind embodied in the old myths—actually seeing it— was more tantalizing than most of them wanted to admit.

Among them came Morgan and her son, angry like Guenevere to have been brought under guard. She protested that as high priestess she was an officer of the state, or should be regarded as one, and Arthur met her with carefully studied obliviousness, pretending it was all for her own protection. She demanded the best rooms in Camelot, to no avail. Mordred sniveled and wiped his nose on his sleeve a lot.

Then came Mark. Both Arthur and Merlin were expecting him to be raging, but he feigned not to have noticed that his escort was really a guard.

"But, Arthur, there's something you must consider."

"And what is that, Mark?"

He lowered his voice. "Something dangerous is afoot."

"You want to warn me?"

"I do. You must not permit it."

"What the devil are you talking about, Mark?"

He narrowed his eyes. "I think you know perfectly well."

Arthur made his face a blank. "No. Honestly. Tell me."

"You can't guess what I mean?"

"It isn't like you to be so cryptic, Mark. If you have a point, make it."

He whispered heavily, "Merlin."

"What? What on earth could Merlin be doing that you have to warn me about?"

"This scheme of his, this plan to waken the dead. It is dangerous."

"He knows what he's doing, Mark." He couldn't resist adding, "Do you?"

"What is that supposed to mean? I'm not meddling with dark forces."

"Aren't you?"

It caught Mark off guard, and he stammered for a moment, trying to recover his composure. "Arthur, listen to me. Merlin is going to do something momentous. Something that has never been done, not in all recorded history."

"He's studied the appropriate texts. He knows what he's doing." Offhandedly, he added, "The gods will guide him— and protect the rest of us."

"Please, Arthur, stop him from doing this. We could all end up in the worst peril."

"Mark, it's been announced. I can't very well disappoint all the nobles in the country, can I?"

Mark was losing his resolve to argue, but it was clear he

was nervous, not to say frightened, which struck Arthur as a good thing. "This is perilous, Arthur. You know all the old legends about sorcerers who meddle in things they shouldn't. When they lose control, everyone suffers."

"Why, Mark, you sound genuinely afraid."

"And so I am. You should be, too. You let that old man play with these forces, we'll all have to pay."

Arthur thought to himself, *good*. But all he said was, "I really don't see how I can stop it. Too many people would be disappointed." He rubbed his hands together and grinned like an eager schoolboy. "Besides, I want to see it myself."

"May I have permission not to attend, then?"

Abruptly, Arthur turned king again. "You may not. I want you there." Then he smiled warmly. "If something awful does happen, I'll need you."

Grumping, clearly unhappy, Mark went off to his quarters. And Arthur went straight to Merlin's tower to tell him about the exchange. "He's worried about your 'miracle,' not about any plots or killers being exposed. That's good."

"Mark has always been superstitious. Er, excuse me, prone to believe in things."

"He's human, that's all."

Merlin ignored this; it was the wrong time to get into a philosophical debate. "So we have all four of our suspects where we want them."

Arthur gaped. "You want Pellenore in the castle walls, leaping out and terrifying people?"

"At least we know where he is. Besides, he hasn't actually hurt anyone, has he?"

"Except my boys."

"You think he slaughtered them but has turned docile and harmless?"

"Yes. That would be odd in an ordinary murderer, Merlin, but hardly in a madman."

"If you'll excuse me, Arthur, I have to go take an acting lesson."

"Act—?"

"Tomorrow night I shall give a performance for the ages. No Greek in the Odeon at Athens portrayed Hercules more convincingly than I shall play the magician."

"Well, you certainly talk like a Greek. Why don't you speak plainly, so people know what you're talking about?"

Merlin smiled and made a slight bow. "The result of years of practice at court."

And so more and more people flowed into Camelot, all of them in a festive mood. Soon the castle was filled to bursting, more so than it had been when the Stone of Bran was to have been unveiled. Servants were overworked; outriders went to the neighboring towns and villages, recruiting workers for the duration of the seasonal festival and offering generous wages. Food was brought in from every available source, and Mark's people in Cornwall sent enormous quantities of wine. Knowing the nature of Arthur's court, it would certainly be needed. Every available space in Camelot was decorated, with holly and other evergreens, with candles or both. No one complained about cramped quarters this time; it was Midwinter, the year's brightest holiday.

The first night, Arthur summoned everyone to the Great Hall. A platform had been set up against one wall—the same platform that had been erected the night Borolet died and the Stone of Bran and Excalibur were stolen. But this time there was only one throne on it, Arthur's; the symbolism was impossible to miss. Scores of torches lit the hall brilliantly; it might almost have been daytime. Musicians played, singers caroled, mummers put on little skits for the amusement of the crowd and servants passed about with trays of meat and cakes.

Then, to a loud brass fanfare, Arthur entered, wearing Excalibur around his waist. He made a speech welcoming everyone to Camelot for the festivities. "Let us rejoice," he concluded, "that this gathering will end on a happier note than our last one."

The assembled knights and lords drank a toast to him, a second to his health, a third to his reign . . . Before long the customary court drunkenness was evident to everyone.

People were buzzing with speculation about Merlin's purported "miracle"; no one seemed to be talking about anything else. And through it all, Merlin and Nimue, who abstained from drinking, circulated among the crowd, keeping a careful eye on their suspects.

Then it was time for business. Arthur sat in majesty on his throne, brilliantly lit by torchlight, and summoned his most important vassals to himself, Morgan, Mark and Guenevere among them. He required each of them in turn to recite the oath of fealty to him, while kissing Excalibur's blade, and swear their oath by the gods. Morgan did so casually, almost offhandedly, as if such an oath hardly mattered. Mark grunted and did it perfunctorily. Guenevere did it slowly, with ill grace, and so softly as to be barely audible. But each time the oath mentioned allegiance to Arthur, she added, "And due caution regarding his armed guards."

Then all the other assembled vassals recited the oath en masse, while Arthur scanned the audience carefully to make sure they were all doing it.

Business ended, Arthur clapped his hands for more

wine, and servants with trays of goblets and wineskins appeared. More came with cakes and tarts. The musicians struck up a lively dance. The formal part of the evening was over, and everyone enjoyed the revel. Before long people were pairing off, and couples slipped out of the hall, either furtively or openly, depending on their inclinations.

By an hour past midnight the hall was empty except for the musicians, packing up their instruments. The floor and tables were littered with scraps of food, empty cups and the like, which would be cleaned up in the morning. Once the players left, two servants went about the hall, extinguishing torches one by one. Merlin stood against the wall watching. He had noticed nothing in the behavior of the suspects that told him anything at all. But tomorrow would be the night.

Then he noticed a slight, almost imperceptible movement of a section of wall not far from where he was standing. He waited quietly, patiently, till the last of the torches and candles were put out. The only light came from the adjoining hallways. One of the servants approached him, a puzzled look on his face. Merlin held a finger to his lips and gestured to him that he should leave. Clearly puzzled, the man went. Merlin was alone in the darkened Great Hall. He pressed himself flat against the wall and waited.

Again the wall moved; he could barely see it in the near-complete darkness, but the sound of stone scraping on stone came to him clearly. Someone stepped out of the wall into the hall.

"Pellenore. Hello, Pellenore."

The old king jumped, startled. "Merlin?"

"Yes, of course. You've been leading the king's men on a merry chase."

"No one could know Camelot as well as I do. There are

blind alleys, dead ends, even pitfalls . . . I hope no one has been hurt."

Even though they were speaking softly, their voices echoed faintly in the hall. Merlin took a few steps forward, cautiously. "Everyone keeps forgetting this was once your castle. You oversaw the construction, didn't you?"

"Mm-hmm. Arthur will never make this place completely his."

"I think he's beginning to understand that, though not in the way you mean."

"I hate it when you're smug, Merlin."

"I know, I know. Everyone does. What can I say?"

"Is there any food left?"

"I imagine so. If you scavenge about the hall I'm sure you'll find some good meat and some of those honey cakes Arthur can't resist."

Pellenore began moving from table to table, piling plates with what he could find and munching as he went. Merlin watched him, outlined dimly in the light from the corridors. "Sooner or later he'll catch you, you know. You can't live in the walls forever."

"I can until he realizes I'm not the one who killed his sons."

"You know they were his sons?"

"You'd be amazed how well voices carry here. I've been eavesdropping on him every chance I get. You're a fool to think you can trap anyone with this stunt you're going to pull."

"Let me worry about that, will you? What else have you heard? Has Mark said anything incriminating? Or Morgan, or Guenevere?"

"They're royals—they're politicians. Scheming is what

they do. Everything they say is incriminating." He bit into a joint of beef he'd found. "I'm happier living in the walls than I ever was outside."

"Will you stay there, then? Even after we've found out the culprit? Will you live in the walls of the castle like a phantom?"

"I've been a phantom ever since Arthur took it from me, Merlin. And you know it."

"I could sound the alarm. Call the guards. End this now."

"Where do you think you could imprison me that I couldn't escape from?"

Merlin shrugged. "Arthur has other castles."

"Leave me to my own devices, will you, Merlin? I'm happier."

"Tomorrow night. I shall unmask the twins' killer tomorrow night. After that, you will have no reason to remain in hiding."

"Suppose I tell you the beasts can't find me when I'm behind the walls?"

"Suppose I remind you that you told me once you are only mad in one direction? And that direction is not into the walls."

"Besides, Merlin, I prefer dragons to Arthur and his family and his courtiers. I could kill them all, you know. I could emerge from the castle walls while they're asleep and do them in."

"You make my mouth water, Pellenore. But you mustn't do that. It's taken all my powers of persuasion to keep them from tearing open the walls to find you as things stand. If you were to do a thing like that . . ." He spread his hands wide apart in a gesture of helplessness.

Arms laden with plates of food, Pellenore moved back to the door he'd entered through. "I could do it. You know it. I could kill them all and never be caught."

"Them? If you're going to kill anyone at all, why not go for the ones who've been plotting treason?"

"Good night, Merlin."

"Good night. Sleep well, Pellenore, if you can. And drop any idea you may have of regicide, will you?"

The old king pulled the door shut behind him.

Merlin moved to the spot and ran his fingers along the wall. There was nothing detectable, not the least seam or crack. A moment later, from behind the wall, he heard the sound of stumbling and plates clattering to the floor, and Pellenore's voice cursing.

First thing in the morning, Merlin was up and about. Nimue joined him. "I'm nervous, Merlin. The more I think about this, the more dangerous it seems."

"It is dangerous for both of us. But I can't see that we have any choice, not if we want to restore order here."

"Even so. I'm having second thoughts, more and more of them."

"Everything will be all right. Arthur will be armed, and he will have guards posted. We'll be safe."

"How many guards?"

"As many as can be, without arousing suspicion."

"Suppose that isn't enough?"

"Suppose fire rains down from the sky and kills us all?"

"Point taken. But Merlin—"

"Come on. The refectory should be crowded enough. Let us begin."

Glumly, reluctantly, she followed him to the dining hall. It was full of people, many of them plainly feeling the effects of the previous night's drinking. Merlin was pleased at this. "We don't want anyone too terribly attentive or thoughtful—certainly not any of our suspects."

Off in a corner of the refectory were two men, dressed in dingy clothes, clearly not nobles or even servants; these were laborers and it was unmistakable. Merlin approached them and shook their hands, and they all sat down together.

Their conversation was loud, uncharacteristically so, and people all around eavesdropped, most of them not trying to hide the fact.

"You understand what you're to do?"

"Yes, sir," said one of the men. "But—"

"Good. And you know which one I want, right?"

"Yes, sir."

"Excellent. The other one was mutilated beyond hope. He would hardly be an apt subject."

"But, sir, we've never done this before. It's ugly; it's not right."

"It is for a good purpose. You may rest assured of that."

"No good can come of a thing like this."

"It will."

This exchange had piqued the curiosity of everyone within easy earshot, which was precisely what Merlin wanted. "Have you had a good breakfast?"

"Yes, sir."

"Good. Then go, now," he told them. "The ground is frozen. It will be hard work, and it may take a good part of the day. I will see that the king rewards you amply."

"Thank you, sir." The two men rose and left.

Guenevere and Lancelot had been eating a few tables away. The queen could not restrain her curiosity. She got up and crossed to Merlin. "Fraternizing with the lower orders, Merlin?"

"They are good men, and I am no snob."

She bristled at the implied criticism. "What was that all about?"

"Nothing, Guenevere. I was just taking care of some preliminaries for tonight."

"Preliminaries?"

"Necessary steps. These things cannot be done haphazardly, you know. Everything must be arranged properly."

Lancelot joined them. "What things? Who were those men?"

"Why, I thought you would recognize them. You've seen them before. And you've given them enough work."

Guenevere snapped, "Don't be coy with us, Merlin. Who were they?"

He smiled. "Why, the royal gravediggers, of course."

"The—!"

"I don't believe I'm hungry, after all." He smiled at them. "I'll just be going. Enjoy your meal, Guenevere." Walking away, he added, as if it were an afterthought, "You too, Lancelot."

For the rest of the day the castle was abuzz with gossip about Merlin, Arthur, the gravediggers and anything else that could support more than cursory speculation. Everywhere either Merlin or Nimue went, people plied them with questions, all of which went tactfully unanswered.

Merlin noticed that Morgan and Mordred remained in their rooms all day, having meals brought to them instead of dining with everyone else. "I don't know whether to find it suspicious."

He decided to pay them a visit. Beaming, overflowing with hearty good will, he went to Morgan's chambers.

She was in a foul mood. "These rooms are drafty. I'm freezing."

"This is a castle, Morgan. What do you expect?"

"If you're going to work miracles with that damned crystal skull, why don't you bring on spring?"

He was smug. "In time, Morgan."

"In time spring will arrive on its own."

"Such skepticism from the high priestess. I am shocked."

"What do you want here, Merlin?"

"Why, no one's seen you all day. I only wanted to make certain you are all right. And where is that handsome son of yours?"

"Mordred is reading. He has a new copy of Lucretius." She added pointedly, "A distinguished skeptic from the ancient world."

"I am perfectly aware of who he was, thank you. But— should you encourage your son to doubt? He might get into the habit."

She had had enough of this. "I want to know what you're up to, Merlin. I'm told you were conspiring with the royal gravediggers this morning,"

"Up to? Conspiring?" He was all sweet innocence. "Why, I am simply doing the king's bidding. He wants a spectacular miracle to impress everyone with his power. The Stone of Bran will make that possible."

"Nonsense. Arthur wants to use the religious impulses of his people to strengthen his position in the country. But neither he nor you is used to doing that. You may find you're getting into more trouble than you realize."

"Is that a threat, Morgan?"

"Let us call it a friendly admonition. I hardly have to

threaten you. Neither of you understands what you're doing." Her voice turned hard. "Abandon this foolishness. Do a few conjurer's tricks and send them all home. There will be no resurrection."

"Will there not?"

"No." She was quite serene in her confidence.

"But, Morgan, the people have been promised a miracle."

Mordred came in; he had clearly been eavesdropping. "A miracle? There is no such thing, Merlin, and you know it perfectly well. The idea that a bit of polished rock might restore life to the dead . . ."

"Not might—will."

Morgan stood. Tall and imperious, she pointed a finger directly at Merlin's head. "Stop this charade. Announce the truth."

"The truth? You mean the 'truth' that only a priestess can work wonders? Really, Morgan, your threats are so toothless."

"They are not. You know perfectly well what I mean."

He got wearily to his feet. "Have you brought your chest of poisons, then?"

"Chest of—" She batted her eyelashes like a demure girl. "Why, sir, I possess no such thing. But if I did . . ."

"Yes?"

"I would make certain I knew what I was meddling with." Her voice took on a hard edge.

"I see. Yes, I suppose you would." He started to go then turned back to her, grinning. "Have a pleasant day. And you too, Mordred. If the cold becomes too much for you, let me know. There are shawls and blankets I can send. Older women are so frail."

"Get out of here, you horrible fraud."

"Yes, ma'am. I'll see you at court tonight."

• • •

That evening there was a huge feast in the dining hall,
which was decked out with evergreens and hung about with
large colorful banners and tapestries. Musicians played,
mimes performed, jugglers juggled. Roast beef, goose,
mutton and veal were served in huge quantities. More to the
point, wine, mead and ale flowed like water. This was stan-
dard at the Midwinter feast, but Merlin suggested that keeping everyone well lubricated would be an advantage.

There was a small head table at which Arthur and Merlin
sat. It was on a dais, high enough for Merlin to watch everyone but not so high as to be intimidating. Guenevere, Morgan and Mark and their people were seated at tables just
below Arthur's. Arthur was dressed in his best finery and
wore Excalibur at his side; it was the tangible sign of
his kingship and had been polished to a shimmering bril-
liance.

Merlin noted with satisfaction that Mark was drinking
heavily. So was Lancelot; and Guenevere downed more
than her share of mead. Only Morgan seemed to be abstain-
ing. She sat beside her son, eating fastidiously, not talking,
not looking around the hall even occasionally.

Merlin commented on it. "Such self-possession doesn't
seem quite human."

"That is my sister you're talking about." Arthur bit into a
flank of beef. Then glumly, he added, "Well, half sister.
She's always been that way. I think if she smiled or showed
pleasure she'd vanish in a puff of smoke."

For an instant Merlin was tempted to ask Arthur about
the incest rumors about him and Morgan, but he decided not
to do anything that might disrupt the king's mood.

At one far corner of the refectory, the two gravediggers

sat, eating and drinking heartily like everyone else. Noticing them, Arthur nudged Merlin with an elbow. "Look. They're getting drunk."

"Like everyone else in Camelot."

"Except you and my sister. Have they done what they should have?"

"Everything is in readiness, Arthur, yes."

"People have been coming to me about this all day long. Mark approached me three times, begging me not to let you do this."

"Mark is a superstitious gull. Which is exactly what I want."

"So three of your suspects will be in the Great Hall. But what about the fourth?"

"Pellenore? He will be there, too, only not in plain sight."

Arthur narrowed his eyes. "You know where he is."

"No. I wish I did. I'd give anything to know the hidden parts of Camelot the way he does."

"I keep expecting him to pop out of a wall and hack someone's head off."

"He's harmless, Arthur."

"No one human is harmless." Saying this, Arthur startled himself. "Good heavens, I'm starting to sound like you."

"You could do worse."

"Eat your goose and be quiet. You're lucky I find this miracle of yours useful and desirable. Otherwise I'd never let you toy with three people I know to be innocent."

"Of course, Arthur."

When everyone had finished eating—and had had time to drink still more—Arthur announced that the evening's entertainment and ceremony would begin shortly in the Great Hall. He urged them to bring whatever was left of their dinners, and their drinks, and adjourn there.

Humming with anticipation, they did so. People filed through Camelot's halls in small groups or singly; pages lit the way with blazing torches. The musicians led the way, still playing lively music, though the tone grew successively more somber as everyone reached the hall.

The hall itself was lit brilliantly, more so than anyone could remember seeing before. Hundreds of torches and candles glowed fiercely; it seemed there was one in every possible space along the walls.

A platform—the same one that had been used on the night of the first murder—had been erected, and a row of more torches glared along its perimeter. Merlin had instructed several of the servants to sprinkle lime into the flames to make them burn even more brightly. But there was only one throne on the platform this night, Arthur's, and it was set off to one side. Clearly he considered what was to come sufficiently important to remove himself from the center of things.

As the crowd filled the room, more servants with still more beverages entered and began to circulate, followed by more with generous supplies of Arthur's honey cakes. It was all terribly festive; everyone seemed in a jovial mood, except Morgan and her son; they stood against the wall opposite the stage and watched everything and everyone with plain disapproval.

On a signal from Arthur, the servants extinguished all the lights in the room but the ones lighting the stage. It was time for the promised spectacle to begin.

First came the play. Arthur introduced Samuel, who in

turn announced that his company would play *The Fall of Troy*, a stunning new drama by Dares the Phrygian and Dictys of Crete based on the eyewitness accounts of the fabled city's fall. "We have performed this to acclaim in all the important courts of Europe. And we are privileged to present it here for you tonight."

Merlin and Nimue took places not far from Morgan and Mordred, hoping to overhear whatever they might say. But the crowd was too loud, too boisterous for any individual voice to carry very far.

The actors took their places, and, lit harshly by the torches around the stage, Samuel recited the prologue. "And we shall see, both man and wife / the city's fall, the end of life."

Merlin leaned close to Nimue and whispered, "Let us hope we don't see the end of Camelot, too."

"Be quiet, Merlin. I want to hear the actors."

The audience was predictably rowdy and ill-behaved, talking and laughing loudly as the performance progressed. But as it went on and got darker and more serious, they began to pay attention. In particular, the boy actor Watson, playing the tragic Trojan queen Hecuba, caught their attention. When he recited his speech mourning the deaths of his children, his husband and his city, there were even people weeping.

"You see the power of dressing as the opposite sex?" Nimue whispered to Merlin.

"Nonsense. They are drunk, that's all."

"Piffle."

Throughout, Merlin kept a careful eye on the suspects. Guenevere and Lancelot were seated at a special table close to the stage. She was not happy, and not paying much attention to Watson and the others. She was, after all, the queen, and she was seated among lesser persons. Lancelot was drunk and kept nodding off, which seemed to annoy her even more.

Mordred and Morgan stayed near the farthest wall from the stage. It was clear they saw themselves apart from the rest. Or at any rate Morgan saw herself that way and Mordred went along. She was not a mother to upset.

And Mark, also drunk, kept lurching through the audience, muttering to one person or group after another. Wrapped up in the play, they shushed him. The expression on his face was not happy.

Britomart joined Merlin and Nimue.

"Have you seen anything, Brit?"

"Yes, a boy pretending to be a sad woman."

"You know what I mean—anything suspicious. What is Mark saying?"

"He is complaining about your mystical show. He thinks something dire will happen, and he wants to find a way to stop it."

"And what did you say to him?"

"I told him to relax, that religious displays of the supernatural are simply more theater."

"Cynic."

"That is exactly what he said."

"I haven't seen Petronus," Brit commented.

"He is making himself scarce," Merlin told her. "The last thing he wants is an encounter with Lancelot. He will be here when he's needed."

"Needed?"

"He is practicing with the lenses for tonight."

"Lenses? Merlin, this sounds sillier and more desperate the more I learn about it."

When finally the play concluded, the audience applauded and cheered wildly. Samuel took center stage for a bow, but the crowd wanted young Watson. Glumly, grudgingly, Samuel let the boy take the glory.

Meanwhile, Merlin moved through the audience in the direction of the offstage space where the actors were. His turn in the limelight would be next.

When the applause for the boy finally died down, Arthur took the stage again and thanked the company for their splendid performance. "What we saw tonight redounded to the glory of England, the fairest country on the face of the earth." He went on at length about the flower of England and the coming period of prestige and leadership on the stage of Europe.

Offstage, two of the young men in Samuel's company helped Merlin into a sorcerer's robe, embroidered with stars and mystical symbols, and a conical wizard's hat. Samuel watched, beaming; if things went well, his company would soon have a patron at court. To one of his dressers, Merlin whispered, "It is terribly lucky you have this costume."

"We use it in one of our comedies, sir."

"Oh. Well, let us hope tonight's events do not play that way."

Onstage, Arthur concluded his speech by talking about the Stone of Bran and the might and the glory it would soon bring to "our fair island." He acknowledged Percival, who was in the audience, and gave him full credit for finding the sacred relic. Then he intoned, "It is time for us to witness its power."

The musicians struck up a somber march, a nearly hymnlike melody. Almost involuntarily the crowd parted and Greffys entered, accompanied by a dozen of Arthur's most trusted guards; Arthur was taking no chances with the safety of his squire this time. On a red velvet cushion embroidered with gold, Greffys carried the Stone of Bran before him. Their little procession made a circuit of the hall, permitting everyone to see the stone close-to. Then they advanced to the foot of the stage.

During this, Petronus had entered the hall and made his way unobtrusively to the side of the stage. As Greffys and the guards climbed to the platform, Petronus produced a pair of large lenses Merlin and Samuel had given him. He held them carefully before two of the torches, and the lenses focused their light and directed it to the stone. Suddenly, it seemed to everyone watching, the Stone of Bran began to glow brightly, almost ethereally. As Greffys moved across the stage to Arthur, Petronus changed the angle of the lenses so that the light followed and the crystal skull seemed to burn with a supernatural light.

When Greffys was beside him, Arthur took the stone in the fingertips of both hands and held it aloft. "Behold the Stone of Bran, the gift of the gods!" The crowd gasped and applauded vigorously.

Then Merlin, in his magician's robes, slowly, solemnly mounted the platform and crossed to Arthur. He made a slight bow, first to the king then to the skull. Then he turned and faced the audience. "Let the wonders begin," he intoned, and the audience fell into a hushed silence.

Petronus adjusted his lenses so that the beams shone on both Merlin and on the stone. Merlin made a slow, deliberate, majestic bow to the audience. Then, with equally deliberate slowness, he removed his pointed hat. With a flourish he showed it to the audience so that they could see that it was empty. Then he took the stone and touched it to the hat, held the hat in one hand and from it produced a live rabbit. The animal struggled to escape his grip. He let it drop to the stage and it scampered away, frightened and confused. It ran, improbably, in the direction where Morgan and Mordred were standing. Mordred caught it and handed it to his mother, who cradled it in her arms till it calmed down.

In the wings, Samuel beamed. Merlin had worked the trick he'd taught him perfectly. Someone in the audience shouted, "That's it, Merlin? That is the great wonder we've been promised?"

Instead of answering, Merlin raised a finger to his lips and gestured to the door nearest the stage.

A young woman with blond hair, wearing a low-cut snow-white gown, entered the hall, eyes lowered, and walked to the stage. Behind her came Greffys, carrying a large saw. Finally, the two gravediggers entered, carrying a large wooden coffin. This was all so unexpected, the crowd fell silent again.

The girl in white climbed to the stage, followed by the others. The gravediggers let their coffin rest on two wooden trestles and made a quick exit. Merlin assisted the woman into the coffin, where she lay down, and he closed the lid.

In the audience, Mark gaped at her. Was she the same woman who'd come to him that night at his own castle? Could Merlin have been behind her presence there, then? Drunk almost to a stupor, he tried to think clearly and make sense of it, but it was no use.

From a corner of his eye, Merlin watched Mark. The show seemed to be having the desired effect on him. Once again he took the Stone of Bran and with a flourish passed it over the coffin three times; then another three times he tapped the lid with it. And he took the saw and began to cut it in half, and the woman with it. People in the crowd gasped; Mark gaped.

When the coffin was cut clear through, Merlin and

Greffys moved the two halves apart, then slid them back together again. Waving the stone above it one more time, he opened the lid, and out stepped the young woman in white. The audience cheered and applauded. Mark blinked and tried to focus, uncertain whether to believe what he was seeing.

Morgan, standing at the back of the audience, was bored. She leaned against the wall and yawned. She handed the rabbit to her son and whispered something to him; he also yawned.

On his throne at the side of the stage Arthur watched alternately his minister/magician and the audience, and he smiled serenely, pleased that Merlin's worst expectations had not come to pass. No one was reacting adversely to the show; the killer was not a member of his court.

But there was something else happening in the audience; and Merlin was so focused on Mark he didn't notice. Lancelot slowly, gradually began to shake off his alcoholic haze. And as his senses returned, or began to, he glared at the boy holding the lenses. It was his former squire, the one who'd deserted him without permission, without even saying a word.

Unsteadily, he got to his feet, pushed the people around him away and drew his sword. "Traitor!" he bellowed. "Turncoat!" And he began to lunge at Petronus through the crowd. "I'll kill you! You'll join the other two in the underworld!" The boy, terrified, dropped his lenses to the stage and scrambled underneath the platform. Nimue left the stage quickly and joined the actors in their waiting area.

Guenevere shouted in alarm, "Stop! Lancelot, stop this!"

Half a dozen knights caught hold of Lancelot and restrained him. But he fought them, shouting at the boy, struggling against their hold and still trying to brandish his sword. Finally, one of them wrenched it free of his grasp and it clattered loudly onto the stone floor.

Arthur stood. "Hold that man! Do not let him go!"

At the rear of the hall Morgan stirred for the first time. She stood erect, watching what was happening, and she smiled slightly and whispered something to Mordred.

Finally, Lancelot seemed to lose energy. He became quiet and permitted the knights to place him in his chair once again. Guenevere placed a hand on his arm and murmured something to him, and it quieted him even more.

From the stage Arthur said, "You six—place him in his seat and see that he stays there. Keep him there forcibly if you must. Let us hope this was the final outburst. This is a solemn occasion. I will not have it disrupted. All of you, be calm. Remember the dignity of our court." And he resumed his throne.

Merlin had watched all of this carefully. That it was Lancelot not Mark who had exploded surprised him. But despite the mention of "the other two," Lancelot's anger was at the squire who'd left him and seemed unrelated to the murders. But the evening's signal event was still to come. Or so he hoped.

Gradually, the crowd quieted. Lancelot sat glumly, showing no sign he would make more commotion. Merlin stepped to the floor, bent to look under the stage and gestured to Petronus to come out. "It is over, Pete. Come out now."

Warily, the boy did so. When he was out from under, he looked at Lancelot and was somewhat reassured to see him quiet. With Petronus back in place, the performance could resume. Merlin remounted the stage.

"And now," he announced, "for the greatest wonder of

all. You have seen a woman torn in two and restored to life. Now you shall witness something even greater."

He clapped his hands loudly three times. The musicians struck up a low, sad melody like a funeral march. Two of the young actors in Samuel's company entered the hall again, this time carrying a pallet between them. On the pallet was what seemed to be a body, over which was stretched a linen shroud or winding-sheet. Petronus focused light on it and made it seem to glow softly. Behind the actors the two gravediggers followed.

Slowly, solemnly, the two actors carried their burden to the stage. Merlin gestured to them to rest it on the trestles; they did so, bowed to him and left.

The air in the hall was tense with anticipation. No one talked or made a sound. Virtually no one moved. All eyes were on Merlin and the shrouded—what?

"I believe you all recognize these two men," he said to the audience. "They have been the gravediggers at Camelot's cemetery for years." The two men, apparently abashed at becoming the center of attention, shifted their weight awkwardly and uneasily.

"Gentlemen," Merlin addressed them, "you have this day performed an extraordinary task at the behest of King Arthur and myself."

They lowered their eyes and muttered, "Yes, sir."

"The king has asked to you perform the reverse of your usual function and to exhume a body which you buried some time ago."

"Yes."

"The earth is frozen and this has been difficult work. But you have accomplished it. And you will be properly rewarded."

The younger of the two said, "Thank you, sir."

His companion added, "It *was* hard work, sir. Every muscle in our bodies is aching."

"I am certain the king appreciates your labors. But now it is time to explain to the assembled court precisely what your task has been. Could you please say whose body it is that you have been required to exhume?"

No one in the Great Hall moved. People leaned forward to hear more clearly. Lancelot squirmed in his seat. But Merlin kept a careful eye on Mark, who was looking increasingly upset.

On the stage the elder gravedigger shuffled his feet and said, "It was the squire, sir. The king's late squire."

"Which one? Could you please tell us which it was?"

"We don't ever know their names, sir. We just dig the holes and fill them in afterward."

A few people in the audience laughed nervously. Mark inched forward in his seat.

Merlin went on. "But there were two of them. Both of the king's squires were killed, one after the other. And— you placed them in the same grave?"

"Yes, sir. One of them was horribly mangled, sir—cut to pieces. That's the one that's still at rest in the graveyard. This is the other one."

"This is the body of poor murdered Ganelin, then?"

"Like I said, sir, we never know their names."

"I see. No, I suppose there is no reason why you should. And has the frozen earth preserved the body?"

"Yes, sir. He looks the way he did the day we buried him."

"I see. Thank you very much."

Looking at each other, puzzled by what was going on

and why they'd had to speak before the audience, the two men climbed down from the stage and left.

Merlin took up the Stone of Bran, which was still brightly lit. He held it high above him then slowly lowered it and touched the head of the shrouded body with it. Three times he passed it over the length of the boy then he touched it to the head once again.

Slightly, almost imperceptibly, the body twitched.

In the audience some people gasped; most were transfixed by what they were seeing and fell perfectly silent. At the side of the stage Arthur sat and watched, mesmerized.

They watched as the body moved again, first the arms, then the legs, stretching slowly as if waking from a long, deep sleep. Petronus pointed his lenses at it, and the shroud caught the light and glowed ghostly pale.

An arm, caked with dirt and blood, reached out from beneath the shroud. Merlin stepped forward and took the hand in his, and the corpse sat up, still wrapped in its shroud.

"Please," Merlin said gravely, "tell us who you are."

And a voice came clearly through the cloth. "I am Ganelin, squire to King Arthur of Camelot. I am cold."

"Ganelin, do you understand what has happened to you?"

"Yes." The word's final *s* was long and drawn out, almost a hiss. "I have been foully murdered. I have lain in the earth these many weeks, in the icy, frozen earth."

Merlin helped the boy to his feet, the winding-sheet still wrapped around him. And Merlin kept a careful eye on the audience, to gauge reactions. Morgan was watching the stage carefully, studying it as a conjurer might study a rival's tricks. Mordred stood at her side, wide-eyed, not moving. Mark was glowering and trembling in his seat, whether with rage or fear or some combination of the two,

Merlin could not tell. Guenevere held Lancelot's hand tightly.

"Tell us, Ganelin," Merlin intoned. "Did you see the face of the the the one who killed you?"

"Yesss."

There was not a sound in the Great Hall. Not the least movement, except for Mark, leaning forward in his seat, fingering the hilt of his sword, and Lancelot pulling free of Guenevere's hand and inching forward in his chair like a man preparing to bolt and run.

"Name him. Tell us, Ganelin, who it was. Who killed you and your brother?"

"Ohhh." The corpse groaned. "I cannot. It is too painful."

"I have restored your life. Now I command you, by the Stone of Bran. Name your murderer!"

Suddenly with a loud roar Mark pushed through the audience and leaped onto the stage, brandishing his sword. "No! You are dead. Do not speak my name. Do not profane it with your moldering lips!"

He lunged at the boy, and Merlin pulled him out of harm's way to the side of the stage. Mark swung his sword at Merlin and he ducked.

Arthur jumped to his feet and drew Excalibur. Instantly, the two men, Arthur and Mark, were locked in a duel. They circled one another, they threatened, they slashed. Mark lunged and his sword hit home in Arthur's left arm. Blood flowed, but Arthur recovered himself quickly. He rushed at Mark and knocked him to the stage, then stood over him with Excalibur poised directly above his throat.

More knights rushed the stage, surrounded the prostrate Mark and caught him. He struggled, shouting, "No! This is unholy! The dead cannot speak to the living. The dead cannot *indict* the living. This is blasphemy!"

"Take him away," Arthur said quietly. "To the dungeon. Lock him away." With Mark still struggling fiercely against their hold, they did so.

Away from this action, Merlin placed an arm around the boy in the shroud. And slowly the shroud fell away, revealing him to be the young actor Watson.

The audience, still in shock from Mark's attack and capture, took a moment to react to this. Then, as they gradually realized who the "dead" boy really was, soft, nervous laughter began to spread through the hall. Merlin made a gesture to wave everyone out of the hall, and slowly, by twos, threes and fours, they began to leave.

Nimue, dressed again as Colin, climbed to the stage and put her own arm around the boy. "Go ahead, Merlin. I'll take care of him."

Merlin crossed to Arthur. The king was still excited, still breathing heavily and plainly tense in every muscle. "Arthur, it is over. You can relax now."

"It is not over. I want to know why he did it. Find out for me."

"Calm yourself. We have him. Everything will come out in time."

"Merlin, this is not what I wanted. Not what I tried to build."

"You've said that before. Let me look at that wound. Can you make it up the steps to my tower? I have a salve that will help, and bandages."

"It isn't bad. A lot of blood but not much pain." He took a deep breath and looked into Merlin's eyes. "I'm the king. Why can't things be as I want them to be?"

"Perhaps because kings are only human beings with circles of metal on their heads."

Arthur finally let himself relax. All the energy seemed to

leave him, and he slumped. "Nothing that glib and cynical could be true."

"Do you want me to lecture you on the nature of truth?"

"For God's sake, Merlin, no."

"Then come with me and let me see to your arm."

TEN

KING AND COUNSELOR

Merlin had slept late this morning. After Mark was arrested, Arthur had ordered even more feasting than usual for the rest of the Midwinter Court, and Merlin, in a jubilant mood, had quite uncharacteristically drunk two cups of wine—not much by Camelot's standards, but more than he was used to.

So he woke to find Nimue standing over him, shaking him. "It's nearly noon. Don't you think you should get up?"

"My head is going to explode. Go away and leave me to die."

"No one can find the king."

"Arthur?"

"He's the only one we have."

He sat up and rubbed his eyes. "Blast whatever demon first fermented wine." He looked at her suspiciously. "Why aren't you hungover?"

"I only had one goblet of hock. I know my limits." She put on her best sarcastic grin. "I live a life ruled by reason."

"Be quiet." Roc and the other ravens were scratching for food on the stone floor. "Go and get them some bread crumbs or something, will you?"

"Yes, sir."

She started to go.

"Wait. You said Arthur is missing."

"Yes. We've looked everywhere. No one can find him at all."

"I can't tell you how much I hate court life."

"Do you have any idea where he might be, Merlin?"

"I think I might. I'll have to go and see."

"I'd brace myself if I were you." She reached for the door.

"Stop. What are you talking about?"

"Your reputation. Bye, now."

"Stop. Damn it, who taught you to be so smug and sarcastic?"

She stared at him. "Heavens, I have no idea."

"What are you talking about? What about my reputation?"

"Your reputation as a wizard. After last night, people are more convinced than ever that you have mystical powers. Everyone's saying so."

"That isn't possible, Nimue. They saw that the living corpse was really an actor. I demonstrated the foolishness of believing in superstitious nonsense. It was Mark's downfall."

"You also sawed a woman in half and reassembled her, remember?"

"A conjurer's trick, no more." He stood up and stretched.

"Wine never used to make me stiff and sore. It must be something Mark's vintners did."

"It couldn't possibly be old age encroaching, could it?"

"Haven't you ruined my day enough already? If you keep needling me, I may saw you in half for real."

"I'll see you later, wizard."

"Wait. Are they really saying that about me?"

She nodded.

"Damn. Do you . . . do you still want to study with me, then?"

"Of course I do. You're the only one I know who's more disagreeable than myself. Besides, I've told you a dozen times, I like being Colin. Do you still want me for a student?"

"Yes, naturally."

"I guess I'll stick around then. Try not to limp too badly, will you?"

Before he could say anything she was out the door.

Eight inches of snow blanketed the countryside. But thankfully it had stopped falling. Yet there was an icy chill and a bitter wind. In moments when the clouds parted and sunshine broke through it was possible to see ice crystals swirling in the air.

Arthur stood in the snow at the burial ground, perfectly still, staring at the graves of Anna and the twins. In the whole landscape as far as he could see, there was no movement. Then a field mouse scampered across the surface of the snow, and an owl swooped down from a nearby tree, fell on it and killed it. Its blood stained the snow. The bird took it and flapped away.

Merlin came up behind the king, leaning heavily on his

cane. Arthur heard his footsteps crunching in the snow. "Merlin. I didn't know you came here."

"I don't. I've been looking for you. So has everyone. You should let people know where you will be."

"Is something wrong? Something else?"

"No, of course not. But you are the king, after all. People grow uneasy when you can't be found. We've been looking everywhere. Some people are quite certain you've disappeared into another of those damn hidden passages of Pellenore's. At least it has distracted them from chattering about my supposed magical powers. I seem to be the only one who thought to look here."

"Clever man. You know me. No one else does."

Merlin shrugged. "Isn't it my job?"

"Is that all? Is that the only reason? Don't be glib. Please. I need a little quiet support. So they all think you're a genuine wizard now."

"I don't understand it. My fraud was so obvious. It was supposed to accomplish two things—to entrap Mark and to show the rest of them how foolish superstitious belief is."

"My friend the magician."

"I've taught you better than that. Kings don't have friends, only courtiers."

"Your cynicism is never quite convincing, Merlin. Why is that?"

Uncomfortable with this line of talk, Merlin switched subjects. "The actors have left. There is a festival in Bath they hope to make."

"You paid them?"

"Quite generously. They put a great deal on the line for us."

"Yes."

"As they were leaving, the boy Watson threw his arms

around me and said, 'You are the best not-a-wizard I've ever known.' I didn't know how to take it. Was he being sarcastic, do you think?"

"With his arms around you? No, Merlin, sarcasm is your department. It's so natural to you, you become puzzled when there is none."

"Everything human is a puzzle, Arthur. At least he knows sham when he sees it. Everyone else has convinced themselves I'm a powerful sorcerer." For an awkward moment he fell silent, then he said, "Mark is dead."

Quietly the king responded, "Oh."

"You don't sound surprised."

"My kingdom is the kingdom of death. Haven't you noticed?"

"Everyplace human is the kingdom of death. England is no place special."

Arthur glanced at him then turned his gaze back to his sons' graves. He and Merlin fell into a long silence. At length, the king said, "You have such a dark view of mankind. I don't think I envy it."

"The result of knowing too many people. I sometimes think it was a mistake to spend all those years traveling the world." He put on a tight smile. "But I'm sure it has made me a better minister for you. I would be doing you a disservice if I told you people are all to be trusted."

"Tell me what happened to Mark."

Merlin bent down and ran his fingers through the top of a snowdrift. "This is half ice."

"I know it. Did he commit suicide?"

"Fall on his sword like a good Roman? No, nothing so noble. I had been interrogating him. Why did he do it? What impulse could have moved him to do such awful things? He said he wanted his kingdom back—and more. He wanted England."

"I wish he had taken it."

"Stop it, Arthur. You'd be dead now. Executed. He said he had been trying to foment a rebellion but no one would support him. They all had their own agendas. Morgan told him she hoped you would make Mordred your heir."

Faintly, Arthur registered surprise. "There was never any chance of that. The boy has good in him, I suppose, but he's no king. Whatever was good has been curdled by his mother, or would have been eventually."

"And Guenevere was plotting her own insurrection with the help of her father. She would never agree to support Mark in his bid for kingship."

"Ah. So we can count on my wife's mad self-interest."

A gentle wind began to blow. Merlin glanced upward and saw that dark clouds were building.

Another mouse scurried across the snow, this one unmolested by predators. Arthur watched it, pleased in a minor way. "Killing two innocent boys was a blow to my prestige, in his mind?"

"Evidently."

"My poor sons. And their poor mother. But how did he find out they were mine?"

"You won't like it."

"Tell me."

Merlin inhaled deeply. "You told him yourself."

"I never did any such thing."

"One night when you'd had too much to drink, you burbled it to him. Told him what fine sons they were and how they would make splendid heirs."

"Oh." Softly he repeated, "Oh. Good God. I killed them."

"No, Arthur. You did no such thing. It was Mark."

"I sealed their fate."

"When Mark went to steal the stone, Borolet was there, so Mark disposed of the witness to his crime and his rival to the throne in one stroke. And when Ganelin began to guess that he was the killer . . . that only gave him one more reason to eliminate the boy."

"All for a chunk of crystal."

"For a kingdom, Arthur. After all, you killed to get where you are."

"Those were wars, not a knife in the dark."

"Even so."

"I was hoping you would tell me something to brighten my mood."

"I'm sorry, Arthur."

"Tell me about Mark's death." The king had been avoiding the subject for days. "What happened?"

Merlin brushed the snow from a nearby grave marker and sat on it. "I had been questioning him all morning. He was exhausted and becoming less responsive. I decided to get myself something to eat and to send him something, hoping that a break and a hot meal would make him more cooperative. So I went to the refectory where, naturally enough, everyone plied me with questions about him. A few of the knights were upset that he had been arrested."

"He is a murderer. And he tried to kill again—in front of an audience, no less. They'll realize that imprisoning him was the only possibility when they've had time to think."

"Knights—not exactly known for thoughtfulness, are they?"

"Go on with the story and stop trying to get a rise out of me."

"When I went back to his cell to carry on the interrogation, he was missing. I realized at once that he must have found one of Pellenore's secret passages. In fact the entrance to one of them was open a few inches. I called for one of the guards, we took torches and we swung it wide open and went in.

"But it was a blind alley. Ten yards in front of us we saw Mark, lit by his own torch, clawing at the wall frantically, trying to find the way to open it. 'Mark,' I told him, 'it's no use. Only Pellenore knows these corridors.'

"He turned on us with a near-savage snarl. 'You can't keep me here. I am King Mark of Cornwall, not a common criminal.'

"Saying nothing, I stared at him.

"'I will not be held!' he bellowed. And he came running at me, snarling. My guard drew his sword, and Mark hesitated but kept coming.

"Suddenly, a door hidden in the wall sprung open. Pellenore leaped out, sword in hand, and struck Mark down. His arm and his head were nearly severed. Pellenore turned to us, wide-eyed, and said, 'The beasts. They are one fewer now.'

"Then he stepped back into the wall and it closed. We rushed to the spot, but there was absolutely no sign of the smallest crack, even. An awful gurgling sound came from Mark, the kind you must have heard on the battlefield often enough, and he was dead." He looked at Arthur and spread his hands apart, letting the empty air between them express what he was feeling.

Arthur remained perfectly still for a long moment. "And so justice has been done."

"Justice? You call death at the hands of a madman justice?"

"Mark would happily have let Pellenore be blamed for his crimes. So it is a kind of justice, I suppose. The evil has been rooted out. By you, Merlin. And I owe you a great deal. England can return to normal now, to harmony and the kind of society I want. There will be no more crime, except perhaps of the common, obvious sort. It is over."

Slowly, Merlin stood up. The cold stone had made his back stiff. "Do you really believe that?"

"I have to. I am the king. England is mine."

There was more wind, stiffer than before, and snow started falling. Merlin stretched, trying to work the stiffness out of his back. "Do you ever read Sappho, Arthur?"

"Are you trying to be funny?"

"No, it was a foolish question. But she was a wonderful poet with a stark, dark vision. She once observed that the gods believe death to be the greatest evil."

"She had a point."

"But she added that the only reason they think death evil is because they themselves don't die."

"There are times, wizard, when I worry about you. Let's get back to the castle. I'm cold."

Merlin hooked his arm through Arthur's, and the two men walked slowly in the direction of Camelot. Merlin said softly, "Now, Your Majesty, about that school for the squires and the pages . . ."

THE END

The Constable Evans Mysteries
By Rhys Bowen

"A consistently satisfying mystery series."
—*Omaha World-Herald*

penguin.com

M257AS0208